FURY RISING

A FURY UNBOUND NOVEL
BOOK 1

YASMINE
NEW YORK TIMES BESTSELLING AUTHOR
GALENORN

A Nightqueen Enterprises LLC Publication

Published by Yasmine Galenorn
PO Box 2037, Kirkland WA 98083-2037
FURY RISING
A Fury Unbound Novel
Copyright © 2016 by Yasmine Galenorn
First Electronic Printing: 2016 Nightqueen Enterprises LLC
First Print Edition: 2016 Nightqueen Enterprises
Cover Art & Design: Ravven
Editor: Elizabeth Flynn
Map Design: Yasmine Galenorn
Map Layout: Samwise Galenorn
Print Layout: Shawntelle Madison

A Nightqueen Enterprises LLC Publication
Published in the United States of America

Welcome to Fury Rising

*My name is Kaeleen Donovan. I'm a Theosian—
a minor goddess. They call me Fury.*

*By day, I run the Crossroads Cleaning Com-
pany, and I also read fortunes and cast hexes at
Dream Wardens, a magical consulting shop. But
by night, I'm oath-bound to Hecate, goddess of the
Crossroads. Hecate charged me from birth with
the task of hunting down Abominations who come
in off the World Tree and sending them back to
Pandoriam.*

*When the Thunderstrike—an ancient artifact
from the time of the Weather Wars—is stolen by
the Order of the Black Mist, Hecate orders me to
find the magical device. The chaos magicians are
out to upset the balance that Gaia instilled during
the World Shift.*

*But I soon discover that the leader of the Black
Mist is out to do more than stir up trouble—he's
looking to bind the world to the Elder Gods of
Chaos, with himself on the throne.*

*Caught between two rival forces, will my
friends and I be able to survive as we search for
the Thunderstrike and attempt to stop a war that
could bring about the end of civilization?*

Map of the Seattle Area
Post-World Shift

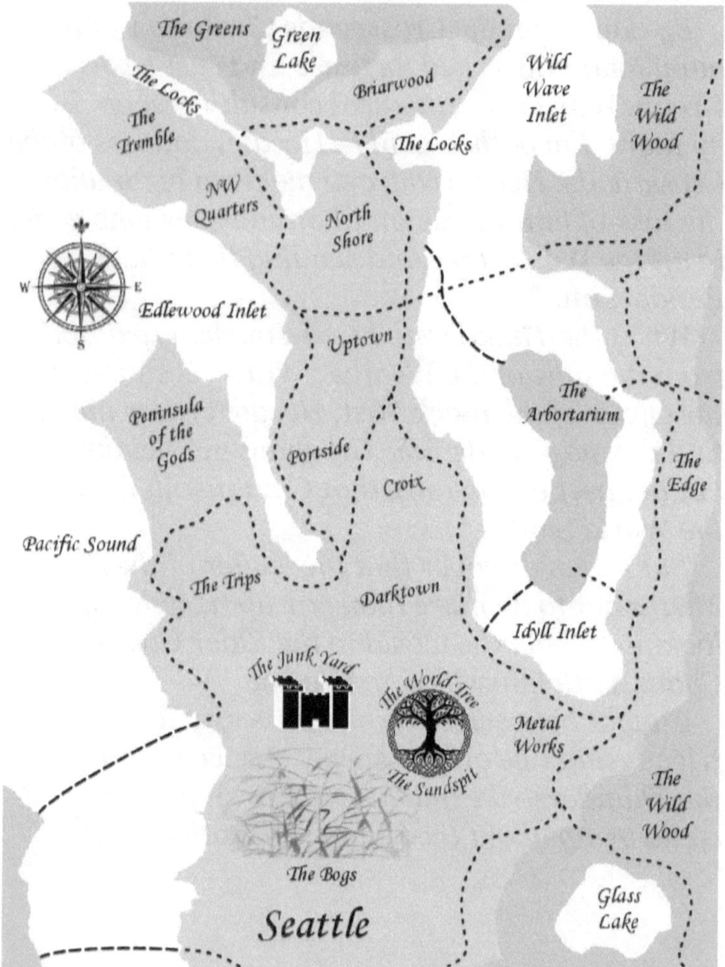

The Greens

Green Lake

The Locks

Briarwood

The Tremble

Wild Wave Inlet

The Wild Wood

The Locks

NW Quarters

North Shore

Edlewood Inlet

Uptown

The Arbortarium

Peninsula of the Gods

Portside

The Edge

Croix

Pacific Sound

The Trips

Darktown

Idyll Inlet

The Junk Yard

The World Tree

Metal Works

The Sandspit

The Wild Wood

The Bogs

Seattle

Glass Lake

To Bend →

The Beginning

The end of civilization as we knew it arrived not with a whimper, but with a massive storm. When Gaia—the great mother and spirit of the Earth—finally woke from her slumber to discover the human race destroying the planet through a series of magical Weather Wars, she pitched a fit. The magical storm she unleashed change such as never before had been seen. The resulting gale ripped the doors on the World Tree wide open, including the doors to Pandoriam—where the Aboms—chaotic demons of shadow and darkness—live, and the doors to Elysium, where the Devani—ruthless agents of light—exist.

In that one cataclysmic moment, now known as the World Shift, life changed forever as creatures from our wildest dreams—and nightmares—began to pour through the open doors.

The old gods returned and set up shop. The Fae and the Weres came out from the shadows and took up their place among the humans. The Theosians began to appear. Technology integrated with magic, and now everything is all jumbled together. Nothing in the old order remained untouched. The world might appear to be similar to the way it was, but trust me—under that thin veneer of illusion, nothing has remained the same.

Chapter 1

My name is Kaeleen Donovan. They call me Fury. I'm a Theosian. I walk in flame and ash, on a field of bones. Some nights I think I'll burn to a crisp under Hecate's moonlight. Other nights...are easier.

I pressed myself against the crumbling brick, breathing softly. A trail of ivy came tumbling down the side of the wall, covering a wide swath all the way to the ground next to me. One tendril reached out and tapped me on the shoulder and the patch of green opened up, offering me the chance to slip inside, out of the wind, but I pushed it away. Wandering Ivy was unpredictable and you couldn't trust it, any more than you could trust the wide fields of vegetation outside the city boundaries. And since we didn't have the resources to eradicate it down here in Darktown—or even keep it in check—most of us just left it alone and watched where we sat or leaned.

The moon was hidden, her light barely visible, masking both street and burrow-lane, but I could sense the clouds coming in. The low rumble of thunder in the distance announced they weren't too far out, but for now, the clear skies meant it was perfect drone weather. And *that* meant the Corp-Rats would have their sky-eyes out in full force.

In fact, one had started to follow me a few minutes earlier, but when I ducked beneath the overhanging eaves of the 22-U, the mini-mall that housed several small businesses, it backed off. Luckily, the drones weren't allowed to maneuver down to street level. There was too much danger that somebody would attempt a disable-and-grab, especially down here in Darktown, so the Devani kept their patrols limited to watching over us from above. They wouldn't respond if something went down, anyway. Nobody gave a damn what went on in this sector of the city—not unless it looked like a riot that might threaten to spill through the borders. And that wasn't likely to happen. As long as people weren't outright starving, and they were kept busy by long-hour shifts and an abundance of Opish and Methodyne, apathy tended to rule.

Another minute, and the sky-eye zipped past and kept on going. I waited until it was out of sight before I relaxed and sucked in a deep breath. It wasn't that I was doing anything wrong, per se. Not yet, at least. But the less I crossed the Corp-

Rats' radar, the better.

Theosians who caught their attention often vanished without warning and I didn't intend to be one of them, especially since my chips had been altered and if they did an in-depth scan on me, they'd find out that I was living off-grid, in a roundabout manner. With luck, the Devani would be running on their usual schedule, which meant there shouldn't be another fly-by in this area for at least two or three hours. Breathing a little easier, I stepped back into the burrow-lane and headed toward the Sandspit.

Darktown's linkup to the Monotrain was erratic at best during the day. At night, it was catch as catch can, so I picked up my pace. Public transportation didn't always make it this far, and it wasn't for want of tracks.

As I jogged along, I pulled out my phone and tapped ENCRYPT. Tam had tricked it out for me, so I could send brief messages that couldn't be intercepted.

"Heading to the Sandspit. Something's going down there tonight—I can feel it, but I'm not quite sure what it is. I'll send Queet with news if we find anything." Phones didn't work near the Sandspit, so once I arrived there, I wouldn't be able to call him.

"Be careful, Kae. The Spit has been very active lately. If you even *think* you need help, send Queet my way immediately." Jason was a hawk-shifter and a magus. He could talk to spirits when he chose to open himself up.

Pocketing my phone, I glanced up at the sky.

The clouds were starting to roll in fast now. The storm was going to be a nasty one. The wind picked up and the scent of rain was heavy.

The Pacific Northwest had always been drizzly, but once the World Shift happened, Seattle was lucky to see full sun for more than a handful of days during the summer. In winter, the downpours turned to heavy snow and ice. In fact, everything had changed since the World Shift, including the weather. The greenhouse effect and global warming? Gone with an angry wave of Gaia's hand. The pendulum had swung the other way and temperatures had grown colder in the north and hotter toward the equators. It was like Gaia had given the finger to humans and decided to shift the weather patterns according to her whims.

With a sigh, I zipped up my jacket and braced myself against the rising wind. I had patrols to make, rain or not. And the fact that I was wearing a pair of leather shorts didn't matter. I couldn't wear pants—it interfered with my magic. So I just had to suck up the autumn chill and deal with it.

I was about two miles away from my home when I reached the edge of the Sandspit.

The Sandspit was a two-hundred-acre vortex of wasteland, bordered by Darktown on the north and the Bogs to the west. Gaia's rampage had swept through with a vengeance. The magical storm she created had raged through every section of the land. A particularly nasty lightning strike had ripped apart this area of the city, and that lightning was infused with her anger.

When the bolt struck the train yards, it had

driven deep into the ground with a massive jolt of magic. *Poof*...in a blink, all the tracks and trains vaporized as the Sandspit formed. But while the area looked pretty much like a hill-and-valley stretch of dunes, it was far from being just a pile of sand. Rife with wild magic, the Spit was a dangerous place. At times odd creatures ventured out from shifting portals that opened from Seattle's World Tree, which was smack in the middle of the patch of magical dunes. Other times, a small whirlwind would spring up, spreading sand and random spells every which way. But no matter what was going on, you could count on it as being dangerous.

Over time, the Bogs had built up on the west side of the Sandspit. They were a dangerous, wild space of cold marsh, tangled trees, and quicksand. People who wandered in there often never came out, and nobody sent search parties looking for them.

To the east stood the Metalworks, the industrial district, but the majority of people who didn't have to work or live in the area avoided the Sandspit whenever possible.

Most people. My mother had traveled through it on her way home one night when she was pregnant with me and that's how I ended up a Theosian. She stumbled into a swirling pool of wild magic and in that brief time, the energy shifted something in my DNA and *boom*...one minor goddess coming up.

The Sandspit was partly enclosed by a tall chain-link fence to keep people from accidentally wandering through, but every time the Corp-Rats tried to barricade it entirely, the fence would mysteriously corrode or break or vanish, leaving the Sandspit accessible again. After a while, the Regent got the message and while the chain fence still stood, wide gates left access on all sides.

Standing near the edge, I cautiously looked around. I wasn't sure what had called me out yet, but I had learned never to ignore my gut. I shaded my eyes, trying to see through the gloom. Finally, bored and yet antsy, I slid down to sit on the ground, back against the fence, my sword across my legs. Whatever it was, I would wait it out for as long as I could. I sure as hell wasn't going to go poking around in there on my own. I'd rather sit here all night, if necessary.

Using whisper-speak, I asked, "Queet, are you with me?"

"I'm here." His voice echoed into my thoughts. Nobody else could hear him unless they were tuned into the spirit realm or he chose to make himself heard.

Relieved, I let out a long breath. Queet was usually nearby, even when I couldn't see him, but hearing his voice made me feel easier. I might complain about being connected in the head with a spirit guide, but truth was, he made my job—and my life—easier, even though neither of us liked being yoked together. Being a Theosian wasn't easy. At least, not for me. I was indentured to Hecate. Hecate, the Goddess of Dark Magic and the Crossroads. My magic was that of cold flame and moonlight, of ash and bone and death.

"Fury? Don't get too comfortable." Queet sounded concerned.

I tensed. "Do we have an outlier?" I tuned in and sure enough, my alarm bells began to ring as my Trace screen opened up.

"Yeah, an Abom."

At the same moment he spoke, the creepy-crawly feeling flared in my gut. Queet was right, an Abomination was near. *Well, hell.* That meant we were in for trouble unless we could head him off at the pass.

"Where is he? I just caught his Trace."

"He's on the north side of the Sandspit. He's headed back toward the center of Darktown. Fury, he's in-body."

An *in-body* Abom? They were usually rare. "Do you think he noticed my footprint?"

"I don't think he's made you. But Fury, Tommy-Tee is out on his corner tonight. Smack in the middle of the Abom's path."

Double hell. Tommy-Tee was a sitting duck. Hell, the poor guy could barely handle life, let alone take on an Abom. But fucked up or not, because of his musical bent, Tommy-Tee had enough energy to attract the creature's attention. It would drain him dry and toss the shell. And that wasn't acceptable. Down here in Darktown, we took care of our own, especially those who couldn't look after themselves.

I pushed to my feet. "Which direction? Guide me."

"If you head west along Industrial Drive, then swing a right into the first burrow-lane, then a left at Silverfish's stall, you'll be on his back."

Crap. That was near Jason's shop—Dream Wardens. And Up-Cakes, his sister's bakery.

"You'll have to use your *blur*, though, in order to catch up to him."

"That's why I wore these shoes, ghostling." I smiled in the darkness. It drove Queet nuts when I called him that, but I couldn't help myself. He was always so very serious that sometimes I just wanted to shake a smile or laugh out of him.

"Just go." Queet didn't like being a spirit guide—he had told me that time and again. But that was okay, because I didn't always like having him for one. Since we had to work together, though, we made the most of it. And truth was, if we had just been able to pal around? We would have gotten along fine. It was the bound-at-the-skull thing that was an issue.

As I headed toward the burrow-lane, the rain started. It pelted off me, giant stinging droplets that bounced off as I sped up my pace, swerving to skirt a massive pile of rubble. Darktown was full of ruins, buildings that hadn't survived the World Shift. Cleanup had stopped at the borders. Croix? Uptown? North Shore? Even Portside was nice and tidy, but in our district, we were left to cope with the decay. At least we weren't as bad off as the Tremble, though.

At top speed, I was a blur of motion—running about four times faster than any human. I came to the burrow-lane and skidded to the right, veering into the narrow passage. As I ran, I talked to Queet. Whisper-speak was easy on the lungs, a talent almost every Theosian possessed.

"Aboms almost always come in on the astral. I wonder what lured this one to cross over in-body."

"I don't know, but wrap your mind around the fact that this one is as corporeal as you are, and he's a bruiser, so be careful. He's likely to knock you for a loop unless you go about this right, Fury."

I always took Queet's warnings to heart. We might chafe at working together but he was smart. And when it came to Aboms—he knew what he was talking about.

Abominations were soul-eaters. They had no conscience when it came to their victims. But in-body? They were far worse. They'd been known to devour their victims down to the bone, as well as drain their souls, usually while the quarry was still alive and could feel it. When they came in-body, they often took on human form, but once they took hold of their victim, all bets were off and they reverted to their natural shape. Which was usually some sort of hideous beast.

At least I was armed. I'd tried stunners and several other weapons, but very little fazed these creatures but magic and brute force. And while magic was my forte, I carried three very important weapons—my sword, my dagger, and my whip.

Xan, my long, ornate sword, was razor sharp. She wasn't exactly legal, but down here, in Darktown? Nobody, not even the Devani, were going to put up a fuss. When Hecate had presented her to me, along with the matching dagger, she had given me the name of the sword. She sealed Xan into servitude for me, enhancing the sword's abilities to strike my opponents and to bite them deep and hard.

"There, make a left." Queet appeared in a flurry of mist next to me. Nobody else would recognize the mist for what it *really* was. That is, no one except another Theosian, magus, witch, or Psi. And right now, it felt good to know that somebody had my back, even a spirit guide.

I swung a hard left out of the burrow-lane, onto Sidewinder Street, the main street in Darktown. Up ahead and across the street was Dream Wardens, and the lights were still on. Next door, Up-Cakes was dark. In the center market, most of the stalls were closed, including Silverfish's Hemporium, but up ahead, on the corner, I could see the faint shape of someone playing guitar. *Tommy-Tee*. And headed his way, halfway between us, was the lurching figure of the Abom.

From the back, he *did* look like a bruiser. The Abom's current vehicle was six feet high, bald and brutish and wearing a pair of jeans and a leather jacket. That in itself was unusual. Mostly, when the Aboms came over in-body, they chose a Suit as their host, attempting to garner an edge via their three-pieces and shiny shoes. But whatever the case, the Abom was on the hunt and he was headed right for Tommy-Tee.

The Abomination's signal lit up my Trace with a neon frenzy. From where I was, I could smell the faint scent of char. They all reeked with it—an acrid scent of burning flesh and wood. My instincts kicked into high gear. Time to hunt and destroy. Hecate was leaning over my shoulder—I could feel her whispering to me through the dark of the moon, through the tattoo on my neck—triple snakes for the Triple Goddess—wound into an intricate pattern. Venomous images embodying my shadow magic.

I'd have a better chance of taking the Abom down if he didn't know I was coming, but it was only a matter of seconds before he picked up on me, and then my advantage would be long gone. And in *that* body? He wasn't going to be easy to handle. Not here, out in the open.

"Queet?"

"Here. What do you need?"

"He's big and he's strong. I need to meet him on the Crossroads."

"Fury, that's a big risk. You know what shifting over to the Crossroads does to you. The aftereffects are nasty. Honestly, are you telling me that you are willing to risk yourself for Tommy-Tee? Think about it."

"I don't have *time* to think about it. Look—he's fucking *huge*. He's at least a foot taller than I am, and the minute he hears me breathe, he'll turn. Then, I won't have a clear shot to his soul-hole. If I have to fight him here, it's going to be bad. *Real bad.* If I take him to the Crossroads, I'll have my full power there."

A half-beat. Then, "Go. Do what you need to. I'll contact Jason as soon as you cross over and meet you there."

I surged forward and within seconds, I raced past the Abom, past Tommy-Tee, and was standing in the middle of the intersection. Thank gods there was no traffic.

"Hey, freakshow! How about a real dinner?" I waved my hands and shouted at the bruiser, trying to get his attention.

Startled, I heard Tommy-Tee stumble over a chord as he lost his place in his song.

The Abomination turned my way. The next moment, he broke off stalking Tommy-Tee and made a beeline for me, darting into the road at breakneck speed.

I waited, biding my time, breath pent.

Tommy-Tee was too fried from years of being hooked on Opish to understand what was going on. He took a step toward the edge of the sidewalk.

"Queet, do something. Keep Tommy-Tee off the road."

Queet swept past—I could feel the gust—and he slammed into Tommy, knocking him back with the force of his currents. Having a spirit guide who could mimic a poltergeist was handy at times.

Tommy-Tee landed on his butt on the sidewalk and I took that moment to make my move. The Abom was almost within arm's range of me. I swept my arms up, clasping my hands together over my head. A flash radiated as I closed my eyes and focused on my destination. The street shifted and blurred, melting around us, as the world lurched and then—we were on the Crossroads.

Chapter 2

So, the Crossroads. A misty, fog-shrouded place where all worlds met. At the Crossroads, worlds merged and met, and possibilities multiplied.

Plenty of Elder Gods worked only from the Crossroads, and every one of them had his or her own space, including Papa Legba. From the beginning, I had thanked the Fates profusely that I wasn't bound to *him*. Strong and alluring, he was also deadly. The Greeks could be rough, but I remained grateful I had been thrown in their camp rather than sent the Santeria/Voodoo route. My path was steeped in death enough as it was.

I was standing on a barren intersection of three dirt roads, with endless fields stretching all three directions. Next to a low cauldron in the middle of the juncture stood a sign. I knew what it said. I'd been here before.

STAND AT THE CROSSROADS
STATE YOUR CLAIM
TO SEAL THE DEAL,
STRIKE THE FLAME.

I wasn't here to make a deal, so I ignored the little voice spurring me on to tempt the Fates. Nope, I was here to keep my nose clean and focus. I was here to send the Abomination back to where it came from and that's all I was going to do.

And there he was. Opposite me, near the edge of one of the fields. He looked confused, which gave me an advantage. I wasn't about to wait for the shock to wear off. I had to get behind him while I could. The one vulnerable place on Abominations who were in-body was their soul-hole, a spot at the back of their necks where they had infiltrated their host. Whoever had lived in this body was long gone, sucked dry by the Abom.

Queet appeared by my side. He was translucent, but on the Crossroads, I could see him clearly. He moved toward the left of the *Y*.

The Abom cocked his head, staring at him, looking more confused than ever, which wasn't surprising. Queet's energy signature packed a buttload of astral resonance. Which was all jargon, meaning Queet presented as a juicy morsel that would tempt any Abom out on the hunt for food. He'd make a tidy appetizer.

We waited to see if the Abom would be stupid enough to take the bait. Abominations generally fell in two categories. On rare occasions, we got a live wire, super smart. In those cases, it usually came down to a life or death match. Much more commonly, we got hold of the ones who were so focused on their hunger that it made them reckless. Queet was setting himself up as a target, giving me a better chance to slip around behind.

I forced myself to wait.

Patience. The Abom will move past you and you will attack. You know how to send them back to Pandoriam. You've done this before. Breathe... just breathe slow and soft and easy.

The waiting was hardest. Every time I thought it would get easier, but it never did. Spirits were bad, but Abominations were far worse. I'd dispatched dozens of these creatures over the years, but it never got any better. I was the best in the business, and still, the fear always scrabbled at my throat as I headed into the confrontation.

Come on, I thought. *Move. Go for it.*

The Abom paused, glancing at me. I slid my hand up to my neck, around which a golden pendant in the shape of an "F" hung, dotted with rubies. It, too, had been a gift from Hecate. She had given it to me when I turned twenty-one. I wrapped my fingers around it, feeling the power grow within the necklace.

Wait...breathe...breathe...

For a moment I thought he was going to ignore Queet and charge me, but then, Queet sent out a flare, his aura sparkling around him in a blaze of fire. That seemed to decide the Abom. He charged.

Poised to swing in behind him as he went past,

I began whispering the charm.

"Three roads meet, three roads divide.
Swept apart by Hecate's tide.
Dog and lion, snake and moon,
I summon forth Hecate's boon."

The power leaped from the necklace to my hand and I grasped the hilt of my sword, swinging the blade up and round as it blazed with a crimson light. I leaped behind the Abom, a blur of motion. Out here on the Crossroads, I was lightning fast and the powers of being bound to Hecate reverberated through me. If I could hit his soul-hole dead center with my blade, I could short-circuit him and send him packing back to Pandoriam.

Queet swirled into a tall vaporous funnel and swept toward him as I connected my sword with the base of his neck, hitting square in the center just below where his cervical spine connected to the skull.

The Abom let out a scream as a wild, twisting vortex of icy-cold flame flowed through me. The energy wracked my body even as I drove the blade into his soul-hole. A thousand pinpricks rattled my nerves and it was as though we froze, held in stasis by the force of the magic itself. Then, slowly, the magic began to weave its way over his body with a web of deep indigo sparks, creating a glowing fishnet to bind him up.

Hecate was riding me hard. She always knew when I was out calling on the Crossroads. She didn't question, merely reached out and touched the connection that bound us together. In that single touch, the magic flared higher and harder, and the Abom let out a screech that echoed through the barren Crossroads. Then in another fraction of a second, there was nothing left as he turned to ash. A gust of wind picked up the light feathers of the charred body and fluttered them away.

The breeze died as I stood, panting, my sword dragging beside me. My hands were a blistering lattice of welts. I felt like I'd grabbed hold of a live wire, shuddering under the weight of a million sparks racing through me. My ears rang and I could barely see anything beyond the flash of light that had temporarily blinded me. The only thing holding me up at that moment was the fact that I was on the Crossroads and not back home. But in the back of my mind, I knew I couldn't stay here long—it was dangerous to linger.

But I couldn't leave quite yet. As I turned, I knew who would be standing there. Sure enough, there she was. Hecate, wearing black leather pants and a crimson bustier. A crimson cape fluttered from her shoulders. Her hair cascaded down to her knees, jet black, and her eyes were the color of twilight. Across her forehead, she wore a circlet of three silver snakes, entwining to hold aloft a shimmering black moonstone cradled in a crescent moon. That symbol had been tattooed onto my neck, marking me as hers.

"Come see me tomorrow. There are worrisome things afoot. You're overdue for your monthly check-in, anyway."

I had expected the chiding. "I'm sorry. I've been..." But there was no way to end that sentence so it would excuse me. It didn't matter if I'd been sick, or tired, or just stubborn. Every month, every Theosian was bound to meet with their Elder God.

In Seattle, we met with them at the Peninsula of the Gods. I'd been punished before for breaking the rules. It occurred to me that the first time around had been bad enough, so maybe I didn't want to push it a second.

"Sure. What time?"

"I'll text you in the morning. Otherwise, you won't be able to remember after this. Meanwhile, I know you're hurting for cash, so I'll engineer a job for you. Take it. Beggars can't be choosers, and the networking you establish will help with what is coming down the road. That much old Pythia has allowed me to know." She paused. "The Oracle is in a testy mood lately."

Another pause and a frown. "Fury... You realize that I don't throw you willy-nilly into danger for fun. You are bound to me. All my Theosians are agents of divine justice and you all seek out the dangers of the world who seek to upset the balance."

I nodded. Hecate was harsh, but she wasn't unfair, and more than once, she had let me skip out or screw up on something that a number of the other Elder Gods would have punished me for. The one time she had taken me before Themis to be punished was the one time I tried to walk away from her. I had been fifteen. Hecate had no choice in the matter.

"Yes, Lady. I know."

"Good. Now, get off the Crossroads. You'll need help getting home. Queet, I know you're there. Show yourself."

Queet appeared, looking disgruntled. He disliked the Elder Gods even more than he disliked being a spirit guide. "Yes?"

"Help her get home safely, whatever it takes. And make sure she's awake by 8:00 a.m. tomorrow. She won't remember this very well, I'm guessing, given the extent of the magic that ran through her body, but she needs to be up and over to see me. Now, off before you both feel the effects from staying out here too long." And *blink*...she was gone.

Queet swept over to my side. He couldn't shore me up, I couldn't lean on his shoulder and let him help me home. But he forced me to stare into his eyes.

"Time to go home, Fury. Come on. You can do this. It's time to go back. I'll summon Jason the minute we hit the other side. He's not far, he won't take long to reach us."

I wavered, a wave of confusion washing over me. The Abom was gone. Hecate was gone. I couldn't stay here, but somehow, the opening to Seattle seemed lost in the mist. As I searched for it, Queet pointed it out. He reached inside my mind and flipped a switch, and suddenly I could see what I needed to do. Shaking, I followed the flicker of light—a flowing green arrow of energy was how I saw it—and the next moment, everything shifted and once again, I was standing in the middle of the street.

Solid ground felt too real to me, too substantial. My knees began to buckle. Queet was once again a misty vapor floating around me.

"Queet... Queet...?"

"Are you okay? Fury? I'm going for Jason." Queet's soft voice surrounded me. He couldn't do much except cushion my energy on the astral plane, but even that little bit helped. One step at a time, I struggled over to the sidewalk, forcing my feet to move. Every muscle in my body hurt so bad I could barely think. Every drop of energy I had in reserve had vanished.

Tommy-Tee was standing there, guitar in hand, staring at me. "Fury? You need help, man? You want some Opish?"

I shook my head. "No." My voice sounded like a croaking frog's. "I need to get home, Tommy. I don't know if I can make it by myself. I need help to get home."

Dropping to my hands and knees, I rested my head against the sidewalk. Being on the Crossroads always sapped me, leaving me a cold, whimpering mess. If I hadn't had to fight the Abom, I could have dragged my butt home, but the energy I had expended on the creature had wrung me dry and there was no top-off at the astral filling station before leaving.

Tommy-Tee put down his guitar and knelt

beside me, rubbing my back. I wanted to shake him off—any touch at this point was irritating, but I couldn't even do that. I whimpered as he muttered, obviously worried.

"Fury, are you okay? Where were you? What was that thing that was coming after me?"

I wanted to beg him to shut up. Even the distant rumble of traffic and the hum of the neon lights were too much for me to handle. But I could barely open my mouth, let alone speak. I managed to curl into a ball on the sidewalk, holding my head, and Tommy-Tee just sat beside me rubbing my back. He very kindly picked up my sword— ignoring the burns that must have hit his fingers as he touched it—and slid it back in the sheath hung over my shoulder.

I don't know how long I stayed that way—it couldn't have been more than five minutes—before I heard Jason's voice.

"Kae? Kae... Talk to me, Kaeleen."

I was having trouble focusing. A blur of two faces looked down at me. One, I knew, was Tommy-Tee. The other, I surmised, was Jason.

"Jason, man. Fury's fucked up. She needs to get home." When Tommy-Tee was worried, I knew I was bad off.

Jason. Thank gods it *was* Jason. "Help... please..." I managed to croak as I started to shiver in the chill of the night.

The next moment, I felt myself being swept up—I was in somebody's arms. I was coherent enough to know that it had to be Jason because Tommy-Tee could barely carry his guitar. The

Opish had eaten away at him so much over the years that physically, he wasn't even as strong as a feeble old man.

"Let's get you back home. Queet let me know what was happening."

I tried to nod and say yes, but it came out a garbled "Uh..."

"Queet, go ahead and unlock Fury's door. I know you can do that, so get a move on. I'm taking her home now." And we were moving. I closed my eyes, the swaying motion of Jason carrying me oddly comforting, but at the same time, I felt vaguely nauseated. He kept quiet, though, knowing too well how much sound affected me at this point. Then we were in a vehicle and it moved slowly but surely. It could have been a car or the Monotrain, for all I knew.

After a while, his voice cut through the fog again. "I'm going to carry you up the stairs now, Kae, so you may feel like you're being bumped around a little. I'm sorry in advance."

And up we went. The swaying became a series of jolts, but I managed to keep myself from crying even though every shudder felt like it was pummeling me with a sledgehammer. My muscles ached, my stomach was knotted, and I had the migraine from hell blowing up in my head. But then, it finally stopped and I heard the squeak of my door, and we were inside. A moment later and the movement stopped. I was on my bed—I could tell that much from the familiar feel of my comforter.

"I'm going to get your clothes off you now

and tuck you into bed. Queet said you were out on the Crossroads. Don't bother trying to answer—you don't have to. I know the smell of char. Abomination?"

"Mmm." I could manage that much now that I was home. My head was beginning to spin, though, and it wouldn't be long before I passed out.

"You have a message on your phone. Want me to read it and tell you what it is?"

My phone...a message...that's right, I always put it on mute when I went out hunting. "Mmm." Again, the one word I seemed to be able to master.

There was a brief silence, then Jason's hushed voice. "Fury, Hecate texted. She wanted to remind you that she's going to call you tomorrow morning."

I tried to say something. I tried to feel anything other than nauseated. But as the room began to swim for real, I gave up. I managed a "Wake me?" but before I could hear what Jason answered, a chasm opened up below me, and I went tumbling into the deep black void that claimed me every time I fought out on the Crossroads.

Chapter 3

Early morning brought with it the numbing chill of rain and wind. I had a mild hangover from being out on the Crossroads, but as usual, I woke early and managed to drive some of the pain out of my shoulders beneath the steaming shower spray. I dressed quickly—a burgundy corset, leather shorts, shiny black buckle-boots with chunky heels that laced up to my shins, and my leather jacket. I couldn't wear anything that might interfere with reaching for my whip.

Along my right leg, from mid-outer thigh, coiling down my leg to end right above my ankle, was the tattoo of a flaming whip. Only it was no mere tattoo. When I needed to, I merely slapped my hand against my thigh and the whip appeared in my hand, a coil of energy that took form when I needed it. Hecate had tattooed it there, herself, when I faced my mother's killer. I could never lose it. Nobody could ever steal it, for the astral weapon would vanish if anybody else ever tried to take hold of it. It was the perfect weapon.

Restless—the next day after being out on the Crossroads always left me at loose ends—I skirted the vendors setting out their wares for the day in the Market Square. The center of Darktown, the Market was where everybody gathered. In summer, on the few hot days we had, the kids would break open fire hydrants and dance under the spray of water, but now we were into early September and autumn had closed in fast and furious.

The play-girls were already leaning against light poles, eyeing the growing throng like so many vultures. Pickpockets were out looking for easy marks, and the Nancies paraded on display as if for an invisible beauty crown. And, of course, there were the bogeys, but they kept to themselves. As I passed by a small group of them gathered on the street corner they gave me a silent nod and I raised my hand in return greeting. Most of them came out of the Junk Yard, but the shadow men knew who I was and what I was capable of. I didn't bother them, they didn't bother me, and we left it at a nice little truce.

Moving through the cacophony of sound and movement, I blinked against the rising smoke of the food stalls. It blended with a hundred different perfumes, urine from the burrow-lanes, smog and exhaust, to create one exotic fragrance that permeated the streets of downtown Seattle.

I paused for a moment and leaned against the

side of a Moroccan restaurant. The smell of spicy couscous and lamb drifted out, and my mouth began to water. I hadn't eaten since lunch the day before, and that had only been a hot dog and a shake. The thought of stopping in for a quick breakfast crossed my mind, but then I nixed the thought. I was running low on cash, and I could always bum a muffin and coffee from Shevron at Up-Cakes.

Besides, Hecate would kick my ass if I didn't take her call when she rang. I promised myself that I would come back and pick up some of the lamb along with some apricot delight once I'd managed to find another job. I had almost run through the money from my last contract.

I gazed around the streets, scanning the crowd to make sure there weren't any Aboms around, but my Trace screen told me that the coast was clear for now. There had been an upswing in activity from the World Tree the past couple of months. While not all were Aboms, there were other creatures just as unwelcome and just as dangerous. Ker demons, for example. Three of them had crossed over a few days ago and vanished into the crowded city.

"Hey baby, how much for a go-round?"

Startled, I whirled to find myself facing a nondescript Suit. *Slummer.* He fingered his money clip in plain view, pegging him for an outlier. Anybody who lived in Darktown knew better than to flash cash around. His gaze darted nervously from me to the play-girls and Nancies lining the street. Most likely, he was afraid of being caught, but he shouldn't have worried. The sky-eyes seldom showed up in the Market during the day. Too many chances for somebody to try to take one down, and that was an expense the Devani didn't want to incur. They had learned the hard way to leave the streets in Darktown and the Trips to the bogeys. Nobody with any sense went into the Trips at night unless they lived there.

I glanced down at my outfit, wondering what about it screamed *hooker* to him. Yes, I was showing some skin, but not like the play-girls. But the dead giveaway should have been my sword, sheathed in the scabbard slung over my shoulder. Sex-for-sales didn't tend to carry large, ornate, prickly sharp blades when they were working. They were usually packing, yes, but not so obviously.

I brushed him off. "I'm not selling what you're looking for."

He tugged on his tie and cleared his throat. "You sure? I can pay—"

I stared at him coolly and then grabbed his collar, shoving him up against the wall, hard. The shadow of fear clouded his eyes as he realized just how strong I was. *Good.* He needed to learn a lesson before somebody *really* nasty got to him.

"You see my sword here?" I pointed to the hilt of my sword with one hand while holding him firm with the other.

"I thought it was a prop," he squeaked out.

"Trust me, it's not. I could cut you in half." I suddenly smelled urine and realized he had peed himself. "Are you afraid?"

He nodded.

I could have let go, but I wanted the lesson to sink in. "Then you're not entirely stupid. You *should* be afraid. But you're lucky that *I'm* the one you stumbled onto and not one of the bogeys. The shadow men don't like strangers, and *their* play-girls are usually armed with steely knives and bowie clips that they'll use without hesitation on the likes of you."

A tendril of Wandering Ivy reached out from the swath covering the side of the building, tapping him on the shoulder, and his eyes grew wider. He squirmed harder.

"Please, let me go. It's going to choke me."

"And that would break my heart *how*?" But I loosened my grip, letting his feet hit the ground again. I held firm to his collar, ignoring the tendril. I could tear it away if the ivy got pushy.

"While we're on the subject of stupidity, you might want to tuck your cash out of sight. You're in Darktown, for fuck's sake. Use your common sense. Daylight won't protect you here. Neither will the Devani. Meanwhile, there are plenty of thieves around here who wouldn't think twice about dragging your sorry ass into one of the burrow-lanes and snagging that windfall. Now, why don't you run on back to Croix or Uptown, or wherever it is you're from, and if you're still horny, call one of the sky-high girls. Don't come here again. Slumming's not a hobby for the weak of heart. Or for Suits."

I let go and he backed away, his face a mask of fear as I motioned for him to run along. He turned, scuttling off toward the Monotrain platform. He'd probably be safe enough without an escort but, for his sake, I hoped I had thrown a good scare into him. Next time, somebody bigger, badder, and meaner was going to find him first, and if it was a bogey, he wouldn't be nearly so generous.

Turning my attention back to the street, I crossed over to Prickle Street and headed toward Dream Wardens. The doors were unlocked and as I pushed through, a wave of asafoetida assailed my senses. The resin was pungent, but the smell made me feel at home.

Jason was bent over one of the workbenches. He glanced up at me, arching an eyebrow as his gaze slinked over my body.

Jason Aerie had wheat-colored hair that fell to his butt. He kept it braided most of the time, and his eyes were a brilliant green. He wasn't a pretty-boy, but he was striking, with a firm jaw and an aquiline nose. The fact that he was built didn't hurt, all muscled but not hulking. He usually wore snug jeans that hugged his butt, a long-sleeved sweater, and motorcycle boots made for actual use rather than looks.

It occurred to me that he was too handsome for his own good, or rather, for mine. Jason was engaged to a Corp-Rat named Eileen, an uncommon match, but there you had it. Sometimes opposites attracted. But they did have something in common—they were in the same Cast—hawk-shifter family. I didn't have much to talk about with her, other than the fact that we both cared about Jason. To be honest, I had harbored a mild crush on him for years. But since he was also one of the best friends I had, I made sure to keep any and all attraction under wraps. I wasn't into breaking up love affairs. Love was too rare to tamper with when you found it.

"Kae, how are you feeling this morning?" Jason was one of the few people who still called me by my name. Most people called me *Fury*, but Jason chose to help me remain connected to a time when I had just been Kaeleen Donovan, before my mother died and I had taken on the full mantle of divine demon hunter and dark moon witch.

"You don't want to know. Ugh, I had horrible dreams." I shrugged off the sheath holding my sword, propping it against one of the chairs, and slid out of my jacket. I still felt like I had been punched in the gut—another lovely side effect from being out on the Crossroads.

"You look like you lost a bet with a bottle of vodka." But the smile fell away as he realized I wasn't returning it. He wiped his hands on a cloth and stepped out from behind the counter.

I wandered over to a well-used sofa against the opposite wall. As I dropped onto the welcoming cushions, I leaned my head back. Every ache and pain running through my body began to clamor for attention and I realized I still wanted to sleep.

"So what's next?" he asked.

"I wait for Hecate to call. I'm not sure what's up, but she told me that there's something going on. At least I got the Abom." I grinned at him.

"And you did a good job of it, by the way you looked last night. Kae, I don't envy you," Jason said. "Honestly, I don't know how you manage to navigate through the minefield of being a Theosian. Especially running off-grid. How you remain...*you*...after you've faced some of the assignments you've been given confounds me. I don't know if I could do it."

"Facing my mother's murderer was harder than any Abomination I've had to kill." I held his gaze, feeling both jaded and very young at the same time.

"I know, kiddo. I remember."

Jason had taken me in from the time I was thirteen, after I had been forced to watch my mother die at the hands of a ruthless serial killer. He had given me a place to stay, fed me, sent me to school, and made sure I got my ass to my lessons with Hecate. Thirteen years later, when I was twenty-six, I tracked down my mother's murderer and cursed him for life. I had wanted to kill him, but Hecate had other plans. That night, I took the name *Fury*. It fit.

And Jason? He had never turned his back on me, and I would never turn my back on him.

"I'm not a kid anymore and you know it," I said softly. "I'm thirty now, and Hecate expects me to do what she asks. Failure is not an option, and there's no getting out of the gig when you're born one of the Theosians."

He laughed as he pushed himself off the sofa and returned to his work. "Kae, I'm a hawk-shifter. I'm two hundred and twenty-four years old. Minor goddess or not, you're still a kid to me. Get used to it." But he hesitated, and I felt his gaze lingering on me for a moment. Then he went back to his work.

"I have to finish making this spell powder. We're out and people will be coming in today looking for it. Apparently, it's Bonny Fae week."

"Oh, crap." The Bonny Fae came into Seattle from the Wild Wood twice a year. When they did, it seemed like every eligible man or woman in the city wanted to catch their attention. Dream Wardens sold a lot of love and lust spells during this time. The fact that potions and powders seldom worked on the Fae didn't seem to harm business. People believed what they wanted to believe.

"That means everybody and their brother's going to be walking around under a glamour spell, doesn't it?"

"Oh, it gets better. Not only are the Bonny Fae in town, but the Portside Festival begins tomorrow afternoon. I can use the extra manpower if you want to put in a few hours for me." He rolled his eyes, but I knew full well that Jason loved the pageants and festivals as much as the rest of us did. He just put on a good front of being world-weary.

"As long as I don't have to simper over Tam." I grinned at him. Tam O'Reilly was our techno-witch. He was as brilliant as they came, and he was one of the Bonny Fae. At the other end of the spectrum, we had Hans. The brawn of Dream Wardens, he was a Theosian like me, a motorcycle nut, and yoked to Thor. His girlfriend was in training to be a Valkyrie.

"Tam loves it and you know it. Anyway, don't you want to catch yourself a gorgeous husband?"

Now he was just goading me.

"When and *if* I look for a husband, my hunt won't be cloaked under a spell or illusion. There's only one reason to get married—if the couple can't keep their hands off each other. And even then, I'd think twice. From what I have seen, most marriages aren't destined to end well." I didn't add that I had noticed that while Jason was engaged, he and Eileen hadn't set the date yet, and they seemed in no hurry to do so.

"Well, most marriages that actually work are usually based on some sort of economic incentive." He glanced at the clock. "You should call Hecate. She'll be waiting."

"She said she'd call," I muttered, but I pulled out my phone. I texted her that I was awake and up, but there had been no answer as of yet. "She knows I'm ready when she is. Until I hear from her, put me to work."

Even as I was speaking, the shop door opened and three young women wandered in. They were giggling and dressed in Lamar's—one of the trendiest designers, whose unmistakable style was cropping up all over town. That alone pegged them as outliers to Darktown. Almost nobody who lived south of Croix had the money to buy high-end

Jason was still tied up with finishing the spell powder, so I approached them, looking forward to helping them as much as a dentist's appointment.

"May I help you find something?"

The center one—a blond bombshell—blushed. "We're looking for..."

I *knew* what they were looking for. "Let me

guess. You heard the Bonny Fae are in town and you're looking for something to make yourself more attractive so you'll catch their eye?"

Jason had just finished, and now he cleared his throat. As I glanced at him, he scowled. I let out a sigh and plastered on a smile.

"Perhaps you'll allow me to show you something in a glamour spell?"

Inwardly, I cringed, but I was a pretty good actress when need be. I had no problem helping people who genuinely needed help. In fact, I was more than willing to go the extra mile, especially if they were looking for protection spells or healing magic. But dabblers annoyed me.

Jason and I had argued the point over and over. His stance was that he was here to serve, not to judge. But I knew damned well that he felt the same way I did. He was just better at hiding it.

The girl bit her lip. "Yes, if it's not too much trouble."

I sucked in a deep breath and let it out slowly. "No trouble at all. Please excuse my churlishness. I had a late night and very little sleep." I gave her a tired smile and she relaxed.

They followed me over to the other counter. I set out several options—all of which Jason had finished making the night before. He usually sold several thousand spells of one sort or another during Bonny Fae week.

"We have scrolls, but scrolls are better if you are already familiar with magic. Should I assume you aren't?" I smiled to take the potential insult out of my voice.

The girls nodded. Their spokeswoman gave a little shrug. "We're students at University Hall. I'm majoring in business, Cindy is studying home management, and Alisa studies social dynamics. We don't have much time for extracurricular activities."

I glanced over at Jason, who was obviously listening in. He cringed at the word "extracurricular" but merely gave me a nod of encouragement. As much as I wanted to tell them to go back to the university and find themselves husbands as quick as they could because they were probably going to need them, I restrained myself.

"This might work better." I set out three little bottles of oil. They were decorative and looked like cut crystal, but were actually just glass. During Bonny Fae week, Jason could charge three times what he normally did for them, at half the cost.

"This is glamour oil. You dab a drop on your pulse points before you go out. We don't guarantee it will attract the person you're looking for, but it *will* add to your personal magnetism and charisma. Though I doubt if any of you need much help."

Jason was right. A smile went a long ways, and so did a compliment. In the end, not only did they each buy a bottle of the oil, but I was able to steer them to music and tarot cards and blank journals. In other words: anything they couldn't screw up too much. As soon as they shuffled out the door, I groaned and dropped on the stool behind the counter. The shop was momentarily empty.

"I *really* hate Bonny Fae week. Portside

Festival is bad enough, but at least the shoppers aren't looking for ways to manipulate somebody into marrying them. Do these girls even realize *what* it's like to marry outside their race? Humans do *not* live in the same world as the Fae, regardless of how glamorous the tabloids make it sound."

"You're preaching to the choir, sugar. But there's not much I can do about it. And if *I* don't sell it to them, somebody else is going to. I might as well make money *and* ensure they get quality products." Jason paused as his phone rang.

As he moved away to answer it, I glanced over at Hans. He had come in while I was helping the girls. "What's your opinion? Should we really be selling these girls love potions?"

Hans shrugged. "They're adults. If they don't know what they're getting into, then it's their own fault for not doing the proper research. And really, is it any of our business what they want to do with their lives? That's one thing you need to learn, Fury. You can't make life choices for everybody. When you think someone's making a mistake, sometimes you just have to let them burn their fingers."

"He's right," Tam said from behind me as he emerged from his computer cave—aka the break room.

"You're Bonny Fae. What's your take on this?"

Tam ran on a moral scale a lot more ambiguous than Jason's. His kind had emerged out of the woodlands after the Weather Wars and after the World Shift. I had no idea if they had entered via the World Tree or if they had always been around, and I doubted if there was anybody alive who knew. Except, perhaps, the gods.

"The Bonny Fae come to town looking for mates to keep the bloodline from growing too inbred. Since Fae blood breeds true, and trumps human blood, it doesn't matter whether the mother or father is human. As long as one parent carries the Bonny Fae genes, all children will carry them and breed true."

"Do most of the marriages last?" I still had my doubts. Moving into a different culture was hard enough, but to marry into a people who weren't even your species seemed an uphill battle.

"I'd say about a third of the marriages actually work out. If they don't, the union is dissolved, but all children stay within our realm. We free those spouses who choose to leave and charm them so they won't mourn the loss. Most of the failures are due to the human partner missing their old life. Life in Briarwood isn't for everyone."

"It's very different, isn't it?" I had no clue how the Fae actually lived, but I had a feeling it wasn't anything like life in the city.

"Very. Also, just so you're aware, we can see right through glamour spells so all the magic in the world isn't going to do anybody any good if we don't find them suitable. That's a fact Jason better hope that nobody figures out. It would put a deep dent into business." With a faint wink, Tam headed to the counter and handed Jason the invoice for his morning's service call.

Jason scanned the paper, putting his phone away. As he scribbled his initials on the paper, he absently said, "Eileen can't make it today, which is just as well. I don't think I have time for lunch. So how did the session go?"

"About as good as you would hope. The woman has a number of *catchalls* attached to her. I removed as many as I could, but she's going to need a couple more sessions, and then she's going to have to learn how to ward against them. I don't foresee that going well, given she lives in a nest of toxic people. Fury, you might cadge a job out of her by clearing her house. If you can clean out the energy there, she might have a chance to set up boundaries and wards."

"Give me her number and I'll call her," I said as my phone signaled a text message. I pulled it out and glanced at the screen. *Hecate.*

GET YOUR ASS OVER HERE NOW.

I glanced over at Jason, grimacing. "I just got summoned. I think she's pissed. I just hope I'm not the cause of it. I'd better get it over with."

Jason nodded. "Let me know how it goes. If you have the time, I think I can book you a couple readings for this afternoon. And Kae—" He paused, then flashed me a smile. "Good luck."

"Thanks. I think I'm going to need it. Something has her in a snit." I headed out the door, suddenly wishing for a flurry of young women looking for husbands to give me an excuse to avoid the coming meeting.

Chapter 4

Seattle occupied a wide spot on the inlet, sprawling between the mountains and the Pacific Sound, which came in off the ocean. Unlike a number of cities around the world, Seattle had managed to stand during the Weather Wars. Even though it had taken a beating, over the centuries it had rebounded.

The city planners wanted to preserve the delicate balance that had evolved. Smooth metal and glass met marble and fresco in a mashup of futuristic and ancient design—at least in the upper-crust areas. Darktown was still filled with the rubble that had come in on Gaia's wrath and had been written off, along with the Trips, the Sandspit, the Junk Yard, and the Bogs.

But even through the rubble, Seattle—like other world cities of its type: New London, Elder Moon, Bifrost, Paris, and Black Forest—

had become a thriving center of culture and community.

When I needed to meet with Hecate, I headed toward the Peninsula of the Gods, better known as the *PotG*.

The Peninsula of the Gods was located near the southwestern edge of the inlet, primarily to assuage the priests who worshipped the water deities. The planners were smart. The placement also tended to keep any magical pyrotechnics away from the central city, should neighboring temples get into a skirmish. Pantheons were grouped to avoid conflict. As a proverb went, *When dealing with the gods, one deals with danger*. The Convocation of Gods had done their best to iron out treaties and codes of conduct among themselves.

The PotG occupied several miles of paved land rectangular in shape and tiered on all sides like rice paddies. Each temple had green space around it for gardens. The entire sector reminded me of a series of mini-parks surrounding gleaming structures. Or at least, most of the temples gleamed. Some were formed of marble, others carved from giant blocks of granite, others were chrome and glass, but they all housed the emissaries of the gods.

The tiers were wide and steep, but flight after flight of staircases were interspersed between the temples, descending through the tiers. Spacious moving sidewalks ran in long ovals, circling each tier. On all four sides of the Peninsula of the Gods, mini-malls containing food courts, restrooms, and elevators offered supplicants a place to eat, rest, and access—an important factor for those who couldn't manage the stairs.

At the bottom, a center pond caught the runoff from rain that trickled down through gutters along the stairwells. Pumps had been installed and during rainy season, the excess could be siphoned off to avoid flooding. The water was routed to chambers where it was recycled into use for city parks.

I passed by the Temple Valhalla. A group of priests brawled on the lawn. Chances were it was battle practice. They kept in top shape and, though they drank themselves under the table on a regular basis, they were a good group. Because of Hans, we had been invited to more feast days than I could count. I had staggered away from the Peninsula of the Gods far too many times after a night partying with the Viking wonders.

Naós ton Theón, the temple of the Grecian gods, was located on a middle tier, near an elevator landing. Though I usually took the stairs, I was still sore. I decided to give myself a break and ride down. I didn't want to strain myself on the steps.

"Tier Three," I said when the elevator asked for my destination. I leaned against the side of the car, the steel cooling my forehead. I was wearier than I realized. Usually I could weather a long day followed by a long night, but the Crossroads had left me drained. The ride was short, but by the time the doors opened all I wanted to do was go home and fall back into bed.

"You with me, Queet?" I hadn't heard from

him since last night.

A shift, then a whirling sparkle racing by told me that he was around. "Ready as I'll ever be. She summoned me, too. Said I needed to hear what she had to say."

"Hmm...this should prove interesting."

Naós ton Theón was to the right, about half a block down the path. I passed the Coliseum, where the Roman gods hung out. A long line at the door caught my attention, but then I remembered that today was Saturday, and there was some sort of festival to Saturn going on.

Working my way around the crowds, I continued along the broad city street. Each tier had a railing to prevent people from falling—or being pushed—over the edge and as I walked along on the narrow sidewalk to the outside of the moving walkway, I stopped to peer over the side at the fountain below. A chill wind blew by and I inhaled the scent of brine and ocean water. It smelled like home. Really, when I thought about it, the Peninsula of the Gods was the one place I actually felt like I belonged.

Up ahead, Naós ton Theón gleamed against the sun. Built of cool marble, it had gray veins running through the stone, giving it a luxurious, mottled look. The Temple rose four stories into the air. As I ascended the steps, forgoing the moving ramp, it struck me just how different life had to be now compared to when the gods were first worshipped. Some days, I wondered what it would have been like, belonging to Hecate back in the time when Greece first rose to prominence, but

I never really went anywhere with the thought. I liked modern life, even though I was living in the squalid part of the city.

At the entrance to the Temple I got in line at the M&M detector. *Metal and magic*. There was always the danger some zealot from another pantheon would come crashing through, hell bent on creating trouble. The priest manning the detector motioned to the scan board in front of him.

"Left hand, please."

I placed my left hand on the flat screen. My chip would work on most scan boards, at least initially, but if they tried to track me, they'd find the altered code and that would be trouble. But the temples were good about never misusing their technology. It was the government that fell down on the job.

A moment later it beeped, bringing up information on his monitor. "Kaeleen Donovan, aka Fury. Theosian, aligned with Hecate. Weapons?"

I slid my sheath off of my back and handed him the sword, then pointed to my left thigh. He withdrew Xan from her sheath while the other priest unsnapped the thigh band and withdrew my dagger, examining it. His hand brushed my bare skin, but he was a professional and there was nothing about the touch that made me uncomfortable. The guardian priests were well-trained.

They scanned both blades.

"Please step through the detector."

I walked beneath the archway. A light flashed green.

"I'm not picking up any hidden charms. Do you have any magic to declare?"

Which meant, in layman's terms, was I packing anything that could be hidden from the detector? If I lied and they found out, I'd be banned. I felt in my pockets to make certain that I hadn't inadvertently brought any charms along.

"Nope."

"You can go through." He handed my sword and dagger back to me. I slid them back into their sheaths and he waved me on.

As I headed toward the elevator, I heard him whisper to his coworker.

"That's *Fury*," he said in a low voice. "Hecate's favorite."

I couldn't hear what the other guard replied as I crossed the hall to the elevator and punched the button. But if I was Hecate's favorite, it was news to me.

The great hall of Naós ton Theón gleamed in shades of ivory and gold. Statues of the gods lined the hall, a bench beside each one for supplicants to sit and meditate.

Each god had their own chamber, complete with offering font and gallery. The main gallery was used for large gatherings and holidays. Draperies embroidered in ivory and gold sectioned off areas of the main hall, sweeping down from the walls, tied back with golden tassels. The temple seemed fairly empty, but here and there a supplicant sat near one of the statues. A woman was weeping next to Hera's statue. By the gray shawl draped around her shoulder, I pegged her for a recent widow. Either that, or she had lost a child.

The elevator doors opened, and, as I entered the car, I silently wished her peace of mind. I knew what it was like to lose someone. You never fully got over it. As the doors shut, I flashed back to events that I tried to leave in the past, but never fully went away.

I was thirteen, and it was a chill winter night. My mother had taken me to a factory party with her. It was near Solstice and the Metalworks, where she held a job for ViCad Corp, threw a huge holiday party for all the workers and their families every winter, complete with a buffet, pageantry, and games. When my father was alive, we went as a family, given he had also worked for ViCad. But now, it was just my mother and me.

It was icy cold, with six inches of snow on the ground, and we were waiting at a Monotrain platform. But the train had broken down—the trains back to the Trips, where we lived, always had problems any time an ice storm hit. The readerboard flashed that it would be another hour before it arrived.

"We can't just stand here. We'll walk." Marlene, my mother, glanced up at the sky. The storm had lifted, and stars twinkled down at us through the icy night.

I didn't want to walk but kept my mouth shut. Marlene did her best to keep our lives together, even after my father died from blue-lung disease. ViCad was known for its poor health practices for its workers, but times were rough and jobs scarce, so neither one of my parents objected. And the fact that I was a Theosian brought in a little extra cash. ViCad had a vested interest in keeping the parents of Theosians employed, hoping at some point to use our powers.

She crossed her arms, tucking her hands under her armpits as we picked our way through the frozen slush and ice. "Damn, it's cold out here." Her breath hung in the air, freezing into vapor.

I was cold, too, but she had managed to buy me a new coat and a hat, and my boots were new, so I wasn't going to complain. It was the end of the month and food was scarce until payday, but the party had offered a good chance to fill up our pockets with finger foods to tide us over until her next check. I had at least ten biscuits, three apples, and a half-dozen pastries hiding out in my backpack.

I stomped my feet as we stopped by a lamp post to catch our breath.

She flashed me a rueful look, her teeth chattering. "I'm sorry, honey. I just don't want to chance freezing if we stayed at the platform and the next train didn't come either. I can't afford a cab. We'll try another Monotrain platform when we make it to Darktown."

I shrugged. "Whatever. I'm cold but it's okay. I've been colder. I can walk if you can."

"Thank you for being such a good sport. Did you enjoy the party?" Marlene beamed at me.

It seemed important to her, so I nodded. "Yeah, good food. It was pretty." The decorations had been a muted glow of gold and silver and red against the walls, and the tree had looked real enough to me. Nobody ever cut down trees for decorations anymore. Gaia had put an end to that along with a number of other activities.

"I promise, we'll be home soon and I'll heat up some soup and we'll curl up and watch a late movie. I have the day off tomorrow."

Marlene wrapped her arm around my shoulders and I leaned against her. I loved her, and though she wasn't ever fully sure how to cope with having a daughter who was a Theosian, she did her best. When my father had died of blue-lung disease when I was five, she picked up the pieces as best as she could and shouldered on for the both of us.

"I wish Terry was here," she said softly, staring up at the sky. "He always loved the holidays."

I gave her an absent nod. I didn't like thinking about my father. His death was ugly, and I hated the coughing and hacking up dark blue mucous—one of the main symptoms of the magically induced lung disease. He had taken a shortcut through the Sandspit one too many times. So I had taken to telling people that he had been a soldier, killed in a faraway war.

Just then a car pulled up. Marlene leaned down to peek in the window. A moment later, she turned back. "He says he can give us a ride. What do you think?"

I frowned, closing my eyes. A dark shadow hung over the car and it chilled me to the bone. "No. I don't want to get in."

Marlene nodded. She didn't fully understand my powers, but she didn't question them, either. She turned away from the car, but the door slammed open against her back, knocking her to the sidewalk. She landed with a hard thud. A man scrambled out before I could reach her. He scooped her up and shoved her in the back seat as I was across the sidewalk in a blur, slamming against him. But he was too big and burly for me to unbalance, even though I was a Theosian and already stronger than most of my classmates.

"You want to come, too, little one?" he said in a low voice, gripping my wrist with one hand. He lifted me up and tossed me in with my mother as if I were a bag of old clothes. I landed on top of her and rolled away, trying not to hurt her.

The next moment, the door slammed shut and he slid into the front seat. I started to scream, but with the windows closed, I realized nobody could hear me. At this time of night, there was almost no traffic down in the Metalworks.

"Mom? Mom!" I turned my attention to my mother, trying to wake her up, but either he had hit her really hard or he had managed to drug her when I wasn't looking, because she wasn't coming around. At that moment, he flipped a switch and a window rose between the front and back seats.

Unable to wake Marlene, I tried the doors again, but the handles had been removed. The car had been retrofitted so that the backseat was basically a holding tank.

I closed my eyes, trying to summon Hecate, but nothing happened. There was no spark when I reached for it. Next, I tried to sense my mother's spirit, but again—nothing. *An anti-magic zone.*

Cursing, I rummaged through my backpack, looking for something hard enough to break the window. No luck. But then I remembered my mother carried a small hammer in her purse. It was a multi-tool that she carried because of her job. I grabbed her purse, found the tool, and began to pound on the side windows.

Four blows later, I realized the glass was shatterproof, so I started working on the window separating us from the driver.

He glanced in the rearview mirror, scowling, and I realized he was actually driving the car—it wasn't an automatic. Very few people bothered to learn how to pilot machinery anymore. He casually flipped a switch and his growling voice filtered into the backseat.

"Put it away, girl. That won't do you any good. Just sit back and enjoy the ride." At that point, he flashed me a sick smile as we turned down a dark street on the outskirts of Darktown. Crap. We were headed toward the Junk Yard.

The Junk Yard.

A huge, gated enclosure that ran twenty blocks long by twenty blocks wide, the walls were made of reinforced steel. In the distant past, the Junk Yard had been used to corral refugees from the South American Mas-Lian jungle. They had fled from

Carpaxia, a corporatocracy determined to grab as much land as they could.

The refugees were Jagulins, a shape-shifting race with the ability to shift into big cats. As the armies of Carpaxia swept through their country, razing their forests to use for agriculture, the Jagulins fled to any country that would take them. But the Regent of Seattle had made one big mistake. The steel walls didn't set well with the Jagulins. They were uncomfortable enclosed by concrete and metal, and soon, they had moved on to other places, leaving the compound empty.

The city sold off their Junk Yard apartments, touting the "gated community" aspect of the area. But what they failed to foresee was the fact that the UnderCult had been looking for a place to hive together for a long time. The Junk Yard began to fill up with thugs, drug lords, dark magicians, and mercenaries, the area taking on a life of its own. By then, the Regent had to decide whether to demolish the fortress or leave it stand. The cost was high either way.

So the Junk Yard stood. As I grew older, I began to realize that leaving it standing was a way for the city council to keep an eye on the groups they were afraid of.

The car eased between the barbed-wire gates that were open from sundown to sunup, turning right at the first street. I clutched the multi-tool, opening up the one actual blade it had. It wasn't much, but it was better than nothing. The driver pulled into a burrow-lane, jumped out of the car, and quickly slammed the door, locking it remotely.

I struggled, trying to smash the window again, but then a soft hiss echoed through the car as gas began to pour out of the vents. The next thing I knew, the world went black.

I woke up to find myself tied to a chair in what appeared to be a dusty basement, lit by a single bulb in the center of the ceiling. My bag was on the ground next to me. My mother was naked on a table, unconscious and restrained. The man was standing over her.

He wore a shiny apron and gloves over dirty jeans, and looked to be bare-chested. I tried to memorize what he looked like. The scars on his head looked like they had been inflicted from a brand, probably a prison brand. Goggles rested on the top of his head, and in one hand he held a scalpel. The dim light glittered off the blade.

"What do you want?" I knew better than beg him to let her go. There was no mercy in those glittering and cruel eyes.

He traced my mother's bare breasts with his finger, smiling faintly, and bile rose in my throat. I wanted to slap him, to smack him away from her. Without looking up, he said, "I'm going to give your mother a lesson she'll never forget." And then he glanced over at me, a twisted grin on his face. "And lucky girl, you get to watch every thing that I do."

My mother stirred. He slapped her face, hard.

"Kaeleen? Kae?" Her voice was thick. He had

drugged her, all right. "Where's my daughter?" Panic filled her voice as she struggled against the restraints.

"I'm all right. I'm over here." I wanted her to hear me, to know I was okay.

"Shut up, bitch." He pinched her nipple so hard she screamed. "I'm going to clean you up, you dirty slut. And then I'm going to tend to your little girl. When I'm done with her, I'll give her the same treatment I'm about to give you."

He clicked a remote and turned on a classical violin piece. Then, covering his eyes with the goggles, he brought the scalpel down and the blood sprayed. As my mother screamed, a red mist began to rise, cloaking my vision. Everything slowed down, the world shining through a crimson filter. As her screams filled my ears, he turned up the music to drown out her screams.

Furious beyond anything I had ever felt, I let out one long shriek, screaming for Hecate.

I woke up, lying on the sidewalk in front of a magic shop. A tall man I recognized as a friend of my mother's was staring down at me, a horrified look on his face. Jason knelt and gathered me in his arms. He carried me into the shop, where I passed out again.

The next time I woke up, I was in a bed, with Jason's sister watching over me.

"Mom?" I knew the answer already, but I needed to hear her say it, to know that it was real.

"We found your mother, sweetie," Shevron said. The heartbreak in her voice said everything I needed to know.

I struggled to sit up, squinting. My entire body felt numb. I glanced around and saw my bag on a chair near Shevron, along with my mother's purse. Then reality hit me in the gut. I leaned over the edge of the bed and threw up.

Shevron held my shoulders until the foam and vomit had vacated my stomach, and then as she wiped my mouth and gave me a drink to rinse, I passed out again.

Later that day, I found out that someone had found my mother's body in a gutter. It was charred to a crisp. The Devani's report noted a fire reported in the Junk Yard but the bogeys took care of their own problems and no official response was mounted. Shevron called in a doctor, but I was unhurt—physically.

Marlene's name was added to the list of the Carver's victims. There were twenty names on the list, too many to ignore. But Seattle was a big city and nobody could seem to find him. Jason wouldn't let me go to the authorities to tell them my story. He warned me that they would take me away and that the Devani would control my every move from then on.

So I kept quiet. Jason took me in and enrolled me in a school in Darktown. Nobody ever made the connection. Tam extricated my chips from the back of my neck and he managed to reprogram them. They retained my name, but my ID number was different and he programmed in a different background. He also negated the tracking system. It was as though the old Kaeleen Donovan had vanished, as far as the government was concerned.

I never knew how I escaped the Carver and the Junk Yard, nor how I managed to land on Jason's doorstep. It was a black area that I preferred to leave untouched. It would be another thirteen years before I saw the Carver again. And by that time, I was itching to face him.

Chapter 5

Hecate's office was on the third floor. She usually met with me once a month, more often when she assigned me to a case, but I was overdue this time. Truth was, sometimes I rebelled just to feel like I had a say in my own life.

"You with me, Queet?"

"Yeah, I'm still here. I'd rather not be, you know."

"I know, I know. Hush up." Queet got on my nerves, but he had just as little say in his destiny as I did in mine, and I didn't blame him for being churlish. It was one thing to be pushed around when you were alive, but to find yourself conscripted into service after you were dead? Not so fun.

I pushed through the double glass doors, striding into the reception room. Coralie, a young woman with golden hair and wearing a white one-shouldered dress, sat behind the desk. She looked up as I slowed my pace and crossed to stand in front of her.

"Fury, hello. Are you here to see Hecate? Hi, Queet." She stared to my right, and I noticed that a misty form was standing beside me. Here, in the heart of the gods, spirits couldn't hide themselves.

"*Uh huh*. Hi, yourself." Queet's voice echoed in the room.

Ignoring him, I leaned forward, glancing at the screen. "Yeah. She told me to get my ass over here, so I figure it's important."

Coralie tapped my name into a computer and looked at the screen. She turned to me with a broad smile, the kind of smile that says *I've done this a thousand times today and I'm getting tired of it*. "She's expecting you. I'll let her know that you've arrived. If you'll take a seat, please." She gestured toward the waiting area.

I eased myself into an overstuffed armchair, crossing my legs. Hecate would let me stew as long as she wanted to. I had learned early on that "Hurry up and wait" was a fact of life in service to the gods.

The office was decked out in gold and pink and ivory, the soft gold carpet plush under my feet. The walls were pale, a muted rose, and the waiting area resembled nothing less than a high-priced salon. I wouldn't have been at all surprised to hear soft wet-dream music playing in the background, but instead there was the soft whir of air-conditioning.

I leaned my head back against the chair, closing my eyes. I wanted nothing more than to take a nap, but it wouldn't be seemly to nod off while I was waiting for one of the Elder Gods. Even though I was dreading the upcoming meeting, I relaxed into the cushions. Ten minutes later, I was having trouble keeping my eyes open. I yawned, about to get myself a drink of water, when Coralie suddenly looked up.

"Hecate will see you now. You too, Queet. You remember where her office is?"

I let out a sigh. "I remember. You don't need to direct me."

I slugged back the water, then headed around the corner and down the hall. At the first intersection, I took a right. Her office was at the end of the corridor, next to those of the Fates. She worked with them off and on.

Hecate was the Goddess of the Crossroads, the Mistress of Dark Magic, the Mother of Phantoms. She ruled in the shadows. She also watched over the oppressed and those on the fringe. Most of us who lived in Darktown fit that category, when I thought about it.

I stopped at the last door on the left, knocked once, and then entered the room. Queet followed in a swirl of mist.

Hecate's office always surprised me. Before I met her, I would have expected to find her office dark and filled with gloom and doom, cobwebs and cauldrons. Instead, the walls were pale ivory, the carpeting dark blue, the leather furniture was antique white, and the desk—a rich, lustrous pecan. A series of pastoral landscapes decorated the walls. Thriving plants filled the room with oxygen, smelling very deep and green and woodsy. Opposite her desk, in a wall case, Hecate displayed her swords and sickles. I admired the blades every time I showed up for a meeting. I loved blades, actually, and in addition to the ones I used in her service, I had a tidy little collection stashed in my apartment.

Hecate herself was another matter. No gloomy robes for her. Today, her hair was fashioned into an upswept chignon with braids dangling from the center. She was wearing her usual black leather pants. But her bustier was plum with white polka dots, and over the top, she wore a black leather blazer.

I knelt in front of her, inclining my head to touch the floor. "My Lady of the Dark Moon."

"For fuck's sake, stifle it. Get up. You know I don't like groveling." She was sitting on the edge of her desk, staring at me with pursed lips. She didn't look happy, but at least she didn't look like she was out for blood.

"So. First, you did a good job on the Abomination last night. I'm very pleased by how you are faring in that department." The sudden praise shocked me. Hecate wasn't given to easy compliments. As if to prove my point, she added, "You look like something the cats dragged in. Don't you ever sleep?"

"You know what the Crossroads do to me. *Every* time." I always seemed to arrive after a rough night. I wasn't sure why, but that was just the way things seemed to play out. I took a seat on the sofa opposite her desk.

"Yes...well...make use of this." Hecate handed me a box filled with chocolates. "Zeus was in a good mood and he decided to give everyone gifts. It's not a good idea to admit that you don't like chocolate when the *god of the realm* decides you should."

I gazed at the box warily. Five pounds of exquisite chocolate, by the looks of it, but I was cautious. Zeus's gifts were tricky. "They aren't cursed, are they? I mean, he's not going to show up in my bedroom in the middle of the night and try to play footsie, is he?"

At that, Hecate slapped her leg and laughed. "Oh, Fury, I do love your sense of humor. But no, I wouldn't worry if I were you. Hera keeps pretty close tabs on him lately. She's not thrilled about the influx of Theosians into the pantheon, all those lovely young women who have joined Olympus as minor goddesses. But no matter, I doubt he would try to bed you anyway. Zeus tends to like his women a little more...*pliable*...than you. All I ask is that you put the box in a bag when you carry it out. Actually, I have a shopping bag you can use. I just don't want it to get back to him that I gave them away."

I accepted the box and popped one in my mouth. The exquisite flavor of melting chocolate combined with raspberry filling exploded on my tongue, and I let out a sigh of contentment.

Hecate just stared at me, shaking her head. "I think I could bribe you to do anything as long as I gave you enough chocolate. All right, tell me about the Abom."

Fueled by the chocolate and the realization that she was actually in a decent mood, I told her exactly what happened. "I picked up his Trace when I was about two blocks from the Sandspit. He came in off the World Tree—I'm fairly sure he hadn't been here too long before I found him. He was hungry and went for Tommy-Tee. That's when I took him over to the Crossroads. He was so big I didn't think I could handle him on this plane."

"I see. Well, good enough on that. Have you noticed that there seems to be an influx of Abominations lately?"

I had an answer for that question, too. "Yeah, I have. We generally get two or three a month, but so far, I've taken out seven in the past three weeks."

"That's what I thought." She frowned. "Keep an eye on things and let me know how many come through over the next two weeks. But that isn't why I called you here today. We have a bigger problem, but you'll have to wait a moment. I forgot to bring one of my files in with me." And with that, she quickly exited the office, shutting the door behind her.

I relaxed, stretching my legs out to stare at the tips of my boots. I still felt bruised on the inside from being out on the Crossroads, but it would fade.

"Nice boots," Queet suddenly shouted at me. Or rather, it felt like shouting because he was projecting his thoughts into mine, and the communication was amplified, given where we were.

"Damn it, Queet, don't shout at me. You nearly broke my eardrums." Relenting, I murmured, "Thanks. I found them in a penny-store."

I turned my leg to the side and stared at the whip trailing down to the top of the boots right above my ankle. Like my blades, that too had been a gift from Hecate.

The day I turned twenty-one, she had taken the tattoo gun to me herself, as a rite of passage. I had never experienced physical pain like that before or since. And there it was, a weapon that I could never lose. If someone yanked it out of my hand, it would burn their fingers and appear back on my leg. By the same token, I couldn't wear pants anymore without losing access to it, so I mostly wore shorts and sometimes, a skirt, which made for some cold winters. But I had found that a long cape helped keep the chill at bay without impeding my movement too much.

I popped another chocolate in my mouth and peppermint oozed out on my tongue. Closing my eyes, I melted into the taste. Thanks to being born a Theosian, my metabolism was faster than a normal human's. I needed to eat and eat often to keep my energy up.

"What's keeping her?" Queet blurred in and out. "I have things to do."

"Just *what* do you have on your agenda that is so pressing? A self-help group for the disgruntled dead? Face facts, Queet. You're my spirit guide. Hecate assigned you to me, so *this* is your job. *I* am your job. You're on the clock right now, just as much as I am."

He just muttered. Queet had been a schoolteacher until an Abomination raided his classroom. He had managed to get his students to safety before the Abom began feeding on him. Another hunter—I have no idea who—burst into the room and took out the creature before it could destroy Queet's soul. At that point, the Fates conscripted him and handed him over to Hecate. She had paired him up to act as a spirit guide for several Theosians before me, but none of the couplings had worked out very well.

As I waited, studiously ignoring his irritation, I glanced around the room. I wanted to read, but I had left my tablet at home, so I leaned back and closed my eyes, deciding that if I dozed off, well, I deserved the break.

Thirty minutes later, I sputtered myself awake. Hecate still hadn't returned, so I stretched, yawning, as I shook off the sudden nap.

Ten minutes later, so bored I was almost tempted to start up a conversation with Queet, I upended my bag on the seat next to me. I picked up my wallet. Time to face the truth, as painful as it might be. I heaved a long sigh and opened the black and white double-fold. Pulling out my cash-card, I stared at the piece of plastic. Finally, I gathered my courage and pressed my thumb against the square on the back. A moment later and the digital display lit up. Seventy-two cash and some change.

"Ugh." I stared at the number. "I have to find another client."

"The cupboards are running bare at home,"

Queet said, ever so helpfully.

"I know. Just be grateful you don't have to eat." Granted, all my bills were paid for the month, but I hated being one paycheck away from the street.

"Have you thought of moving back in with Jason? At least you only had to clean the apartment instead of paying rent."

Queet knew how I felt about the subject, but I had to admit, it was a thought. But it was a thought I immediately nixed.

"No, that ended when I was eighteen. Eileen isn't comfortable around me. She was okay with me living there till I reached legal age, but then she got antsy. We're better off living apart, if only for the sake of his love life. I'll figure something out. I'd better—rent will be due again in a few weeks."

As I stuffed my wallet back in my bag and slipped another chocolate in my mouth, deciding to go in search of Hecate, I looked up to find her watching me from the door, a scowl on her face. But she merely crossed to her desk and slid into the chair.

"I told you I wanted to talk to you because there's a problem. Queet, I want you to hear this since you work with Fury. It's a delicate matter, but now...things are breaking open and we have to act immediately."

"Wha—" Melted chocolate dribbled down my chin and I swallowed as quickly as I could without choking, then wiped my face with a tissue. "What's going on?"

She grimaced. "There was a theft a few nights

ago at the World Regency Corporation. Word leaked out. Don't ask me how we found out—we have many spies who walk the world."

"What was taken?" It had to be important for Hecate to get involved.

"The World Regency Corporation has an anti-magic zone at the top of their building. It turns out that they not only conduct private meetings there, which you would expect, but they also store dangerous magical tools. Last night, someone broke into the building and took something that could have a significant effect on the future. Today, the Fates invested me with retrieving it and finding out who was behind the theft. I'm assigning you to help."

I had never been asked to retrieve stolen items before. This all sounded very strange and mysterious. And she still hadn't told me what went missing. "What was stolen?"

"A silver disk, about the size of a bread-and-butter plate. There's a soft sheen to it, almost like brushed silver. The center is raised, like a dome, and it looks like polished chrome. A ring of red lights surrounds the very edge of it. It's an artifact from the Weather Wars, it's known as the Thunderstrike, and it can be used to amplify and control weather." She fell silent, waiting for me to digest the information.

I stared at her, then my jaw slowly dropped open as Queet suddenly appeared, misty but in full view. *An artifact from the Weather Wars?*

"Does the World Regency Corporation know that you know?" I asked.

She nodded. "Not yet, but you know what this means."

My stomach flipped. Weather magic was illegal. *All* the Corp-Rats knew that—Gaia had laid down the law when she opened up the World Tree. Humans weren't allowed to use any form of weather magic, and neither was anybody else. It had almost destroyed the planet, and Gaia was *so over* the vast gales and storms that had rocked her body.

Hecate continued. "It's my belief they'll simply say they found it and were trying to keep it safe. But you and I both know how likely that is. For one thing, any artifacts of that nature are to be turned over to Lightning Strikes immediately upon discovery."

"Yeah, that's going to be one hell of a shit storm when word leaks out."

"Oh, they're going to pay a steep price for it. Even possession of this disk without immediately reporting it is a capital crime. I called Lightning Strikes early this morning. The World Regency Corporation is in line for a royal smackdown and I doubt if they'll survive this. But worse, somebody out there in the city is now in possession of the device." Hecate leaned back in her chair, a grim look on her face.

I processed the information. The ramifications were enormous. The World Regency Corp. would be better off facing Zeus. On a good day, Zeus might have some mercy. Lightning Strikes wouldn't be so compassionate.

Lightning Strikes was a worldwide

organization directly under Gaia's authority. Dedicated to preventing the use of weather magic, the organization was given authority over any country or magical guild when it came to manipulation of the weather. They were above any government on the planet and they were policed by the Greenlings—Gaia's henchmen. Even the Devani couldn't touch them. While Lightning Strikes couldn't monitor every magus or witch, they were extraordinarily thorough.

"What's really frightening is that such an artifact still exists. And it's now in the hands of rogue magicians? Scary times two." I leaned back in my seat, pushing the chocolates aside. "What next? How do I fit into all of this?"

Hecate tapped one perfectly manicured red-taloned nail on the desk, folded her hands together beneath her chin and, elbows resting on her desk, leaned forward. "The Fates say this matter is likely to throw the world out of balance. And if it gets that far, who knows what Gaia might do? Perhaps obliterate all life? Start over completely? Nobody knows because she's the Great Mother. In the end, even if we were to band together, all the gods could not—and would not—stop her. She is the heart and soul of the world. But for now, the Fates say we still have a chance to salvage the situation. We must find the Thunderstrike and destroy it, and we have to find out who stole it and prosecute them as well."

Queet suddenly piped up. "Just how powerful is the artifact?"

"Very, though I doubt if any of us know the

full extent. The World Regency Corporation will try to cover up as much as they can, but Lightning Strikes will get the information out of them. When they are done, that company is going to be a bloody mess."

"I'll be surprised if Lightning Strikes lets them survive. And, of course, you know they'll tell Gaia." I shook my head. "All right. What are my orders?"

"Track down the disk. I don't know how yet, so don't even ask. As soon as I can, I'll dredge up all the information I can. But even more important, I need you to find out *who* stole it. I'm going to do some research and should have more information by tonight or tomorrow. Meanwhile, keep your ears open in Darktown. I know you don't head into the Junk Yard often, and with good reason, but there may be something in the rumor mill there. Perhaps you can ask your friend Jason to have a listen?"

"Am I the only one you're attaching to the case? I need to know so I don't think I'm being shadowed." That had happened once before. Hecate had assigned somebody else to work a case and we had almost taken each other out, not realizing we were on the same side.

"For now, you're it. At least, out in the field. I'm going to ask Zeus's assistant to keep an eye on the weather. We need to be alert for anything out of the ordinary. If the cretins who stole the Thunderstrike decide to use it, there's no telling what ramifications it will have." She paused, a strained look on her face. "I have a feeling we're sitting on the tip of an iceberg, Fury. And I don't know how far below the surface this goes. The World Shift altered life forever. Another...might destroy it for good."

Everything around me seemed to shift sideways as she spoke, and within that one blink, I could sense her fear.

"All right. I'll wait till you contact me. Is there anything else?"

"Yes, actually. Two things." She pulled out her phone and texted me a name. "First, here's a phone number for a job. It's simple, some sort of spirit cleanup in an office building up in North Shore. It will net you some money and shouldn't take long. Sheila will be in her office Monday morning, so call her then."

I stared at the number gratefully, hoping to hell that it wouldn't be another Suit who wanted my services but didn't want to pay. That happened all too often, people of means thinking they shouldn't have to pay for the services they engaged. But I pushed it out of my mind because Hecate was speaking again.

"There's one more thing. This is going to be tricky, but I want you to talk to someone tomorrow. He lives over in Arbortariam. I would visit him myself but he's not fond of the gods for some reason. But he's agreed to talk to an emissary."

I stared at her. The Arbortariam? *Oh. Fucking. Hell.* "I've never been out there. And truth is, I don't want to start visiting now."

"Well, you need to adjust your goals because that's about to change. Contact Jerako. He's one of the Greenlings. They need to know about this now, and he can also tell us if something is changing in the environment, long before the rest of us notice. I had an intermediary set up a meeting for you tomorrow morning at seven a.m."

The Greenlings. Double hell with crap on it.

The Greenlings were Gaia's henchmen and they had singlehandedly destroyed a number of cities during the World Shift. I had never seen one, though I knew of them. They were reclusive, keeping within highly wooded grounds. A number of them lived out on the island of Arbortariam in Idyll Inlet. Ancient beings, they were far older than the Fae, and they were repositories of natural history. They were also dangerous as fuck.

"No more arguments. You are going, because I can't." She stood. "But you have to be cautious on this case. I fear much is riding on it."

"When your friend Jerako finds out there's a weather magic device on the loose, you do realize all hell's going to break free," I mumbled. I knew my history.

"Welcome to my world, Fury." Hecate motioned to the chocolates and handed me a shopping bag. "Here, for your treats."

As I shoved the box in the bag and headed toward the door, she added, "Remember—be careful. You're strong and you're good at what you do, but you're not invincible. And I don't have the power to resurrect you, and I'd rather not have to hand you over to the Boat Man."

With that sentiment ringing in my head, I headed back to Dream Wardens.

Chapter 6

By the time I arrived back at Dream
Wardens, the shop was full. Hecate had texted
me, reminding me again to not be late for the
meeting with Jerako. I let out a muffled grunt, and
reassured her I wouldn't forget. A seven-o'clock
meeting meant getting up at four in order to catch
the Monotrain down to the ferries, but I didn't
bother complaining. Instead, I just planned on
another late night and an even earlier morning.

Jason glanced up as I strode through the
door. His hair had come out of his ponytail and he
looked shaggy and frazzled. He was also wearing
sunglasses—a dead giveaway that he was on the
verge of a migraine. He overloaded quickly when
the shop filled up like it did during Bonny Fae
week. Add the Portside Festival to the mix, and his
head must have been ready to split wide open. As
tired as I was, Jason probably felt worse. I quickly

dropped off my bags in the back and hurried over to him.

"Go take a break," I said. "Tam and Hans can run the register, and I'll take the readings you lined up for me and cover when they need someone to field customers."

"I don't know..."

I couldn't see his eyes behind the wraparounds, but the strain was apparent in his voice.

"Go lie down. You look like hell."

As he gratefully headed into the back, I turned to face the crowds.

Tam was out on the floor, swamped with women. He was a heartbreaker all right, especially when his people were in town. We always played up his Bonny Fae heritage, and he willingly volunteered himself as bait. In fact, I suspected he liked it. The Bonny Fae were proud of their glamour and saw nothing wrong with using it.

Jason had scheduled two readings for me, which would help out. Besides running the Crossroads Cleaning Company—a psychic cleaning company that I ran out of Jason's shop—I also read the cards and threw bones.

The readings were simple. The first—a woman who wanted to know where her sister had disappeared to—was hardest.

"I don't know where Delia went. She's never been gone this long before, and I know she hasn't got a boyfriend or anything like that." Marie couldn't have been over twenty-two, and she was wide-eyed and worried.

I hated this kind of reading the most and it always broke my heart a little. I bit my lip, barely looking at the cards, because I was too busy watching Marie's sister. Delia was standing behind Marie's shoulder, clear as life to me, but she wouldn't be coming home. Her throat had been slashed—I could see the blood oozing down her neck—and she smiled sadly at me.

Using whisper-speak, I asked the dead girl, "Where's your body? Your sister needs to know."

"Up on the Tremble. I took a joy ride with a guy I just met." She paused, then added, "Tell Marie I'm happy, will you? Tell her that I'm okay, and that I'll watch over her? And tell her that the man who murdered me is named Donal Tripoli. He lives in Uptown."

I nodded softly. That wasn't going to be easy. Uptown was where the upper crust lived—that and North Shore. Croix was more middle-class, or what there was left of it. But in Uptown, people had money to buy off the Corp-Rats. Though the Devani, at least, were less likely to take a bribe. They were ruthless in their pursuit of justice, but that meant the government's idea of justice, and the government was ruled by money.

"Marie...your sister...I don't think she'll be coming home. I see her now, with you."

Marie let out a little cry, and at that moment, Delia reached down to wrap her arms around her sister. "I feel her. I can feel her. What happened?"

"I think she was murdered." I wrote out what Delia had told me.

"I can't go to the Devani," she whispered,

paling. "They arrested my brother last week. I don't know why, but I'm scared to tell them about Delia."

I nodded. The Devani seldom gave anybody a reason for detaining them—the government was really good at making people disappear on a whim.

"Listen, I'm going to tell you what to do and you follow my instructions. If you go to the Devani, they may ignore you. And you can't give them my name or they won't bother looking into the case. I want you to contact a friend of mine. His name is Dane, and he's a Theosian like I am. He is yoked to the goddess Tisiphone, and he can figure out a way to help you find your sister's body and bring her killer to justice." I scribbled out the basics on a piece of paper, including Dane's phone number. "I'll tell him to expect your call."

"Thank you." Delia's whisper-speak hit my ears and I looked up to see her smiling. "My brother's dead too, thanks to the Devani. But don't tell Marie. I don't think she could handle losing two of us in the same day."

I stifled my reaction, simply wishing Marie the best. She paid me—twenty cash, which wasn't much but I knew it was all she could afford—and hurried out of the store.

I put in a call to Dane and let him know to expect a call from her. He, like me, lived off-grid, and he was bound to the Furies, to those who had been wrongly murdered. By the time I was off the phone, my second reading was there. She was easier—just a bride-to-be nervous about her husband, but my reading turned up nothing unusual or worrisome, and she left happy. She dropped me thirty cash, along with a twenty-five cash tip.

Sometimes, I thought as I pocketed the money, being one of Hecate's chosen had its benefits, though when I thought about Delia, I sobered. After seeing the excited bride out, I settled into helping Tam handle the steady flow of customers. Hans manned the checkout stand.

I tried to push away thoughts about the Thunderstrike and the Greenlings, immersing myself in the work. An hour later, the store phone rang and I grabbed it so that Jason wouldn't have to pick up.

"Fury?" The broken voice on the other end of the line was shaking.

"This is she. May I help you?" I impatiently looked at the throng at the counter, wishing we could just send all calls to voicemail when we were swamped. But Jason liked his store to have a personal touch, so we answered the phone even when we were busy.

"This is Eileen's mother. Is Jason there?" She hurried to add, "If he is, don't get him yet."

I frowned. Her voice sounded thick with tears. "Yeah, he's in the back resting. I think he's on his way to a migraine."

"Fury, Eileen was..." Again the throaty sob, but this time the pain came through loud and clear. "Eileen was killed an hour ago. She was out flying early this morning and accidentally ran into one of the sky-eyes. She... The drone thought she was attacking it and fired on her. The Devani have labeled it a 'regrettable accident.' "

Fucking Devani. Every day it seemed I found a new reason to dislike them. I leaned against the counter, unable to speak for a moment. Finally, I found my voice. "I'm so sorry, Mrs. Wallace." There wasn't much else I could say.

"I don't know how I'm going to tell Jason. I can barely think." Her voice was breaking.

I paused, then realized what she was asking. "Do you want me to tell him?"

If I could spare Eileen's mother any pain, I would. Eileen had been a smart, funny woman, almost impossible to dislike, and her family was just as likable.

I could sense the relief pouring through the line. "You would do that for me? Thank you, Fury. I can barely..." She paused. "Precinct 37 has more information, though I doubt it will do any good." Tears clouded her words again. "I have to go."

"Of course." I slowly hung up, glancing back at the crowd. I caught Tam's eye and motioned to him, nodding frantically when he shook his head. He frowned, then weeded his way through the customers.

I cornered him against the back wall behind the counter. "Listen, I need you to get these people out of here and lock the store."

"What—"

"Don't argue. Just do it. Trust me?" I stared him down. It was hard to maintain eye contact with someone who could bore holes through your skull with his gaze, but I wasn't about to tell Jason his fiancée was dead with a store full of people around to hear. I'd seen too many rubbernecks in my time, and I wasn't going to subject Jason to that.

Tam closed his eyes for a second before a melancholy look washed over his face. "All right, Fury. Give me a moment here."

He swiftly rounded the counter and within minutes, he was gently herding people to the door, encouraging them to come back tomorrow. I watched as he worked, his glamour coming out strong. He was trim and lithe. At times, he made me think of a sapling. His curling mane of hair frizzed out like branches, tangled in a sexy way. And everybody responded to him like he was a hot knife sliding through butter.

I anxiously watched, hoping Jason wouldn't hear what we were doing. If we were lucky, he had put on his ear buds to drown out the noise. Finally, the shop was empty. Hans locked the door and flipped on the Closed sign. Glancing at the break room door, I was relieved to see it was still closed. I motioned for Hans and Tam to follow me to my nook.

"Sit down and listen. We don't have time to waste." Every minute that passed was one more moment closer to somebody calling Jason to say they were sorry.

"Who died?" It wasn't a rhetorical question or a joke. Tam cocked his head to one side, his gaze brushing me like liquid fire.

I stared at the table for a moment, then said, "Eileen. She was flying and got hit by one of the fucking sky-eyes. Hans, can you go down to..."

I frowned and glanced down at the note I had scribbled to myself. "Precinct 37? They should have more details. I don't dare go, given my chips are altered. I offered to tell Jason. Eileen's mother was in no shape to relay the news."

Tam reached out and took my hand. I closed my eyes as he softly drained away some of the heaviness weighing on my heart. The Bonny Fae liked touch, they liked connection. If a friend was in pain, they did what they could to help.

"Thank you," I whispered, feeling less ragged. "I'd better go tell Jason now. Tam, come with me?" I wasn't sure if his magic would work on a hawk-shifter, but I was hoping for some little miracle. "Unless it's too much to ask..."

"Not at all. I can handle more than you think, Fury. Come, let's get this over with." He glanced at Hans. "Lock up when you go out and set the security code."

Hans nodded, his face a blank mask. But I caught a glimpse of the ache in his eyes. Eileen wasn't really one of us, but she had been Jason's chosen mate, and that was all that mattered. We had lost one of our own.

Jason stared at the floor, unmoving and silent as I gave him the news.

"Hans is on the way down to the police quarters to find out exactly what happened. Eileen's mother is...not coping well, I think." I leaned out to take his hand in mine but he pulled away. Tam gave me a quick shake of the head and I withdrew.

Jason glanced at Tam, then motioned toward the door. "Give us some privacy, Kae."

Tam blinked, but said nothing.

"Of course," I said stiffly, stung by the sudden rebuff. I left the room without another word, trying not to slam the door on my way out. By the time I reached the counter, I was running a mixture of emotions from sorrow to anger. I paused, trying to get my temper under control. The old adage *Don't shoot the messenger* appeared to be alive and well. But as I gathered my things to leave, I forced myself to stop and reason. Jason would need his sister and even though I was pissed, I wasn't going to walk away without doing everything I could.

I quietly let myself out, securing the door behind me. I shoved the key in my pocket and trudged next door to Up-Cakes. Shevron was in the corner, hovering over a tiered cake stand that she was filling with muffins. The store smelled like I had died and gone to lemony-heaven.

She glanced up as I shuffled over to her. "Hey, Fury—" She stopped, setting down the tray of cupcakes. "What the hell happened? You look like you just lost your best friend."

I shrugged, feeling the chip on my shoulder all too keenly. "Shevron, I'm sorry to have to be the one to tell you, but Eileen's mother just called a few minutes ago. Eileen was killed by one of the sky-eyes."

Shevron blanched. "Oh, great gods. How horrible." She swept around the counter, whisking me toward the back. Over her shoulder, she called to her store clerk. "Liza, watch the front?"

When we were in her office, Shevron closed the door and motioned for me to sit down. "Does he know yet?"

I nodded. "I told him."

"Do you know what happened?"

"The rudimentary facts, but I sent Hans down to find out whatever he could. Obviously, I couldn't go. The Devani are calling this a 'regrettable accident.'"

"Regrettable accident, my ass. Those freaking drones are dangerous for aerial shifters. This has happened more than once." She paused, then tilted her head to the side. "Something else is bothering you. I've known you too long for you to hide secrets from me."

"How can you always tell?" I did a good job of hiding my feelings, but Shevron and Tam could always see through me.

She reached over and ran her fingers through my hair. "You've come a long ways from that frightened little girl Jason found on the doorstep in front of Dream Wardens. You've been through a lot and I've watched you handle everything life threw in your path."

I let out a long sigh. "Okay, but it sounds petty and you're going to think I'm an ass."

"Tell me anyway."

"After I told him what happened, Jason wouldn't talk to me. The only thing he did was to order me to leave. He's in there with Tam right now. I know he's hurting but it felt like a fucking slap in the face."

Shevron was a pale woman, her hair far blonder than her brother's. Her rounded face was jarred by the dark blackberry lipstick she wore, and her makeup was one step away from haute-couture odd. But her eyes had the same discerning gaze as her brother's, and the family resemblance was very apparent. Now, it felt like she was looking directly into my heart.

"You know, Fury, grief does strange things to people. They act out in ways you'd never expect. You did, when we first met." Shevron was blunt. That was one of the things I loved about her.

My stomach flipped and I pressed my lips together. I had developed a tough exterior when out in public, but in private I had to let down my guard. Keep too much energy bottled up and it would implode, especially when working with shadow magic. Magic tended to backfire when emotions were repressed, and the last thing I needed was for it to come blasting out at the wrong time, at the wrong target.

"Jason isn't thinking right. Plus, remember, we're shifters. We've lived a long time compared to you. Hawk-shifters, in particular, are notorious for being able to control our emotions, to look at any given situation and follow the threads back. We're aligned with the element of air, which means we are ruled by intellect and thought. But grief can bring the strongest of us to our knees, and in this regard, Jason has always been more emotional than is good for him." The soft smile on her face was the last straw.

"Aw, damn it, Shevron. I feel like a heel for getting angry." I slapped the table, wanting to lash out at something.

"What else is going on, Fury?"

I shook my head. I *really* didn't want to go into it any further. "Don't you need to go over to see Jason? He's going to need you and the last thing I want to do is to make things worse."

"Tam is with him. Now, tell me what's stewing in that fiery heart of yours?" She smiled, and I had the feeling she knew the answer already, even though I wasn't sure what it was.

I closed my eyes, breathing softly. As I sorted through the tangle that my thoughts had become, I realized there was something I was hiding from myself. A feeling...of...*relief*? What the hell was that about?

"Oh hell," I blurted out as I opened my eyes. I didn't want to look at her. But the elephant in the room was loud and big, and I couldn't avoid facing it. "I don't know how to say this."

"Then just say it." She waited patiently.

I stared at the wall. I couldn't look her in the face. Finally, I swallowed my pride. "Maybe...just maybe...I might have a crush on your brother. Or at least I did till he kicked me out a few minutes ago."

She nodded, taking her time. After a few beats, she asked, "Do you think it's more than infatuation?"

I blushed, so embarrassed I wanted to crawl under the table. "I don't know. I mean, I *really* liked Eileen and I never would have interfered in their relationship. But..."

"But the fact that she's gone means the field is open?" There was no judgment, no anger behind her words. I nodded again, waiting for her to read me the riot act. She pursed her lips, then leaned back in her chair, crossing her legs. "Tell me about it."

Now that the gate was open, the words came spilling out. "More than once, I've had the fantasy of what it would be like if she was gone...or if he had..."

"If he picked you instead of her?"

I pressed my lips together, nodding.

"You never fantasized her dead, did you?"

I jerked my head up. "Of course not. No, never. I like Eileen...liked..."

"Then you didn't set the sky-eye after her?" She held up her hand as I bristled. "A stupid question, but to illustrate my point. You need to realize that you had no part in her death."

"No," I answered slowly, beginning to understand.

"Good. Therefore, any connection between your fantasy and Eileen's death is accidental. You didn't wish her dead, or cast a spell, or anything like that. You didn't want her to die any more than you want my brother to be broken-hearted."

Exhaling deeply, I let go of the knot that had formed inside my heart when Eileen's mother had called. "No, I didn't."

"Take it a step further. You care about Jason, but you stay out of his relationship precisely because you *do* care about him. Then his girlfriend dies and you find yourself thinking there might be a possibility...right?"

I blushed. "*This* is why I feel so bad. How can I be such a fucking ass? How can I be so angry at him for asking me to leave when I know he's hurting?"

Shevron stood and took off her apron. "Honey, everything you're feeling is natural. Don't beat yourself up. You aren't rejoicing in Eileen's death. If you were, we wouldn't be having this conversation." She held out her hand and pulled me to my feet, drawing me into a hug.

"I really did like Eileen. I envied her, yes. It's not easy being a Theosian. We're always bound to the Elder Gods, and so often, we live lonely lives. Humans envy or fear us, the government is always looking for a way to use us, and...it's just...it can be lonely. But I never wanted anything like this to happen." I closed my eyes as I leaned against her shoulder.

Shevron took me by the shoulders, forcing me to meet her gaze. "You listen to me, girl. And yes, you *are* a girl compared to my age. The day your mother walked through the Sandspit pregnant with you, she altered your destiny. The rogue magic transformed your DNA. You were meant to be human, but you were mutated in the womb. You carry both paths within you, honey. You're a *minor goddess*. You belong to Hecate. Do you know what that means? You're one of the Divine! Embrace the dark magic in your soul, and revel in it. Quit trying to avoid your nature. Quit trying to play down your talents so you can fit in." She paused, then added,

"Do you remember the cards that the Oracle drew for you at your birth?"

"How can I forget? My mother continually reminded me. In fact, she had a poster of the reading made when I was very young. It hung over my bed for the longest time."

"What were they, again?" Shevron knew very well what my birth-reading was, but I answered anyway.

"The Wheel, Death, and the Queen of Wands."

"Right. *The Wheel of Fortune:* Change happens. If you try to hold it back, the Wheel will run over you, but take control and you'll rise with it, stronger than before. *Death:* Transformation is occurring, with no escape. So embrace it. And the *Queen of Wands*: The queen of flames is the mistress of action. She is fury embodied, and passion and power. It's time to stop shying away from who you've become. You became *Fury* the night you faced the Carver. Claim your name. Revel in what you are. That's the only way you'll ever be happy, regardless of what happens with my brother."

What she said hit home with a thud.

Shevron led me back out to the main shop. "Liza, will you pull together a box of maple bars, éclairs, and donuts? A baker's dozen. I'm going next door and I may not be back for the rest of the day, so you'll have to watch the shop. Family emergency."

As Liza prepared a box of pastries, Shevron turned back to me. "Go wash your face. And remember, I'll be there with you."

She winked, and—feeling like the little sister again—I headed for the restroom, where I splashed cold water on my face.

Shevron had always had my back. While Jason had done his best to make sure I went to school, was fed and clothed, and he tutored me in my magical lessons with Hecate, it was his sister who had tended to my emotional needs. She had guided me through puberty, helped me when I had boyfriend problems—though I always skittish around men. Basically, she became my role model. As much as I had loved my mother, Shevron had taken over and done a better job. She was born to nurture.

I splashed another round of cool water on my face, then brushed my hair back, staring at myself in the mirror. "Remember who you are," I whispered.

Directing my thoughts to the matter at hand— maybe Hans was back with information on Eileen's death—I returned to the front where Shevron waited for me. Without another word, she picked up the pastry box and we headed back to Dream Wardens, to see how Jason was.

Chapter 7

Tam and Jason were sitting on the sofa when I unlocked the door. Hans hadn't returned yet. Shevron silently walked over to Jason's side and sat down, merely offering her hand. He took it for a moment, gazing at her. Then, with a sigh, he let go.

Tam reached over and patted my knee as I dropped into the chair next to him. If he had been anybody else, I would have slapped his hand away, but for once I welcomed the reassurance.

Jason cleared his throat. His expression was a blank slate. I couldn't tell what he was feeling. "I didn't mean to chase you out, Kae. I just needed to process, and Tam...he's good at helping me do that."

Then it hit me. Tam had removed some of Jason's immediate shock. I sidled a glance at Tam, wondering if he was okay. Taking on the emotions of others wasn't easy, and it was a magic I knew I could never handle having. But he seemed calm and collected.

"Not a problem." I felt stiff and awkward, suddenly. My talk with Shevron had only served to make me more uncomfortable. To my relief, at that moment the door opened and Hans let himself in.

We all turned, waiting. Jason tensed.

Hans slumped onto the sofa. "Well, it was a sky-eye, all right."

Jason let out a soft breath. "How did it happen?"

"The Devani wouldn't tell me anything except that she was flying around the top of her building this morning. The drone zoomed in, she 'flew' at it and the drone protected itself. I swung by her apartment, and one of the neighbors confirmed how it happened, though she said the drone was the aggressive one. She saw it happen."

"Damn it to hell. Isn't it enough that the Devani are *always* suspicious of everything? Gods, I wish those freaks would go back to Elysium." I really hated the ultra self-righteous henchmen the Corp-Rats had roped into service as the security force for the country. The Devani came through the World Tree, more spirit than men, with wings that made them look like some sort of winged-shifter mutation. They had no sense of self, really, and did whatever their masters ordered. The Devani lived by strict codes, and were more alien than human. The Conglomerate—the grouping of five corporations that ruled the nation—had become more and more militant, and they gave the

Devani more and more license.

"The Devani make me twitch," Shevron said. "I don't trust them and I never have."

"I have *never* trusted them," Jason said. "In the two hundred–plus years I've been alive, I've always believed they have an ulterior motive." He let out a sharp sigh. "So, did you find out anything else, Hans?"

"The neighbors were far more cooperative than the cops. They said the sky-eyes buzz the building every morning. Usually Eileen waits till a little later to go flying, but she met one of the neighbors on the stairs today and said she had an early meeting and wanted to get in some air time before she went to work."

"We warned her time and again to stop flying in the city. It's too dangerous." Shevron stiffened.

"That's what her neighbor said. Her name is Jessica, by the way, an elderly woman. Anyway, Jessica warned Eileen to be cautious, but she said that Eileen insisted she could avoid the sky-eyes and that she had to fly. She said something about it keeping her sane."

"Yeah...Eileen really would have loved to live out in Bend or some small town like that, but we were going to wait till we got married and then talk about it. Damn it, I wish I would have given in. She wanted to get married this spring, and I told her to wait." Jason hit the cushion next to him, his eyes smoldering.

"There's no guarantee that something wouldn't have happened. The Fates cut the cords when they will," I said, then shut my mouth. I hated that he felt guilty over this, but there was nothing I could say that would make it any easier.

"Her mother is going to be sorting through her things tomorrow. The building already rented out her apartment starting next week," Hans said.

"Figures. Greedy Corp-Rats." Jason frowned. "I'm so glad that her mother wasn't there to see. Terabet isn't strong enough to handle something like that." His face was ashen, but he managed to keep it together.

"Oh, and while I was still at the station, the Devani asked why I wanted to know. I told him I was checking for you because you were too broken up to come down yourself."

After a moment's pause, I sucked in a deep breath. "There's something else, though I don't feel this is the best time to bring it up."

"Please, change the subject," Shevron said. "I think we need to let discussion over Eileen's death sit for a little bit until we've assimilated it."

I glanced at Jason and he nodded.

"All right. This morning, Hecate told me that she's been assigned to a case. Apparently, somebody broke into the World Regency Building last night and stole an artifact from the time of the Weather Wars. The Thunderstrike...it's a magical device that can amplify elemental energy, especially that of storms. Hecate has contacted Lightning Strikes. The Fates have put her in charge of finding the device and whoever stole it. So, yours truly is on the case."

Jason let out a low whistle. "An artifact? *Weather magic*? Crap."

"Yeah, and you know World Regency is going to get slammed. They are trying to claim they found it and were just hiding it until they could contact authorities. Which is, of course, bullshit. We'll see if they get away with it. I wager that by the time Lightning Strikes gets done, the head honchos will be out of business and in prison, waiting execution. But be that as it may, somebody is behind the theft and the Fates insist we have to find out who and get the disk back."

Tam's expression froze. "This sounds like a slippery slope."

"That's not all. Speaking of slippery slopes, tomorrow I'm being sent over to the Arbortariam to speak with Jerako, one of the Greenlings. Hecate wants me to tell him about theft. And you know what that means."

Tam stiffened. "Holy Mother. Yeah, I know what that means." He paused for a moment. "You know, it might behoove you to take me along with you. I've never met one of the Greenlings, but I know about them and I know the proper etiquette."

Shevron raised her eyebrows. "*You've* never met a Greenling? I would have thought that your race interacts with them on a regular basis."

Tam shook his head. "No. The Greenlings are reclusive. They are seldom open to communication and are entirely devoted to Gaia. Fury, I hope you realize what an honor this is. Even the gods are honored when the Greenlings agree to a meeting."

"Well, the fact that I'm being sent in as the bearer of bad news doesn't make me feel very secure. And I've already got one strike against me in that the Greenlings dislike the gods, for some reason. I'm just hoping they don't kill the messenger." I didn't mean to sound flippant, but Tam bristled.

"Don't joke. You may know your history, but do you truly realize just how much power the Greenlings possess? They tore the cities to rubble when Gaia woke up and brought her wrath to bear. They're living extensions of the planet. They aren't mere plant spirits or walking shrubs or talking carrots. They source their power directly from Gaia." He paused, leaning forward till he was staring at me nose to nose. "Tomorrow, you had *better* show respect or you'll find yourself out on your ear, and Hecate will whip your ass. And that whip you wear on your leg is nothing compared to hers, I'll wager."

I straightened my shoulders. "Tam, chill. I have *no intention* of being rude or snarky to Jerako. I don't know what you think I do when I'm out on a case, but trust me, I always take my assignments seriously."

Tam's eyes sparkled with magic as he muttered something and slid back in his chair. "I'm sorry. I just... You're one of the Theosians and sometimes the minor gods take themselves all too seriously. I know you aren't like that...it's just... Fury, I don't think you realize just *who* you are going to be facing. I'm trying to save you some trouble."

"We're all a little on edge," Shevron said, interrupting. She opened the box of pastries. "Which is why I brought these. They won't solve anything, but let's take a moment to breathe and eat. Jason, you too—even though you may not feel hungry, you need the energy." She held out an éclair—one of his favorites—and he silently accepted it.

Tam and I stared at one another for a moment before he offered me a tentative smile and reached out. I took his hand and the tension began to evaporate as he entwined his fingers through mine. A warm glow began to infuse my hand and I realized he was playing fast and loose with his energy. I gently squeezed his palm, then let go. Tam was a sensuous, passionate man, but I knew better than get mixed up with the Fae. *Especially* the Bonny Fae.

"I want a muffin," I said, glancing over at Shevron.

She handed me one. Hans asked for a doughnut, and Tam, a cinnamon roll. We sat there in silence, eating and breathing. After another moment, I yawned. It was barely three p.m., yet I felt like I had been up for hours.

The sugar took the edge off my temper. "Tam, I'm going to call Hecate and ask if you can come with me. You're right. It would be good to have someone there who understands the Greenlings better than I do." With that, I offered the peace branch, and Tam accepted it gracefully. I moved away from the group, popping the last bite of the muffin in my mouth before I dialed Hecate. As usual, I had to leave a message for her—the gods didn't spend most of their time in the temple.

"How are you, really?" Shevron was holding

Jason's hand when I returned. When they were sitting together, it was easier to see the family resemblance.

"My fiancée is dead. How *should* I be? My heart feels like it's been stabbed through. I need to visit her parents. I'll call them tonight. The Cast will gather later for her memorial."

A group of hawks was called a *Cast*, and so were a group of hawk-shifters. Eileen had belonged to the same Cast as Jason and Shevron. The pair had been engaged for twenty years. Hawk-shifters weren't impulsive like werewolves or big cat-shifters. And none of them were affected by the moon's phases, unlike lycanthropes, who were extremely dangerous and a whole different breed. Over the years, growing up with Jason and Shevron, I had gained a sizable insight into the world of hawk-shifters, and it was both intimidating and impressive. They valued intellect over emotion, and tended to take the long view. But I had never seen them deal with the death of another Cast member.

"What do you want us to do about the shop?" Tam finally asked.

Jason shrugged. "Nothing will bring her back. Open as usual tomorrow, I suppose." He looked over at Shevron for confirmation.

She nodded. "Keeping busy is best."

My phone rang and I glanced at the screen. *Hecate.* I moved off to the side to take the call. After quickly explaining what had happened to Eileen, I asked, "So, can Tam come with me to meet Jerako?"

"We'll talk about that in a moment. I'm sorry about Jason's loss. But have you seen the news?"

"No, we've mostly been focusing on Eileen's death."

"A massive tornado hit Bend two hours ago. The town hasn't weathered a tornado since the World Shift—it's not usual weather around here. An eerie green glow was spotted in the area where it originated. A farmer saw it about thirty minutes before the storm struck. I had a talk with the Fates and they concur. This is no ordinary tornado. A member of Lightning Strikes will meet you tonight—I need you over in Bend in three hours. She will meet you at the Casa Café Shop. Her name is Tigra, and she's the one I talked to about the weather disk. She'll be able to ascertain whether weather magic was used to raise the storm. She's a weretiger, so walk softly."

I blinked. "Weretigers are volatile, aren't they?"

"Yes, so watch your step. And take someone with you. I don't want you going alone. But we have another issue. An informant relayed the information to me that an Abomination was spotted over on the south side of town, down in the Bogs. So I'm afraid it's going to be a late night for you. Please check out the report after you talk to Tigra. You should be able to pull the Abom up on your inner Trace."

"What about Tam? Can I take him with me tomorrow?"

"Yes, that's actually a good idea. Jerako might respond better if he's along. I didn't even think about the fact that you work with one of the Bonny Fae." With that, she signed off.

I closed my eyes, suddenly feeling overwhelmed. As I tried to steady my breathing, Tam slipped up behind me and placed his hands on my shoulders. I leaned into his touch as he slowly began to siphon off some of the tension.

"You don't have to do that, you know," I murmured.

"It gives me pleasure," he whispered back. "I'm sorry you felt shut out today. Jason was ready to lose it, and he didn't want to break down in front of you."

"I just wish he hadn't made it sound like I wasn't welcome."

"You could never be unwelcome around him... *or me,*" Tam murmured as he brushed his hand over the back of my neck and another knot eased. "Was that Hecate?"

"Yes. She gave permission for you to go with me. But there's another problem." I returned to the group. "Bad news comes in threes. Two more issues have come up." I told them about the tornado and the Abomination. "Hecate's ordered me out to Bend to meet with a member of Lightning Strikes tonight. I need a ride—I don't have a car. Hecate wants me to take someone with me. Then, after I return, I have to go after the Abomination in the Bogs."

Shevron was about to say something, but Jason cut her off. "Don't even think it. You have Leonard to think about."

Leonard was Shevron's fifteen-year-old son.

I had been living with Jason and Shevron two years when she gave birth to him. Len's father had run off shortly after Shevron announced she was pregnant. Since he wasn't a hawk-shifter, the Cast had pretty much ignored him. Instead, they focused their attention on helping Shevron open her bakery and looked after Len until she could find a good nanny. But being a single mother was hard, no matter how much help you had.

"I'll go with you," Jason added. "I could use a chance to get out of the city. A trip out into the country might do me some good, let me clear my head. Let me wash up and we'll head out."

I glanced over at Shevron, and she nodded her encouragement. I gathered my things.

Tam touched me on the elbow. "Are you all right?" His voice was soft and washed over me like a calming breeze. He was draining off more of my fear and worry, and I didn't have the strength to protest.

"Yeah. Thanks, by the way. I know what you're doing, and I don't understand how you can take on so much pain and manage to remain so calm."

"It's my nature. We can feed on pain and transform it into something delicious."

That was a new one to me and sounded almost vampiric, but I let it go. Some things were better left untouched.

"Listen, can you do some digging while we're in Bend? Check the net. See if anybody in the UnderCult has been in the market for weather magic gadgets. I want to get an idea of what might be going on among the arcane magicians, especially those who refuse to register with the Guild."

The Seattle Magician's Guild required membership of every magus and witch who lived within the city limits. Not everyone joined—since I was running off-grid, I hadn't, and luckily, nobody who hired my services had asked to see my membership card. But most who declined were penny-ante hucksters, and the city turned a blind eye on them. The guild was primarily focused on restraining the magicians who *could* cause a lot of trouble—the ones who had real power and few ethics.

"I've got some contacts in the Junk Yard. I'll work through them. Easiest that way." Tam motioned to Shevron. She approached, a wary look on her face. I knew she didn't trust the Fae in general, but she was always polite to Tam.

"I drew a lot of the initial pain off of your brother, but it will return. He has to walk through it in order to heal, but at least the shock is tempered for now."

She inclined her head, touching the center point of her brow with her index finger, a sign of gratitude among the Cast. "It's true, we hawk-shifters are more analytical than most other shifters, but we aren't immune to emotion. I thank you for helping." She stopped as Jason entered the room again. He had brushed his hair and put on a clean shirt.

I gathered my things and grabbed the box of chocolates out of the bag, stopping suddenly as I found an envelope beneath them. I opened it to find myself staring at a cash card marked for three hundred cash. *Hecate*. She had overheard me talking to Queet.

Suddenly, I felt a wash of gratitude that I was under her yoke. Feeling a little better, I pocketed the money. Calling out, "Queet? You there? Let's go. We're heading to Bend," I popped another chocolate in my mouth. We headed to the parking garage down the street where Jason kept his car. I had a feeling by the end of the day, the candy box was going to be empty. It was just that kind of a day.

Jason's car was a spiffy low-rider wonder, a self-driving model with a manual override option. When the gas and oil crises got too bad, the manufacturers had finally moved beyond electric models, which had proven untenable for the long run, and instead developed a sustainable form of fuel and non-toxic batteries.

Unfortunately, even though agroline was affordable, the government stacked on so many taxes that it was difficult for the average commuter to own a car. Add to that, parking costs were at such a premium that most people just gave up and used mass transit. The Monotrain was the easiest and swiftest way to get around the city.

As we sped along the freeway, I tried to think of something to say. I wasn't sure if Jason even wanted to talk. I glanced over him, trying to gauge his expression, but hawk-shifters were cagey and hard to read. Finally, I decided that he could start the conversation when he was ready. I leaned back in my seat and stared out the window. I thought about trying to pinpoint the Abom on my inner Trace, but we were rapidly moving away from Seattle and he'd be out of range entirely soon.

Seattle sat on the edge of the Pacific Sound. Bend was about an hour inland, southeast of the city, deep into the Wild Wood. In the distant past, the suburbs had sprawled for miles outside of the cities, but eventually both small towns and big cities had became localized, and the natural world was allowed to reclaim the space between metropolis areas.

Lining both sides of the freeway was a thick wall of fir and cedar, interspersed with oak and birch and aspen. The undergrowth was made up of vast copses of fern and huckleberry, stinging nettle and skunk cabbage and all manner of wildflowers and shrubs. Small streams trickled through the foliage, reinforced from the glaciers that rose, icy and sparkling in the western Cascades and their foothills. The water moistened the forest floor, creating ravines and gullies and meadows in the resurgence of the natural world that had taken hold since the World Shift.

The ravines were deep and dangerous, filled with wildlife. Most of the animals would run if you came at them, but the cougars and bears usually held their ground. Hunting was illegal, save for in certain areas that were strictly bordered. Given all the Weres who had appeared when the doors on the World Tree opened, hunting had to be regulated. As a result, the ecosystem had a thriving array of predators and prey.

Dusk was falling. Outside the city, the air cooled quickly, given the absence of concrete, and before long, the evening mist would rise thick and soupy, to drift over the roads.

It'd been a while since I've been away from Seattle and I found myself sinking into a state of relaxation that I seldom was able to manage in the city.

"My family comes out to the woods every week or so, so we can fly." Jason's voice startled me, I had been so wrapped up in watching the miles pass by. "Eileen never could wait, though. She had to fly every day or she was unhappy."

I lazily rolled my head to look at him. He had switched over to manual driving and was focused on the road, but he looked calmer. Cities weren't a natural element for most shifters.

"When was the first time you took wing? I don't think I ever asked you." I figured that if I overstepped my boundaries, he would tell me.

"I was five years old when I learned to fly. I first shifted when I was four. Most hawk-shifters take wing between five and six years old. It's a scary time, and even more frightening for the parents. So much can go wrong when a shifter first learns to transform. That's pretty much across the board for all Weres and shifters."

"I thought puberty was the trouble-time."

"Oh, it's also a bad time. The same hormones that drive human teenagers nuts are even more problematic when you add in shifter DNA. There have been cases when a shifter or a Were went into a hormonal crisis in the middle of transformation and got stuck."

I had never even thought of such a thing happening. "What do you do?"

"It's an incredibly painful situation, and the majority of cases end in death. Usually, the Alpha Mother of the Cast or Pack ends up putting the victim down. No matter how it ends, it's traumatic for the entire extended family unit. The few who survive never forget, and some of them are so traumatized they lose their ability to shift."

"What happens to them?"

He didn't answer for a moment, then said, "They're exiled from the Cast. They wouldn't be able to handle life among those who make the transition successfully. They're usually sent to work among humans who live in the Wild Wood. We place them in low-risk, low-stress occupations."

"Never seeing their family again? Harsh."

"Sometimes being harsh is the best love you can give someone."

"Given how much can go wrong, I must have been easy to handle then, when I showed up on your doorstep." I gave him a sideways glance.

Jason snorted. "Are you kidding? A Theosian yoked to Hecate? I was constantly terrified I'd do something wrong and have the Dark One on my back. Or that the government would come hunting for you."

"Well, Tam took care of the latter, at least. Though I wouldn't take a chance on trying to live outside of Darktown, Portside, or the Trips, even though I'm off-grid. It's too easy to draw attention from the sky-eyes when I'm out on the hunt."

The government not only insisted on chipping all the Theosians to keep tabs on us, they also restricted where we could live. Croix, North Shore, and Uptown were off limits, reserved for human and Were inhabitation only, though allowances were made for the Theosians who rose to stardom because of their powers. Briarwood was mostly inhabited by the Fae. Theosians *could* live out on the Tremble, but that was just asking for trouble. The NW Quarters gangs hated us, though technically, the Corp-Rats didn't care if we lived there. So we mainly congregated in Darktown, the Trips, and Portside.

Occasionally, a Theosian would turn up missing, and nobody would ever find out what happened to them, but we all knew what happened. If the Conglomerate found out that one of us had any strong bent for telepathy or bilocation, the potential for spying on other countries was too great of a temptation. More than one of my kind had disappeared when their powers grew too noticeable. When Tam helped me go off-grid, Hecate applauded the move. I just had to watch myself when I was hunting, and stay away from the sky-eyes when I wasn't in the thick of a crowd.

"The Corp-Rats are always looking for how they can make use of my kind. At least they tend to leave the Weres and shifters alone."

"That's because they haven't found effective

ways of taking us down. Theosians tend to be much more pliable than Weres and the Fae, because you began life as human while first in the womb. But back to your question, do you *really* think you were easy to handle? If it hadn't been for Shevron, I would have gone crazy trying to figure out what to do with you. I'm just glad I found you before some bogey did."

I nodded solemnly. "I'm not sure why I ended up on your doorstep. I think I knew my mother trusted you. I had no idea that I could transport myself like that—I've never been able to do it again without help from Hecate."

"Your sense of self-preservation kicked in. You had just witnessed one of the most horrific things I can think of and you knew you were next. My theory is that you used every ounce of magical energy you had to propel yourself out of the situation. And since your subconscious knew that your mother trusted me, that's probably why you ended up on my doorstep."

I stared out into the approaching dusk. "Do you ever regret taking me in?" It was a question I had never asked, but sometimes wondered.

"Honestly? I do it again in a heartbeat. Kae, *never* feel that you have ever been—or ever are—a burden. I wish the circumstances had been different, but I'm glad you're in my life. Really, when I think about it, you're one of my best friends." He was silent for a moment. "I can't believe she's gone, Kae."

"I know. I want to promise that it's going to be okay, but I don't make promises lightly."

Jason let out a sigh. "I know. I'll be all right, but this wasn't in the plan. This wasn't supposed to happen." After a moment he added, "I *did* love her, you know that, right?

Wondering why he felt he had to ask me, I gave him a confused nod.

"Even though our marriage was arranged when we were children, I really *liked* Eileen. And I would have done the best I could as her husband. Even though I wasn't ready to get married, I would have tried to make her happy."

And right then, I realized that what I had thought was a great love hadn't been quite the match I had believed.

Chapter 8

If I had ever been to Bend, it was when I was little, when my father was still alive and we could afford an occasional vacation to the Wild Wood. All I knew was that it was one of those towns that, if you blinked twice on your way through, you'd miss it. I leaned forward, staring at the lights ahead as we approached the outskirts.

"What's Bend like?"

Jason eased off the freeway, onto the short exit ramp leading into town. "It's a pit stop, really, on the way to Spokane."

Spokane was the other large city on the eastern slopes of the Cascade Mountain Range. The range divided the region into two distinct climates. The western side, where Seattle sat on the ocean's edge, was temperate with lush forest growth, though winters were snow-shrouded. The eastern side, where Spokane watched over the land, was sun scorched in summer and a blowing frozen wasteland in winter. Spokane was a lot more dilapidated than Seattle. It had been hit harder during the World Shift and never fully recovered. It had mostly turned into an agricultural hub, far more agrarian in nature.

The Cascades were volcanic, providing rich growing soil on both sides. Mount St. Helens had erupted a number of times since the beginning of the Weather Wars, as had Mount Rainier. Where thriving communities had once nestled at the base of the latter, the Wilds spread, thriving woodlands growing over the pyroclastic flows that had covered the towns once living there.

Several passes offered travel through the range, winding through the towering mountains, though during the winter months they were usually closed because of the rolling avalanches that thundered down to cover the roads and anything that happened to be on them.

"I've never been to Spokane. I've never been any place other than Seattle, really." The world was huge, but my personal world suddenly felt provincial.

Jason hushed me. "You have lived through things that would have turned some people into hermits. You belong to Hecate. I wouldn't call that sheltered."

With a shrug, I continued to stare out into the night. "I suppose...but I think sometimes that I'm at a disadvantage. I envy you shifters and Weres and the Fae. You can go where you want. Even humans can. You have the chance to see the world as you decide. I don't. Theosians are forever chained to the Elder Gods."

"What do you want, Kae? What do you want out of life? I don't know that I've ever heard you talk about any goals or dreams."

I frowned. What did I want? My job was set from the day I was born and offered up to Hecate. I couldn't come and go at will, unless I vanished into the Wild Wood where the Corp-Rats couldn't chase me. So what did I want? A husband? A family?

"I think...I want to have a little house somewhere out of the city, where I can practice magic, and do what Hecate wills, and maybe... maybe someday the man of my dreams will appear on the doorstep to complete the picture." It was as clear of a goal as I could make, and as I said the words aloud, I realized that yes, I did want something of this nature.

"Really? No life as a priestess in the temple for you?"

I shook my head. "No. I don't like being cooped up anywhere. I guess what I want is what anybody wants. Happiness. Maybe a little freedom, although I do love Hecate. She's always treated me right. Sounds like I might as well be a human, right?" I forced a laugh to cover the sudden hiccup in my heart that told me I really did feel alone most of the time.

"You *were* human once...before you were born." He adjusted the tint of the windshield, turning it up against the sun that was still several hours away from setting. Then, changing the subject, he said, "We're almost there. Where are we supposed to meet Tigra?"

I pushed aside my shifting mood. "At the Casa Café Shop." I checked my phone, glancing at the message Hecate had sent me with the directions to the diner. "It's not far from here, I think. The west side of town, near the freeway exit, on 70th Street. Remember, be cautious. There's going to be debris all over."

"Right." Jason plugged the directions into the GPS and we took the next exit. But as we entered the center of Bend, he eased the car over to the curb and coasted to a stop. The cheerful exterior of the town had vanished, awash in a vast sprawl of devastation.

I found my voice first. "What the hell happened here?" This was no pleasant, *spend-Saturday-morning-at-the-diner* town, at least not anymore. "It looks like a war zone," I whispered. I had never expected anything like this.

As we entered the clearing where the town had stood, we could see that what had been the center square was now a field of rubble. Buildings were half standing, roofs blown away, windows shattered, brick and stone and siding littering the streets. People were sitting on chunks of stone or folding chairs, staring aimlessly as the medics went from person to person checking for injuries. It was as though the tornado had taken a direct path along the street, uprooting everything in its wake. An ugly scar raced through the center of Bend, a gaping wound through the heart of the small town.

"Bloody hell," Jason said under his breath.

As we watched, rescuers dug through the rubble. I wanted to join them, but I had my orders. I tapped Jason on the arm, still unable to pull my gaze away from the destruction.

"We need to meet Tigra. Can you find a way around this to the Casa Café Shop?"

Jason glanced once more at the rescue efforts, looking like he wanted to be out there, too. He nodded and readjusted the GPS. "Yeah, as long as this mess doesn't go forever."

He pulled a U-turn and turned down a side street. Ten minutes later, we found the diner, still intact. Jason parked near the door. The restaurant was full, and it looked like people were gathering in small groups in the parking lot. We were about to head inside when a voice behind me caught my attention.

"You're Fury, aren't you? I'm Tigra." The woman moved toward me, holding out her hand. As I clasped it, I noticed her grip was firm and cool. She was tall and sturdy, muscular as all get out, and her hair was streaked, golden blond with black highlights. Her skin was pale yellow, with faint black chevrons lining the flesh. Older weretigers tended to show their true nature more than the younger ones, and the chevrons would darken with age.

"Do you think there's room in the restaurant for us?"

She shook her head. "I doubt it. We probably couldn't hear over the uproar, even if we could find a table. I had no idea the destruction was this bad. There's a park across the street where we can talk, if you don't mind sitting outside."

We followed her over to the park. The swath of green had remained undisturbed. Here and there, we spotted someone sitting, dazed. The picnic tables were still standing, and the rest area was intact, its roof still in one piece. The trees swayed gently in the wind, but otherwise we would never have known that less than a half-mile away the town had been trampled.

As we settled at a table, Tigra brought out her tablet and began tapping in notes, her fingers flying over the screen. She finally turned back to us. "I take it you've seen the storm's aftermath?"

"When we drove in," I said. "Hecate filled you in on everything that happened?"

"Yes, she called me about the Thunderstrike. I called her this morning to tell her about the tornado." Tigra glanced around, then inhaled a deep breath and let it out slowly as she closed her eyes. I could sense her searching around on the astral plane. After a moment, she opened her eyes.

"The energy around the town is supercharged. While tornadoes leave behind residual energy— most storms have some form of sentience—this one left a magical footprint so big a giant could have made it."

I glanced at Jason, who was taking a few notes of his own. "Then it was magically created?"

"No doubt about it. The storm was generated

by magic." She paused, then cleared her throat. "Here's the thing. Lightning Strikes is aware of a groundswell movement. A number of the more powerful UnderCult magicians are angry over the restrictions on weather magic, as well as several other limitations. They worship Chaos, and they've formed a worldwide order called the Order of the Black Mist."

"Chaos?" Jason asked.

"The primal force out of which came Gaia, Tartarus, Eros, Nyx, and Erebus. Chaos is more of a force than a god. Chaos predates most of the gods. The Order of the Black Mist believes that too much order has thrown the world into a tailspin, and they resist limitation. They work with other forces than meteocramancy, so they aren't simply out to begin another Weather War. This is just a show of force to remind us that they refuse to be controlled. But we have to find that disk and get it away from them before they cause much more damage, because if we don't, Gaia will take matters into her own hands. That means that whoever stole it will be brought up on charges." Her voice drifted off, but both Jason and I could fill in the blanks.

Meteocramancy was expressly forbidden and punishable by death. Usually, it was only an outlier here or there who decided to rebel. But a dedicated movement could do far more damage.

"Does Lightning Strikes suspect any one nation of harboring them? Or of funding them?"

She frowned, then shook her head. "No. They're spread out in pockets across the world. We doubt any government is behind this. The corporatocracies are greedy, but not stupid. Add to that the fact that too many countries are struggling just to keep their people alive. No, we doubt this is an officially sanctioned act. Famine and war have depleted the population in so many places."

"Wouldn't famine be a good reason for invoking weather magic?" Jason asked.

She shrugged. "Possibly, if the famines were due to drought, but most of them are caused by crop poaching and food wars. What magicians the smaller countries still have under their command are focused on protecting food supplies. No, if there *is* any government connection to the Order of the Black Mist, it's well hidden. For one thing, nobody in power is going to want to rock the boat, and if another Weather War breaks out, Gaia will step in and end things."

"True enough that," I said. "A number of kingdoms are barely scratching out an existence. Another round from Gaia would obliterate them."

"Precisely." Tigra frowned. "Two weeks ago, there was a theft in Bifrost, over in Scandnavaland. Four ancient grimoires from the Museum of Magica are missing—four priceless volumes, all on chaos magic. Three guards were killed, and a fourth's body was found two days later. We contacted the Fates, but at that point, they couldn't pinpoint whether this was linked to the Order of the Black Mist or not. Yesterday, they confirmed it. While the Fates still can't read the future—the threads are still unclear—now we know the Order is out to upset the balance."

I already knew that the Fates were involved.

"What about the gods?"

"We have begun talks with the priests of Thor. We'll swing into high gear tomorrow. We have to walk cautiously when approaching the various pantheons to avoid insulting anybody or engaging two gods together who hate each other."

Dealing with the gods required a delicate balance. The Fates were bound by cosmic law and could only intervene when situations grew dire. If they stepped in, the Norns would follow, so it made sense to talk to the Norse pantheon next.

"Well, Hecate told me to help you in whatever way I could, so here I am."

"I'm grateful." Tigra frowned. "Would you—" She paused, staring off into space. "*Hell*. Follow me, please." She was on her feet, racing to her car. Jason and I followed, heading to Jason's car. As Tigra peeled out of the parking lot, Jason and I went zooming after her.

Tigra was a scary driver—and she drove manually. Her car nipped in and out of tight spaces like a metal dancer. She flipped on flashing lights and we chased behind her. Five minutes later, we were on the outskirts of Bend, and she swerved onto the shoulder of the road next to a wide field that sat beneath a tangle of forest at the base of a foothill. The field had a crater in it as large as a small pond that had been blasted into the ground.

Tigra jumped out of her car and headed out into the field, motioning for us to follow. I slung my sword over my shoulder. Jason slid a thin blade into his belt before exiting his car.

The weretiger slowed as she neared the crater, and we hurried to catch up to her. The woman was quick—she had darted through the field faster than a sprinter on race day. At the edge of the hole, she slid to a halt, staring into it with a look of alarm.

"What's wrong?"

She glanced at me. "Tune in. See what you can feel."

I closed my eyes and let the energy in the field wash over me. Next to me, I could feel Jason slipping into trance, as well. He was the first to gasp, and after a moment, I could feel it too—the sensation of creeping worms, long tangling knots of them, dragging themselves out of the crater to slither onto the field. Once they were in the field, they were suddenly airborne, silently streaming past us toward the town. They felt sickly and rotten, like the worms squirming out of a rotten apple.

"What the fuck—?" I was trying to put a name to them but was coming up empty.

"Astrigators. Energy suckers, and they breed at an incredible rate. They piggyback on people who don't have much magical energy and feed on even the tiniest slivers of magic and psi powers. Once sated, they divide like amoebas. I guarantee you that we're infected already. We'll have to go through decontamination before we leave the town."

I shuddered. "I hate parasites." The thought that I was being fed on by a bunch of psychic worms turned my stomach. My dislike of parasites had become almost a phobia over the years, and it was all I could do to remain calm and not vomit up all the chocolate and pastries I had consumed.

Jason rested a hand on my arm. His presence steadied me. "We'll get rid of them. Meanwhile, breathe, and try not to use your powers. It will only attract more of them if you do. Drop out of trance."

As I pulled back my feelers, a cold chill washed over me, a final present from the creepy worms, no doubt.

"How do we go through decontamination, and how soon? I still have work I have to do tonight, and Hecate's not big on patience." None of the gods seemed to be, actually. Plus, I was already tired, but I still had to go after the Abomination down in the Bogs. All I really wanted to do was go home and sleep. I was running on fumes— adrenaline and sugar.

"It won't take long. I've put in a call to headquarters. They'll be here within half an hour. Meanwhile, something else you should be aware of. Astrigators not only drain energy, but they can store it up and transmit it to the person who summoned them. They're a favorite tool for magicians who want to siphon off a great deal of energy without being noticed. The creatures can swarm through a populated area and steal energy. This will allow the magus to use higher power spells—ones that she or he can't normally attempt."

"So you'll have to quarantine the entire town? What about anybody who has left since the tornado hit?" I couldn't imagine what kind of job that would be.

She nodded. "Yes, the *entire* town. I've called in the D-Com unit. They'll be here within the hour. Trust me, they have sirens and know how to use them." She paused. "I need to speak with the Regent of Bend. You two stay here and wait for D-Com to arrive. They'll start decontamination procedures so that you can get out of here as soon as possible. I'll be in touch. I have your number—Hecate texted it to me." With that, she snapped her tablet shut and stuck it into her bag, heading back to her car.

Jason and I wandered over to a rock the size of a bench and settled ourselves on it. I glanced up at the last of the fading light. Out here, the sun set earlier, and night seemed to arrive quickly. I let out a soft breath, trying not to think about the frenzied rush of astrigators who were swarming us even as we waited. The thought of them made me itch.

"What do you think they'll do to us... The decontamination squad, I mean?" I wasn't sure what to expect. "Will we be stuck in some tent and fogged over with some chemical or..." I had no idea how magical decontamination worked.

He shrugged. "I'm not sure. I would use a crystal grid or my wand, but Lightning Strikes is a sophisticated organization. There's no telling what they've managed to come up with. I'm sure it won't hurt," he added.

I shrugged. "I'm not really worried about that."

After a moment, I lapsed into silence, staring at the crater where the storm had touched down. The force inherent within weather magic was terrifying—mind-bendingly powerful.

"Penny-cash for your thoughts." Jason glanced over at me.

"Just thinking about the past—history. Who would be stupid enough to chance setting off another World Shift?"

He leaned forward, resting his elbows on his knees as he stared at the horizon. "A lot of people. Those who think they could possibly manage to come out on top. If the Order of the Black Mist has decided to just basically throw a bunch of wrenches in the works, then they're short sighted and stupid. Not to mention arrogant. But I had another thought. What if they are trying to overthrow the current governments in order to seize control rather than incite anarchy? They—the magicians—used to work behind the scenes for the various kings and lords. Now, what's to stop them from trying to erect their own governing structures?"

"So rather than a corporatocracy..."

"Exactly. A magikosocracy."

"I don't think I've ever heard that word before."

"Rule by magical forces." He pressed his thumbs together, staring at his hands. "I need to talk to the Cast about this, Kae. I'll abide by what Lightning Strikes orders, but I have a really bad feeling that we're sitting on the tip of an iceberg and we're about ready to see the rest of the glacier rise up out of the water. The Cast has to know."

His words resonated too close to the bone. I shivered, staring at the crater again. I was about to say something when the decontamination crew pulled in. Pulling my jacket tighter around my shoulders, I stood and headed over toward them, hoping that we were exaggerating the danger. But somewhere, deep inside, I knew we weren't.

Chapter 9

The decontamination went easier than I thought. We were run through a series of magical scanners. Sure enough, there were dozens of astrigators latched onto both Jason and me. After being sprayed down, dusted with powders, and given crystal elixirs to drink, we walked through the scanners again. Three rounds of this, and we were finally clear of the parasites. Meanwhile, they decontaminated Jason's car and drove it around to where we were waiting on the edge of the town. By that time, the D-Com unit had surrounded Bend with a magical barricade. I could see the wavering force field, and the worried looks of the townsfolk staring at us as we waited outside by the main unit.

"This is like some scene out of a movie." I stared at the line of vans that barricaded the freeway, rerouting people to go around the town. The vans were all marked with a brilliant fork of lightning—gold surrounded by a blue aura, and the words, "LIGHTING STRIKES: Official Vehicle" on the sides. Members of Lightning Strikes were scanning the area for astrigators who had managed to escape before the net was installed, and they were all carrying stunners—weapons that could disable or destroy.

As the team member handed Jason the keys, he said, "Please don't attempt to return through Bend. A detour has been erected to guide you back to the freeway." He abruptly moved away.

As we ducked into the car, I exhaled a long sigh of relief. "I don't know why, but there was a part of me afraid we'd never make it out."

"Me too, to be honest. That wasn't an experience I care to repeat." Jason's jaw was set. He looked almost angry.

"When we get back to Seattle, I need you to drop me off at the Bogs. I still have to go after the Abomination." I glanced at my phone. It was almost ten. "I'd rather go home and sleep, but Hecate wants me to take care of it tonight."

He shook his head. "You aren't going into the Bogs on your own. I'm coming with you."

I frowned. "You don't have to, Jason. You've had one hell of a day." I didn't want to bring up Eileen's death, but it didn't take a genius to figure out that he must be feeling like crap.

"Don't argue." He used the same tone he had on me when I was a teen, and he wanted me to cut out the crap and just do what he told me.

"Yes, sir." I snickered, but then waxed serious again. "All right, but when we get near, you do as

I say. Aboms are my specialty and I don't want you putting yourself on the line as a target. I can't afford to worry about you when I'm trying to focus on it. Queet will be there to help me."

"Deal," he said, and sped up as we headed back to Seattle.

The Bogs were on the southwest side of the city, bordered by the Sandspit to the east, and the Junk Yard to the north. At one time, the entire area had been an industrial area. Rusted heaps of slag metal were the only indication of the trains and light rail and trucks that had come through on a daily basis. The Bogs were chill swampland, marshy stretches laden with quicksand and nettles and poison oak and ivy, thistles and stinkweed. The foliage was thick, and during winter, a heavy layer of snow made the going even more dangerous.

Twice in the past fifty years, the Regent of Seattle had sent in cleaning crews to try to harness the tangle, but both times, the crews vanished, never to be seen again. After the second time, they gave up and left the Bogs to fester and bubble.

A dozen winding trails led through the area, all of them clearly marked. Unfortunately, the markers occasionally shifted positions, but nobody ever figured out how and security cameras never picked up anybody actually moving them. They just seemed to magically change places. But the

Bog-Keepers had been through within the past couple of days, according to the trail notes at the entrance, and so everything should be in order.

Above each of the twelve gates marking the entrance to one of the trails was a readerboard with a warning in bright red lights: ENTER THE TRAIL AT YOUR OWN RISK. SEARCH AND RESCUE TEAMS WILL NOT BE DISPATCHED. The boards also warned of various other dangers found in the Bogs—mostly wildlife of various sorts and UnderCult creatures that had escaped from their enslavers.

"Makes it looks like a regular walk in the park, doesn't it?" I was trying for lighthearted, but my voice fell flat.

Jason glanced at me as we stood at the gate leading to the trail. "I haven't been in the Bogs in years."

"I haven't ever been here, to be honest. But that's going to change now." I closed my eyes and brought up my Trace. Suddenly, a light flared and I could see the blip showing movement deep in the tangle.

"It's still here. I'm not sure whether I should be relieved or depressed. There," I said, opening my eyes and pointing to Trail 7. "It's down that trail."

"Let's get moving. Stick to the path, watch every step. I have a light, but that doesn't mean the going will be any easier." He moved to the front. I felt that I should volunteer, but also realized that Jason was better prepared to navigate.

"You lead, but when I say stop, you stop. I found its Trace." I kept watch to our back and sides, sword out and right hand poised near my thigh, ready to unleash my whip at the first sign of it being needed. "Queet, are you with us?"

"I'm here," came Queet's faint reply. "I'll follow."

A veil of stars dotted the chill night sky as we slowly passed through the gate. Everywhere, we could hear the rustling of plants. Whistles and grunts emanated from all around us—night birds singing, animals whispering through the thick undergrowth, Wandering Ivy hungry for dinner. The trail wound through a grove of cypress and yew trees that rose out of the boggy soil. The scent of green and fetid water intermingled in an icy, cloying mix.

What few lamplights there were along the dirt and flagstone path had mostly shorted out.

"The Bog-Keepers don't come through very often—too many have gone missing. If you read the news, you'll see every now and then reports of another one vanishing. Whether the quicksand takes them, or it's something else, I doubt if anybody knows."

"What about the bodies?" I stuck close behind him. We were walking single file for safety's sake.

"You saw the signs. No search and rescue teams, and no recovery teams either. I'm pretty sure the missing become food for the animals and bog-creatures." Jason shook his head. "Just like the Junk Yard and the Sandspit, the Bogs live by their own rule. Seattle does well to leave it alone."

"The soul of this place is dark and hungry." Every city, every stretch of wood, had its own sentience. Some slept, some rested easy, others were volatile. But every city and town, every forest and desert, and bog and marsh had a soul of sorts.

We were near a curve in the road, which curved to the left after a large stand of yew. I closed my eyes, checking the Trace. There...around the corner, I could sense the Abom. Sheathing my sword, I reached down to my thigh and gently slapped my hand against my thigh. The whip uncoiled into my fingers, lighting up with a pale ethereal fire. I had a better chance of taking the creature on with it rather than a blade, given the close quarters we were in.

"Be cautious. The Abom is near."

Jason edged to the side, his hands working runes in the air. He was prepping a spell, though I wasn't sure what. Not much that a magus his level could cast would work against an Abom.

At that moment, a screech echoed as the Abom came racing around the corner. It hadn't had a chance to take on a human vehicle yet, and instead of coming in on the astral, it had chosen to jump a bog-creature. The squat, gray being had leathery skin and its narrow eyes tilted up at the sides, a faint orange glow coming from within the sockets.

"Queet, stats?" My voice echoed, causing the birds to fall silent.

"No ordinary Abom. The soul-hole is blocked. You'll have to destroy the vehicle to stop it."

Taking it to the Crossroads wouldn't work, given the soul-hole was blocked, and I wasn't near a crossroad anyway.

I raised my whip, but the Abom took one look

at me and did a one-eighty, heading back the way it had come. I loped after it, around the bend, managing to skid to a halt just before I fell into a marshy patch that stretched across the path. The Abom was on the other side.

I gauged the width of the bog. A good ten feet, at least. If I took a running jump, I *might* make it, but I couldn't be sure and I had no desire to land in a patch of quicksand. I glanced up at a branch overhanging the bog from a tree on the other side.

Bringing my whip up, I cracked it overhead to wrap around the branch. In one smooth motion, I swung across the bog, landing on the other side in front of the Abom, who lurched backward. I gave my whip a solid yank and it glided off the tree branch. As the creature launched itself toward me, I jumped to the side. It skidded at the edge of the bog, and I raised my foot and booted it firmly in the ass, knocking it into the quicksand.

The Abom let out a guttural cry, but managed to drag itself out without any problem. I backed away.

Quickly, the Abom opened its mouth and a spray of something pungent came spewing toward me. I darted back another step but not quickly enough to dodge the liquid and a few drops landed on my left hand. The pain was instant and fierce as the caustic acid began eating into my skin. Crap, the bog-creature had an acidic spit, and the Abom had made use of it.

I wiped my hand against my jacket, but whatever the compound was, it wasn't coming off. Blisters began to fester over one of the metacarpal bones, and two oozing holes the size of peas bubbled and frothed.

"Fuck, how the hell do you even have a mouth with that sort of saliva? It's a wonder his jaw doesn't rot off." My hand aching, I extended my whip to the side, then slashed forward to wrap around the demon's ankle. It let out a low growl as I gave a swift tug, bringing it to the ground.

With my left hand I drew my dagger, dropping to my knees beside the Abom. I drove it deep into where I hoped the bog-creature's heart was. As the silver etchings on the blade met flesh, I heard a loud *pop* and the body fell silent. The Abom took flight into the astral and vanished.

I glanced at my hand again—the acid seemed to have stopped eating away at my skin, but the pain was still excruciating, and I could see blood and muscle and the faintest hints of bone beneath where the skin had burned away.

"Damn it, I'm going to need medical attention for this." I stood up, activating my Trace. There was no sign of the Abom—either it had returned to Pandoriam, or it had vanished into some realm I couldn't follow. I let out a long sigh. I turned back to see if Jason was waiting on the other side of the bog.

"Jason—are you—" But I didn't even get the words out before he blurred, then shifted into a majestic red-tailed hawk. He easily glided over the bog to land beside me. Another moment, and he shimmered back into his human form. I had once asked him what happened to his clothes when he shifted and he simply stared at me, grinned, and said, *"You do know I'm a magus?"* And that had been the end of that discussion.

"You're hurt." He stared at my hand. "Did you kill the Abom?"

I shrugged. "I don't know. I wasn't able to catch the soul-hole—it had it blocked somehow—but I destroyed the host's body." I was about to call it a night when a noise from the tangle ahead alerted me. The blip on my Trace screen reappeared. "Crap—it's still here. Incoming."

Jason nodded, stepping out of my way.

"It found a new body. Get behind that thistle-bush until we know what it's wearing."

He obeyed, dodging out of the way as another creature came charging at me around the bend. This time, the Abom was wearing the skin of a pig-headed dog with tusks. As it raced my way, eyes gleaming with the unnatural light of Pandoriam, I raised my whip again and brought it down smack across the creature's face.

"Queet? Soul-hole?"

"It's there, on the top of the head." His misty shape swirled in back of the pig-dog.

I slapped my whip back onto my leg and unsheathed my sword as the Abom lurched toward me. *Closer...closer...a little closer...*and then it was right on me. It struck with its tusks, trying to stab me in the leg. I brought my sword up and plunged it down toward the pig-dog's head. As the blade whistled toward the top of its skull, I could see the soul-hole, pale blue and writhing with energy. I shifted my aim ever so slightly, and the tip of the sword dug deep into the Abom's soul-hole. Xan sang as she hit, sending a blast of energy racing through the bog. As the Abom screeched out its death-wail, its vehicle slowly keeled over.

This time, the Abom was truly dead.

Panting, I knelt, hunching over as the pain from my hand started to eat through my adrenaline rush.

Jason emerged from behind the bush, his face ashen. "Kae...Kae, are you all right?"

I groaned slightly. While I hadn't drained myself by crossing over to the Crossroads this time, the energy it took to channel the force of a dying Abom was tremendous.

"Yeah, as long as we don't meet any more. Take me home. My hand needs medical attention and I need food and a drink."

It was then that I realized I had to get back over the marsh. There was only one way. Jason couldn't carry me in his hawk form. He seemed to realize the same thing.

"Let me get to the other side so I can catch you if need be. And here..." He looked around, finding a stand of Wandering Ivy. He hacked a long tendril off of it, jumping back as the plant lashed out at him, then tied it around my waist. The vines were almost as strong as rope until they dried out. With the other end in his mouth, he transformed back into his hawk form and, carrying the tendril, flew across the marsh.

There, he shifted back. Through my exhaustion and pain, I realized what he had done. If I should lose hold of my whip, he'd keep me from sinking due to the makeshift rope. Wearily, I sheathed my sword, then slapped my thigh again and brought my whip to bear. The pain ripped through my wounds as I grasped the butt of the whip with both hands and swung back over the marsh. Jason caught me, helping me land.

We hurried back along the trail as fast as we could. I was tired, but I'd done this gig too many times before to let myself rest yet, and not in the Bogs. I could muster the energy to get out of the area before collapsing.

Once we were out and back in his car, I fell against the seat as we headed toward my apartment. I thought about stopping in at the temple, but decided it could wait. I had taken down the Abom and talked to Tigra. That was all I needed to do tonight.

As we crept through the streets of Darktown, I stared out into the night, nursing my hand, thinking about the Order of the Black Mist. Abominations I knew how to deal with, but how the hell was I supposed to find a group of magicians bent on defying every rule we lived under? With a sigh, I pushed aside my thoughts. It was enough for one evening.

Chapter 10

As we trudged into my apartment, Queet used whisper-speak so Jason could hear him. "Fury needs food."

Jason grunted. "I'll see what she has in the fridge." He pushed me toward the sofa as he headed into the kitchenette. "Sit. I'll get food and drinks."

I groaned, dropping onto my couch. At least I wasn't hurting as bad as I had coming back off the Crossroads the other night, but that didn't mean that I was comfortable. I peeled off my jacket cautiously, taking care not to drag the material over my hand. Then, I unzipped my boots and slid them off, groaning as I curled up in the corner of the sofa.

Queet swirled into form next to me and sat his misty ass down on the edge of the coffee table. "Too many Aboms, too close together."

"Hecate is right, the activity from the World Tree is picking up. I may have to head into the Sandspit to have a look and see if anything has changed."

The World Tree was an actual tree—or rather network of trees. Areas like the Sandspit dappled the world, and each one had a giant tree in the center of it. Here, it was an oak—in other places it was a tree that fit the ecology. But all the trees were linked on the astral level, and all of the trees were part of the World Tree. Through the branches and trunks were portals leading into other realms.

Queet grew unusually somber. "It's dangerous to get too close. You never know what will come through." He shook his head. "I know you've been there before, but be careful, Fury. You know I have your back if you go, though."

"Thanks. I know we don't always see eye to eye, but with the Aboms coming over faster, and the Order of the Black Mist rising, I have the feeling we may be going even more places we really don't want to." I stared at my hand. "The Abom was bad enough, but what really scares me is that tornado. Queet, you know what will happen if the rogue magicians take this any further."

"I know. I know all too well."

Jason appeared at that moment, two plates in hand. He had made thick sandwiches, piled high with meat and cheese. "You're out of chicken, by the way."

I groaned. "You just cleaned me out of three days of food." When he gave me a pointed look, I added, "It's a tight month, okay?" But then I remembered the three hundred cash Hecate had slipped me and the cash I had made off readings at the shop. I also had a job to call about on Monday. "Never mind, it will be all right."

"If you need a little extra, just ask." Jason pulled out his phone.

"No. I'm not your responsibility anymore." I tried to wave him off, but within less than a minute, I had a text telling me he had transferred two hundred cash to my account. "You didn't have to do that."

"No, but I did, so shut up and eat. Where's your first-aid kit?"

"In the bathroom," I muttered. "Top drawer on the left."

He set his sandwich aside and headed into the bath.

I stood up and opened the curtains. I was on the fourth floor of a brick walkup. My apartment was small—a bedroom, living room, kitchenette, and bath—but I didn't care, because my view overlooked Idyll Inlet, on the northwest edge of Darktown.

I lived in the King's Cross apartment building, directly across from a Monotrain platform. My apartment overlooked the water, and sometimes at night, I would turn off the lights and watch the silver crest of the inlet against the moonlight. The sight seemed to soothe the perpetual fire that burned within me. Jason had once remarked that watching the water tempered me—like fire and snow tempered steel. When I thought about it, he was right. Hecate bathed me in her fire day and night. I could feel her in the tattoo on my neck, in the whip inked into my leg. When the gods came calling, they weren't subtle about it. The water gave me a respite from that continual burning that raced through my blood.

Jason returned with first aid supplies and a basin of water. He set them on the table, then took hold of my left hand as I continued to eat with my right. He examined my wounds.

"We should have stopped at the Care Clinic. This is bad, Kae. Why you aren't on the floor whimpering is beyond me. I think I can manage this, though."

I had no desire to head back out into the night just to see the doctor. "If you can take care of it here, I'd rather do that. I've got some Sleep-Eez, which will help me through the pain tonight." One thing about Sleep-Eez, it came in quarter doses and each dose provided for two hours of sleep. There was no morning-after hangover, either, and it wasn't addictive.

Jason began cleaning my hand. I grimaced, gritting my teeth, but kept quiet as he flushed the wounds with clear water. Then he examined them closely.

"Well, they're nasty, but I think you can avoid infection. We can't let them heal over too soon, though. I'm going to pack them with the antibiotic powder and then cover them loosely for the first day or two." As he tamped the powder into the holes where the acid had burned through the flesh, I let out a sharp yelp. "I know it hurts, but this will help prevent infection."

As he wrapped my hand in gauze, he glanced around the apartment. "Where's the Sleep-Eez? You're going to need it."

He was right. My hand was throbbing and I wouldn't be able to sleep without help. "In the bathroom, in the top right drawer."

While he was getting the meds, I finished off my sandwich. Jason returned and shook out three of the tablets. I placed them under my tongue, wrinkling my nose as they fizzed into a bubbly grape-flavored liquid in my mouth. As the medication began to absorb into my system, I felt my pillows calling me. I let out a soft murmur and yawned.

"Usually this doesn't hit me so fast."

"You don't usually don't get burned by acidic spit from a bog monster."

"Stay here tonight." I blurted out the words before I could stop myself. "I mean...you can sleep on the sofa. It's comfortable. And that way you'll get more sleep than you would if you drive home." I blushed a little, partly because I was hoping he didn't think I meant it any other way and partly because the image of us together in my bed had suddenly flashed through my mind, totally unbidden, but nevertheless, there it was.

He stared at me for a moment, then slowly nodded. "I'll take you up on that. I don't feel like driving home to..." With a pause, he winced, leaning forward to cradle his head.

"I'm sorry." I pushed away my own fantasies to make way for his reality. "I'm sorry, Jason. I wish..."

"I know, Kae. You're a sweetheart and a good friend." He gazed up at me, his cool eyes piercing right through my heart. Never had a compliment stung so much and yet felt so good. I yawned again, suddenly realizing I was about to pass out. "Come on, sleepy girl."

He lifted me into his arms, and as I protested, he carried me into the bedroom. I was drifting off already, and the last I remembered was whispering something to the effect of "This is nice" as he undressed me, slid me under the covers, and tucked me in. Too tired to be mortified, I closed my eyes and was out for the night.

I woke to my alarm going off. I blurrily looked at it. Five-thirty. At first I thought Jason had set it, but Queet was swirling near the end of my bed. "I set it," he said, his voice thundering through my brain. That alone drove the cobwebs out. "Get up. Jason is up, Tam will be here soon, and you need to head out to the Arbortariam."

"Everybody will just have to wait until I take a shower." The Sleep-Eez had soothed my aching muscles, but I felt grimy. I eased beneath the inviting spray, jerking my hurt hand away as the pounding water stung it through the bandages. Using my right hand, I soaped myself with violet-scented bath gel, my all-too-abundant boobs peeking out from the lather. I lathered up my hair, too, washing the crimson and black strands as best as I could with one hand. Finally, deciding I was as clean as I could possibly get, I turned off the shower and stepped out of the stall.

Fifteen minutes later, my hair was dry and I was dressed. Getting on my shorts and bra was a chore given my hand, but at least the tank top was easy. My hair was a mass of waves and I did my best to brush it back into a ponytail. I slapped on some eyeliner, mascara, and lip gloss, and called it good. It was then that I checked my phone and saw that Hecate had phoned an hour before. I decided to call her back after I'd had some coffee and headed into the living room.

Jason was there, along with Tam. Queet was nowhere to be seen. He had vanished after waking me up. The guys had made coffee, and Tam had brought breakfast: pastries and sausage sandwiches and a bag of grapes. As I accepted a mug of coffee, we gave him the rundown of what had happened in Bend and at the Bogs.

"This isn't going to play out well. If whoever's behind this has already started mucking around with weather magic, either they have figured out how to use that disk, or they already knew how to call up storms." He found my plates and portioned out the food.

As we gathered around the table, I gulped down the coffee, burning my tongue in my haste.

"Slow down. We have time," Tam said. "How's your hand feeling?"

I shook my head. "Achy. It hurts, but not as much as last night."

Jason finished his sandwich and held out his hand. "Let me see."

I switched my sausage muffin to my right hand and then let him remove the bandages. The wounds were red and inflamed, although there was no sign of pus oozing out of the holes. The antibiotic powder was still packed inside them, serving to keep them open as it slowly worked on my system. Jason examined my fingers.

"Can you feel this?" he said, wiggling them from side to side.

"Yes, I can feel it, and it hurts. There's a lot of pressure there." I bit my lip, staring at my puffy fingers. "Should I go to the doctor?"

"At this point, I doubt if there's much they can do for you. But the fire in your system can't be helping. You need water to counter the swelling. Healing magic." He glanced over at Tam. "Can you do anything?"

Tam took a closer look. "I have a spell that might offer some relief, but..." He paused, then smiled. "I can help you, but you have to let me kiss you."

I blinked. That was a new one on me. "Say what?"

"A great deal of my magic is transferred via kiss and touch. My healing magic is the magic of the Grove and the Crystal Grotto."

I wasn't sure what the *Grove* and *Crystal Grotto* were, but said nothing as he scooted his chair around, sliding it in between Jason and me. Jason leaned back in his chair, crossing his arms across his chest, watching with a smirk.

"All right." I found myself growing nervous. I wasn't sure why, but I felt like I was about to enter new territory and I didn't like doing so without a map.

Tam caught my gaze, holding it firm. His eyes were silver as the moon and I couldn't look away as he leaned closer to press his lips to mine. A deep shiver raced through me, so deep I almost lost myself in it. I melted into his arms, and he shifted, drawing me closer as a sudden wash of his breath entered my mouth, cool like mint, cool like winter ice. I drifted in the kiss as his energy worked its way through my body, stretching me, embracing me. And then, the wash hit my hand—a rush of rainwater, whitecaps on a mountain stream. It washed through the injury, soothing the pain and relieving the pressure.

Another moment, and he slowly drew away.

I started to blush, but the embarrassment faded as I realized just how much the kiss had helped. I held up my hand, staring as the swelling began to visibly subside as we watched. It wasn't fully healed, but within the space of a few moments, the angry color was almost normal.

"That's amazing." I turned to Tam. "Thank you…" Then, I found myself blurting out, "You have the softest lips."

"My pleasure," he said with a wink. "You have nice lips yourself."

Jason interrupted. "Hadn't we better get going if you are supposed to meet Jerako by seven?"

"I suppose we better." I stood, turning to Tam. "I'm taking my sword. I don't want to chance not having it when I need it." Slinging the sheath over my head, I said, "Let's go. I'm not sure how to get there or how long it takes. I've never been to the Arbortariam before."

"I'll drive you to the ferries. I might as well head into the shop and set up early. After yesterday..." Jason paused.

"After yesterday we *all* need to regroup." At six-fifteen, I followed the men out the door, locking it securely behind me. Jason and I sat in front, Tam in back, as we headed toward the eastern border of Seattle, where the Arbortariam was.

My phone jangled and I glanced at the text. "Hecate wants to see me at noon. I hope we're back in time."

"We should be," Tam said.

We arrived at the docks shortly before the next ferry was scheduled to leave. Jason had very little to say as Tam and I slipped out of the car. He waved, then drove off, speeding into the center of Darktown.

Tam watched as the car disappeared, then turned to me. "He was pretty quiet."

"I think he's still thinking about Eileen. Yesterday when we were headed out to Bend, he told me that it had been an arranged marriage and was doing his best to convince me he would have done right by Eileen."

"Methinks our fair-haired hawk-shifter didn't want to get married and now feels guilty over it," Tam mused. "Whatever the case, he has to work it out. Come, let's go meet the Greenling."

The ferries over to the Arbortariam ran every half hour. We had five minutes to get on board and managed it with seconds to spare. As we stared out over the bow, the dark water churned beneath the boat.

The morning was shrouded with mist, rising off the inlet. At one time, they said, Idyll Inlet had actually been a lake, but between the Weather Wars and the World Shift, all the coastlines had changed. Now, the inlet was a long stretch of water feeding in from Pacific Sound through the Locks. Idyll Inlet stretched along the inner coast, where the Edge was nestled between water and forest. Not many people lived over on the Edge, and those who did were rife with rogue magic. Creatures sidled out of the Wild Wood there, and the rumors were thick about magical valleys deep in the wilds.

The ferry ride was short—fifteen minutes at best—and as we pulled into the docks, the stretch of forest spreading before us made me nervous. It was then that I realized there was a force field—invisible but extremely tangible—surrounding the entire thicket.

"You can see the barrier, right?"

Tam nodded. "Yes, I can. It's very much like the ones that we erect around our barrows in Briarwood. The field surrounds the island, save for a thin strip that circles Arbortariam. If you were to try to walk through it, you'd find yourself turning around and walking the other way. It's extraordinarily powerful." He sounded delighted.

"You're really looking forward to this, aren't you?" Impulsively, I looped my arm around his. "I suppose they'll have someone waiting for us." We were among a handful of people to get off the boat.

Most walked up to the forest and did exactly as Tam had predicted: turned around, walked back to the ferry, and re-boarded.

But as we approached the front of the copse, a figure slowly moved out of the shadows. He had been standing near enough to observe, but had been cloaked—camouflaged, perhaps. He was lithe and svelte, and reminded me oddly of Tam, but with a far more feral feel. Branches rose from his head, but unlike Tam, they were actual branches, not his hair frizzing out.

"I am the one they call Zhan. Please follow me and I will take you to Jerako. Neither touch nor seek to gather any of the plants."

"What about my sword? I promise to keep it sheathed." I expected they might take it until we finished, but our guide merely shrugged.

"It is unimportant. You may bring it with you."

The thought occurred to me that if they weren't concerned about my sword, they must have pretty damned powerful magic to counter it.

He turned to Tam. "Welcome, Bonny Brother. We are honored to greet one from your world." He didn't sound so much honored as intrigued.

But Tam responded graciously, inclining his head. "As am I. I have always longed to meet the Greenlings, and I am grateful for this opportunity." He gave me a little pinch on the elbow as he took my arm to walk me along.

I hastily nodded. "Yes, as am I."

"Then we are all honored and mayhap be moving the meeting along." And with a vague smile that might also have been a frown, Zhan led us into the world of the Greenlings.

Chapter 11

It was as though the force field were a translucent veil that lifted as Zhan led us toward it.

As we stepped through the shimmering veil, I caught my breath. The forest inside the Arbortariam was totally unlike what it looked like outside the veil. The island of Arbortariam had been connected to land at one point, but now it was connected to the Edge by two bridges, and to Seattle proper only by the ferries.

Outside, it looked like a dark forest, sprawling and spooky. But one step through the veil and we were in fairyland. The mood shifted—the Wild was all around us. The trees began to shimmer, as if dusted in miniature stars that sparkled under the silver sheen of clouds, as a light rain began to fall. The air seemed clear here, almost richer in oxygen, and smelled like wet cedar and fir and moss. I thought I heard a stream in the distance.

Everywhere, the dripping rain echoed off the trees, cool and crisp, and smelling like ancient forest. The trees were jumbled, tall and laden with bracken, and oak moss hung from their branches like long beards on old men. Mushrooms sprouted along nurse logs that lay silent on the forest floor, their trunks slowly working their way back to the sludge from which they had first sprouted.

I stopped, overwhelmed by the sheer beauty around me. The very air seemed to sparkle. Suddenly dizzy, I stumbled and Tam caught my arm, steadying me.

"This...what *is* this place?" The words sprang to my lips before I could stop them.

"This is the home of the Greenlings," our guide said, turning with a faint smile on his face. "I am one of their servants. I'm a hedgemite."

Tam stiffened. "Your kind still exists, then?" He turned to me. "We thought the hedgemites had died out eons ago during the Weather Wars." He turned back to Zhan. "I had no idea what you looked like."

Zhan gave us a solemn nod. "We do exist, yes. The Greenlings brought our kind back to life. There were few of us left by the end of the great wars. Thanks to the ancient race, we have recovered. We now serve them as a measure of our gratitude."

I had no idea what a hedgemite was, but figured it would be impolite to ask. I'd save that question for later. "The Arbortariam is breathtaking. I've never felt anything quite like this." I wanted to close my eyes and drift in the energy swirling around me. I felt like I was being gently rocked, encased in soft petals.

"We are grateful for your joy. Joy means so much here. Hedgemites thrive on it."

He turned back to the path and led us deeper into the woodland. Tam reached out and took my hand and I let him hold it. It felt totally natural in this space. His fingers closed over mine and my stomach fluttered. I blinked, wondering if I should pull away, but then my thoughts drifted on to the birdsong echoing through the morning chill and I quit worrying.

We rounded a bend in the path and I stopped, Tam halting beside me. Ahead and to the left, the ground mounded up to form a hill, from which a waterfall trickled down, creating a lazy pool beneath it. The water shimmered with prisms, and I thought I could see women bathing in the pond below but when I blinked, they were gone.

I let out a slow breath. "That veil...it wasn't merely an illusion to fool the outer world, was it? We really are in a different world, aren't we?"

"There are illusions, and then there are illusions," was all Zhan would say. But Tam squeezed my hand and shook his head just enough for me to see. I fell silent, but my sword tingled against my back as if it could hear me and agreed.

We came to a clearing in the woods and Zhan led us into the center of a grove where grass quivered, knee high in the breeze. The clearing sloped uphill on a slow gradient, and in the center, an oak sprang upward a good hundred feet. Beneath the overhanging boughs heavily laden with round-lobed leaves that were turning bronze there sat a tall man, his long legs stretched out in the grass. He was sturdy and completely formed of foliage. His crimson eyes reminded me of holly berries, and as we approached, I realized his legs and arms were actually long, straight branches covered with a thick cover of moss. He was unlike anyone or anything I had ever seen.

"Greenling..." Tam whispered beside me, his eyes wide.

As we approached, Zhan suddenly lost his composure and he stammered as he said, "May I present you to Jerako, Elder among the Greenlings. Jerako, I bring you the Theosian Fury, and her companion Tam, one of the Bonny Fae."

Jerako grumbled something, and then slowly rose to his feet. He was a good ten feet tall, and up close I could see just how intricately the foliage wove together, as though it had been tightly braided. I wondered if he had a heart or an actual brain, or whether his internal organs looked anything at all like ours.

I slowly let Tam's hand drop away as everything else seemed to fade. My entire vision was fixed on Jerako as he loomed over us. He was wild and feral, and the only thing I could focus on were those ancient eyes that flickered crimson, but then they seemed to shift and spin, and I realized that, no—they were orange...then...finally, they were the brilliant pale lemon chiffon of early morning clouds covering the sunrise.

He seemed to loom larger and I realized I had sunk to my knees. Tam had done the same beside me. In the core of my heart, I knew we were facing the beginning of the world, caught up in form. His aura flickered with a magic directly spun from the center of the earth. He was a child of Gaia, stretching back farther than any of the gods, any of the Fae or shifters or Weres.

How old he was, I couldn't say, but the years seemed to whirl past as I gazed into his eyes. His lips, formed of leaves and vines, crinkled into the semblance of a smile and I had the sudden feeling we were still alive only by the grace of his nature. He could wipe us out, stomp us down, tear us to shreds with a single breath. I began to lower my head to press my forehead to the grass at his feet, when he stayed my movement with the tendril of a single vine reaching out to touch my shoulder.

"Stand, young goddess. You too, Bonny Brother." His voice boomed through the air, catching my hair in a breeze. Yet, the words didn't linger—they vanished as soon as I heard them...so quickly that I wondered if I had heard them at all.

Tam held out his hand and I took it, slowly standing beside him.

"So, Hecate bade me talk to you, if I would. Come, let us have a chat." He motioned to the tree. "Join me. This is my favorite spot to sit and think. The grass is soft, the air clear, and the shade, just the perfect amount."

We followed him, silently settling under the oak tree. The grass was wet, but I didn't care. I settled down, lifting my sword over my head to set it by my side, then leaned back, my hands on the ground behind me. A steady *thump, thump, thump* echoed beneath my fingers. The heartbeat of the Earth, a staccato tattoo, trilled through my body as it counted the beat of years passing by. The energy was seductive and frightening in its intensity. It reminded me of a softer, opulent version of my fire, and a quiver in my stomach responded.

Tam seemed to be responding to it, too. He reached out, almost absently, and stroked my arm. A ripple of hunger raced down my spine. I looked over at him, locking his gaze with mine. The silver of his eyes flashed as he smiled. Again, the shiver of desire washed through me, setting spark to the flames. Between him and the energy of the Arbortariam, I was about ready to jump out of my skin.

"Hecate tells me that you have a problem with weather magicians?" Jerako took his time to speak, but when he did, he came right to the point.

I tried to shake away the web of desire that gnawed at me and returned my attention back to the Greenling. "I'm not sure how much she told you..." I stopped, totally out of my league. Dealing with Hecate didn't seem nearly so difficult. She was ancient and powerful, but this creature—he was older than the gods.

Jerako let out a soft murmur. "Why don't you tell me the story from the beginning? It seems the most logical place to begin."

I acquiesced, telling him about the rise in Aboms coming through the World Tree, the theft of the Thunderstrike, the tornado in Bend, and the Order of the Black Mist. When I finished, he simply grunted and leaned back against the oak tree.

Tam inched closer to me. Shaken out of whatever spell had been weaving around us, I cleared my throat and scooted away. He chuckled and slid forward. I gave him a warning shake of the head, but couldn't help but smile. With a shrug, he laid back in the grass, closing his eyes.

We waited. Five minutes or fifty might have passed—time seemed to bend and stretch in the Arbortariam—when Jerako finally spoke again.

"The Greenlings watch from here, and other places like this, and we see the world march by. Civilizations rise and fall, then rise again. They change and evolve and crumble. We retreated at the beginning of the Weather Wars as the scourge of humanity did their best to destroy the planet. When Gaia summoned us, we went to war. Now, we guard over the Wild, always ready to go marching again when she calls."

I shivered. That sounded like a threat.

"Magic is a part of humanity's heritage, a part of the Fae...it is as natural as breathing to some." He paused, then abruptly asked, "Do you know why weather magic is forbidden?"

I shook my head. "We misused it. Gaia forbade its use."

Tam nodded.

Jerako let out a low sound that could have been a laugh or a grunt. "Yes, but do you *fully* understand the history?"

I glanced at Tam, who gave me a hesitant shrug. We waited. This meeting was Jerako's to lead. I wasn't going to step on the Greenling's toes.

"Weather magic decimated the forests, with the governments waging war by launching vast hurricanes and scorching droughts against one another. Famine spread as they lay waste to the natural balance of the planet and sent the world spiraling to the brink of a mass extinction such as never before seen. The gods tried to stop them, but they are limited. But when Gaia awoke from her long slumber and realized what was going on, she roused the Greenlings. We are her arms and legs and we rose by the thousands and went to war."

The thought of a hundred—let alone thousands—of Greenlings marching on the cities was terrifying. I couldn't imagine what it had been like when the governments of the world found themselves directly in the line of ten thousand pissed-off servants of the planet. My expression must have shown on my face, because Jerako let out a dark laugh.

"You begin to understand what it was like. The governments brought their weapons to bear, but we are the soldiers of the planet, and we cannot be stopped. We drove through and shook the walls and crumbled the cities and brought the governments to their knees. Gaia opened the World Tree in her anger. They begged us then to spare them. In return, we exacted their promise to never again allow the use of weather magic. Elemental magic? Not a problem, but never to be used to alter the weather. And so they gave us their word, and promised on their children's lives and their grandchildren's lives. Gaia relented and allowed them live, under the doom of destruction should they ever forfeit on their promises."

I slowly straightened up, as did Tam. "If we cannot find whoever is stirring up trouble..."

"If you do not recover the device, and too much damage is done, we will follow through with our decree. I give you this message to all who might listen: The Greenlings are everywhere. If the perpetrators of the tornado—and those who seek to revive the hidden arts of meteocramancy—are not stopped, then we will once again lay waste to the cities."

And with that, he stood. "As to advice, keep an eye on the weather. Follow the patterns. Do whatever you have to in order to stop them. We will give you time to act, but we will be keeping watch. If you do not counter this threat, expect destruction. A warning, however: Those who work with weather magic are often turned by the destructive power, and they become possessed by the fury of the storms. And that is one fury that you do *not* want to face."

With that, he turned and strode into the depths of the forest.

"Did he just say what I think he did?" I didn't turn, didn't move, simply stared at the vanishing back of the Greenling.

Tam cleared his throat. "Yes, I think so."

I jumped as a voice behind me said, "Trust me, the Greenlings never say anything they don't mean." Zhan stood with crossed arms. His eyes were glowing. "Take his words to heart, O Furious Beauty. He means what he says."

Shaken, I picked myself up off the ground,

brushing the stray grass off my legs and butt. "They could destroy the world."

Tam slid his arm around my waist and I didn't protest. "They can destroy *our* world. Not Gaia— she will continue. We have to find whoever stole that disk and we'd damned well better execute them. The Greenlings are no gentle race like some faerie tales make them out to be. They're ruthless and they won't brook mercy." He tightened his grip and leaned down to nose my hair. "Come, Fury. We have to let Hecate know what happened."

All too aware of how close he was, I nodded. "We have to get back to the Peninsula of the Gods before anything else happens. This takes precedence over everything, because if we mess up, there won't be anything left to protect. Come on."

Before I could say a word, Tam placed a soft kiss on my forehead and again, the ripple of hunger raced through me. I glanced up at him and he lightly brushed my lips with his own, then stood back and took my hand.

We turned to Zhan. "Can you lead us to the entrance? We have to go visit the gods."

And with that, Zhan led us out of the Arbortariam and, all too soon, we were back aboard the ferry, heading toward the streets of Seattle.

Chapter 12

Once we were back in the city, Tam and I caught the Monotrain. Everybody gave us a wide berth due to my sword, which suited me just fine. As we headed to the Peninsula of the Gods, neither of us said much, but my thoughts were racing. Jerako had scared me—and scared me good. It wasn't so much him, but what he represented. The Arbortariam had swept me in, but the thought of the Greenlings rising up thanks to a group of rogue magicians haunted me.

"Are you all right?" Tam lightly brushed my shoulder and I jumped.

Tam wasn't my type. At least, I tried to tell myself that. I had feelings for *Jason*. Jason, who was mourning his fiancée and who had never made a move toward me. But even as I tried to ignore the feeling, Tam's touch sparked off something I had never felt—not on any of the dates I had been on, nor with any of the men I had slept with. I was on a slippery slope, dangerously close to falling over the cliff into the mists.

I did my best to brush aside my disconcertion as we exited the Monotrain and entered the Peninsula of the Gods. We stood for a moment at the top, then clattered down the stairs to the third tier.

Naós ton Theón was busy, and I remembered it was Sunday. Most weekday shift-workers made their pilgrimages on the weekends.

As we approached the line, I grabbed Tam's wrist and bypassed those waiting in front of us, striding up to the entrance reserved for the servants of the gods. I seldom had to use it, but I wasn't about to stand around waiting today. Jerako's warning echoed in my head.

As we went through the M&M detector—once again, with them scanning my sword and passing me through—Tam scowled. His frown deepened as we headed deeper into the temple.

"Your gods elevate themselves outside of nature. All of these temples, all of these monolithic structures, are so alien to my culture."

I blinked. I hadn't thought about it before. "Don't you have gods? I thought your people worshipped the Celts."

"We are descended from the Celtic gods. But do you see temples here dedicated to the Celtic gods? Do you see huge marble structures devoted to the Danu and the Dagda?"

"I don't know if I've ever noticed."

"You won't find them here. Our temples are out in the Wild Wood. They're by the streams and lakes, or buried deep in the mountains. The buildings are made of stone, yes, but they are modest and scaled to fit in their environment." He paused, glancing at me as we strode toward the elevator. "I'm sorry. I'm being disrespectful. Our way is not the only way."

I punched the button for the third floor. "No, I think I understand, but I didn't choose my path, Tam. Like you, I was born to it. But to be honest, I don't think that Hecate gives a rat's ass about *big and pompous*. Some of the gods do..." I glanced around, then lowered my voice. "Zeus and Hera? You'd better believe it...at least from what I've gathered."

He chuckled, letting me take the lead. As we entered the waiting room, Coralie waved and told me to go directly back.

Hecate was behind her desk when we entered the room. She glanced at Tam, arching her eyebrows. "Tam, hello. I trust you enjoyed your trip?"

Tam gave her a deep bow with a winning smile. He had met her before, but never here. Hecate had occasionally dropped in on me at Dream Wardens over the years.

"We just returned from the Arbortariam." I dove into what Jerako had said. Hecate listened, nodding solemnly. "To sum up, if we don't stop whoever is mucking around with the weather, they'll come in and do it for us." I leaned back against the leather sofa. "Last night's Abom was a hard one. It had managed to obscure its soul-hole the first time. Either they're learning new tricks or it got lucky."

"I'll be right back." She tapped swiftly on her tablet. "I promise, I won't be gone as long as I was last time." And with that, she whisked herself out of the door.

Tam looked around the office. "Professional. Not at all gothic."

"No, Hecate's not into dust catchers. At least not when she's here on this plane. In her own realm...well...she's much more...terrifying. Beautiful and dark, like a queen of crystal and obsidian. It's hard to explain but she's both fire and ice. I respond to her flame, but when I'm on the Crossroads, my fire is as cold as her ice."

"I wouldn't cross her, tell you that much." He lowered himself to the sofa, and gingerly sat near me, keeping enough space between us to prevent an accidental touch. "Fury..." Then he paused and shook his head. "Later."

"Good decision." I winced. My hurt hand was starting to ache again. I held it out, staring at the bandage. "More Aboms entering than usual. An order of arcane magicians out to stir up trouble. What next?"

"Don't tempt the Fates by asking." Tam paused, then added, "I didn't put a Come-Hither on you, you know. Please believe me."

I gazed into his eyes, realizing that what I had been feeling hadn't gone away. "I know you wouldn't do that." It was true. The Bonny Fae could be cagey, but Tam and I had known each other too long for me to believe that he would put a Come-Hither spell on me. Something had shifted between us. I wasn't sure what, but now wasn't the time to find out.

Hecate reentered the room. She sat on the edge of her desk. "News, good for a change. Or, at least, I think it's good news. One of the grimoires that was stolen has been tracked down. We have it—as well as the magician who stole it. And the Thunderstrike was spotted in the Junk Yard. I could contact the authorities, but we don't trust the powers in power at the moment. There's some movement going on among the government and the Devani that has us worried. Nothing for you to concern yourselves with. At least, for now."

"Really? I thought all of them were buddy-buddy."

Hecate leaned forward, clasping her hands on her leg. "Jerako is correct. At one time, the Greenlings were poised to destroy what was left of civilization. Gaia extracted a promise from the governments that humans would never again use—or allow the use of—weather magic as a weapon. The gods vowed to uphold Gaia's decree. Weather magic is far too disruptive to the balance. The governments of the world pulled together, but they were run by the richest corporations, and they had incredible influence—just as they do now. The EuroAsiAmerican Alliance took form. Any country refusing to join is kept at an agrarian level, strictly watched for magical and technological development."

"How long ago were the Weather Wars? So many records were lost during the World Shift."

"Long ago. Centuries. It took Gaia one

moment to cause the World Shift, but it took quite awhile for the world's climate to return to some semblance of balance, and for humans to develop sustainable technology that met her approval. It also took centuries to rebuild from the destruction during the Weather Wars."

A grim smile spread across her face. "Before this matter gets totally out of hand, I need to send you into the Junk Yard to see what you can find out about the Thunderstrike. I'm sorry, Fury. I know how much you hate the place, and you have every reason to feel that way."

"Do you know exactly where I should look?" The thought of returning to the Junk Yard made my stomach lurch. I hadn't been there since I had faced the Carver five years ago.

Hecate scanned her tablet. "Actually, yes. Try a nightclub called Phoenix Rising. It's a magicians' bar, so go cautiously, but the fact you're a witch will make it believable for you to be there. Don't take your sword—that would be a dead giveaway. You're too well known around Darktown and the Trips to go in without cloaking up." She glanced at me. "Obviously, you'll have to go in at night, since they lock the gates during the day."

"So what do I do if I run across an Abomination while I'm in the Junk Yard? Should I take them out? I'm just trying to plan ahead."

Hecate shook her head. "No, for now leave them be. In fact, as much as I hate taking away your immediate access to it, wear something that covers your whip."

I had already been thinking about that. "I have

a long skirt with a slit up both sides. It will be a little cumbersome, but I can still manage both dagger and whip."

"Be careful, and do your best to remain undercover." She held my gaze. "I don't like sending you into this situation, but there's really no choice."

I had been thinking about something, uncertain of whether to ask about it. But finally, I decided I needed to know. "Why did you send me to Jerako, if you already knew what the Greenlings would say?"

Hecate laughed, her voice rich and throaty. "There's a method to what might seem like madness. Think carefully, Fury. The governments don't like learning from the past. Now, Jerako will warn the EUAA to work with Lightning Strikes. If I were to go to the Regent of Seattle and tell him that a weather-magic device was stolen, he would nod and make a show of being appalled, and then the report would slip through the cracks because the Conglomerate is as corrupt as they come. They don't take the gods seriously, not truly. Add to that, the government has their fingers deep into the World Regency Corporation's pockets, and you can bet they'll do their best to divert Lightning Strikes from permanently dissolving the company and executing the person responsible."

I was beginning to follow her thoughts. "But if the *Greenlings* warn them that they'll whip their ass if weather magic is used..."

"Exactly. The Conglomerate is terrified of the Greenlings. The Elder Gods? We can cause a fuss and mayhem and destroy some lives. Gaia? She can destroy civilization. They'll do more if they think their asses are one step away from annihilation." Hecate's lips curled in a snarky grin. "And I, for one, won't have any qualms about seeing them squirm."

Tam's eyes narrowed. "I'm surprised they haven't tried to exterminate the Greenlings over the eons. After all, they're the only ones holding the corporatocracies in check. If it weren't for Jerako and his kin, humans would be out to tear apart the world again."

"Not every human is like that, and there are plenty from other races...other species...who are just as short-sighted and greedy." I shook my head. "Even the gods have their troublemakers." Realizing who was in the room with me, I glanced at Hecate, but she just nodded.

"True enough. There are several gods who would love to set up a hellhole on Earth, given the chance. They would happily enslave or destroy anybody giving them trouble. Nobody has a monopoly on being an ass." She slid off her desk and let out an exasperated sigh. "I wish to hell that the Order of the Black Mist hadn't been so stupid."

"How long do you think that Jerako will give us to find the disk?" Tam asked.

Hecate shrugged. "If he's in a generous mood, we may have a month or so. Unless whoever has it goes trigger happy and starts creating storms everywhere. Then, all bets are off and I'd recommend heading out of town."

"Then I'd better find that disk. I'll head into

the Junk Yard tonight." And with that, Tam and I bade her good-bye. Tam returned to Dream Wardens, and I headed home for a nap.

I entered my apartment, locked the door, then opened the drapes. The view of the water always calmed me down. My stomach rumbled—breakfast had been a long time ago, along with my last sip of coffee—so I headed into my kitchenette and scraped together one last sandwich and a handful of chips. Thanks to Hecate and Jason, I could go grocery shopping, but that could wait until tomorrow.

Queet startled me as I carried my roast beef sandwich and cup of coffee over to the sofa. He was sitting—in full misty form—on the edge of the ottoman, staring out at the water.

"What's going on? Please don't tell me there's an Abom near. I don't think I can handle another one this soon." I was thoroughly dragged out.

He shook his head. "No, Fury. Nothing like that. But I do have something to talk to you about. First, though, tell me what happened out on the Arbortariam."

"Let me eat first, okay? I need a moment to breathe." Truth was, I needed more than a moment. Not only was I worried sick about what was going to happen with the Order of the Black Mist, but my reaction to Tam was confusing the hell out of me. I had developed a crush on Jason when I was sixteen, but he had never noticed it.

Or, if he did, he never let on. I thought I would outgrow it, especially given the fact that he was engaged.

But until this week, even though I had dated other men, there had been a part of me dreaming that something would change and we'd end up together. He was handsome and strong and smart. And, to be brutally honest, I suspected I had a bit of hero worship going on.

After all, he had picked me up off his doorstep, a broken and frightened girl who had somehow escaped from a crazed psychopath. He had taken me in, given me a home, helped me learn how to live again. At night, he had raced into my room when I fought the nightmares, waking me as I screamed my lungs out. He had counseled me when I had been depressed, and called in his sister when I needed to talk to a woman.

Most of all, he had encouraged me to grow into who I was, never interfering with my relationship with Hecate. The day I had gone to the Junk Yards to face the Carver, he had backed me all the way and never once questioned whether I was doing the right thing.

But now...in the sweep of a single day, my crush on Jason seemed just that as I found my thoughts turning to Tam. Tam, whose touch had set me afire. Tam, whose eyes were like molten silver, embracing me in their opulent, passionate stare. Tam...who was one of the Bonny Fae and who scared me as much as he attracted me. The Fae lived by their own rules and they didn't care what anybody else thought. Could I withstand

Tam's intensity? Or would my fire clash with his and erupt in a horrible rain of stinging sparks?

I slowly ate my sandwich as I watched the waves of Idyll Inlet whip into white caps. The wind had risen and rain beat down in a silver stream. Finally, I found myself breathing normally again, and I finished my sandwich, wiped my lips, and sucked down the last of my coffee.

Queet waited patiently, which surprised me. He wasn't the calmest spirit in the world. Finally, I turned to him.

"Okay, I've had my breather. What's up?"

"Fury, I know you're a Theosian. I know that you have to do as Hecate bids you. But I'm worried about you." He paused. "Do you remember the first time I appeared to you?"

I frowned, trying to think back, but finally shook my head. "It's almost like you've always been here. Honestly? No. When was it?"

He stared at the floor for a moment before answering. "I came to you the night your mother died. I was sent to you. You don't remember me there, but I watched over you while the Carver held you captive, and I made certain you knew exactly what to do in order to escape him. When you reached out for help, Hecate sent me in."

Letting out a soft breath, I wasn't sure what to say. So I simply waited.

"You haven't been in the Junk Yard in years, not since you faced the Carver and almost destroyed him. Are you sure you want to go in there again? The magicians are going to be powerful, and their kind like to source women for power. You know that they run a network of enslaved women. I'm not sure you can handle being around them."

I frowned, shoving my plate farther back on the coffee table. "You don't think I can handle a bunch of horny guys?"

He let out a sound of exasperation. "That's the thing. They aren't just 'horny guys.' Fury, these are dangerous men capable of sickening acts. I just... want you to be safe."

I smiled. Queet wasn't questioning my ability, he was questioning the men I'd be around. It was true, a number of magicians—especially the ones who overstepped the boundaries—played fast and loose, using women as an extra source because we generally ran more natural power.

"Queet—remember who I am. I'm a Theosian. Can I be hurt? Yes. Can I fight back? You know it. You've seen me bring down Aboms. You've seen the creatures I take on. I have to do this—so much is riding on getting the Thunderstrike back and catching the magicians behind the tornado and the theft. If this Order of the Black Mist is determined to cause havoc, the world will be far more dangerous than it is now. I need to do what I can to stop them."

He caught my gaze and, out of the misty swirl, I sensed a mix of compassion and regret. "You're right. I'm already dead. Nobody can do much to me anymore. Well, actually, I'm not going to bet on that, but if the Greenlings storm the cities, it won't affect me. But you...you belong to the world of the living. Do what you have to do. I'll be with you, as close as I can be without them sensing me. Call me if you need me. Promise?"

I nodded. "I promise. And now, I'm going to get a couple hours of sleep, because I have a feeling tonight's going to tax every reserve I have." And with that, I curled up on the sofa and fell asleep, watching the waves crest against the shore out on the inlet.

Chapter 13

Nobody went to the Junk Yard at night, not unless they were looking for trouble. After a couple hours of sleep, I was ready to rock. I strapped my dagger to my inner thigh so the band would look like a garter from the outside, and I ran a thin layer of makeup over my whip. It wouldn't affect its use, and while it didn't fully cover it, the foundation muted the brilliant colors to a low roar. The magic was still strong, but it shouldn't attract the attention of the casual passerby. My skirt covered up both weapons to a degree, and the slits provided adequate access to them.

As I zipped up my blue leather corset and slid my feet into ankle boots that were high enough to be sexy, but chunky-heeled enough to run in, I wondered how the hell I was going to pull this off. It wasn't like I had any clue of who I was looking for.

Suddenly feeling peevish, I thought about calling off the half-baked scheme, but stopped as I stared out over the inlet. The gods weren't omniscient—none of them. And they weren't omnipotent either. *Nobody* in this whole freaking universe had that kind of power. In some ways, the gods were like humans, like Theosians...like Weres and shifters and Fae. They were just trying to get along in the world.

I slid a pre-paid cash card into a liner that attached to my dagger sheath. I didn't bother with ID. If the authorities picked me up, they'd read my chips—which would lead to a whole different can of worms. And if anybody in the club tried to ID me, they wouldn't have any official documents to go on, unless they had managed to get hold of a chip reader. While that was possible, it was also highly illegal for private citizens to own.

I wanted to wear my pendant, but that wouldn't be a good idea. So instead, I fastened a silver chain around my neck that would keep the bloodsucker types at bay. Vampires were rarely seen in public, but going into the Junk Yard? Anything could happen there.

Finally, I slugged back an herbal mixture that Tam had sent over while I was asleep. It would make it hard for anyone to charm me. Theosians weren't easily charmed anyway, but this would almost guarantee nobody could slip me a magical drug, or try to mesmerize me. As for regular drugs, some of them would work on me, some not. There wasn't much I could do except keep my eyes open.

As I stood at the counter, staring at the pale

blue bottle the potion had come in, I realized I didn't want to go. It wasn't due to fear. It wasn't due to being afraid someone would recognize me for who I really was. No, the two times I had been in the Junk Yard, I had come out with my emotions charred to a crisp, forever changed.

"Are you sure about this, Fury?" Queet whispered from my side. He knew what I was feeling.

"I have no choice."

"Then go, and Hecate be at your back. I'll go as far as I can. Call me if you need me, I'll be listening. So will Jason and Tam. They'll be on the outskirts, waiting. All you have to do is call to me and I'll tell them to come running."

And with Queet's promise ringing in my ears, I headed downstairs to make my way to the Junk Yard. The last time I was there, I had rained down hell on earth. But it hadn't been enough to erase the memories...or the cause of them.

He was in the Junk Yard. I was standing on the outskirts of the gated enclosure, gearing myself up to enter. I glanced up at the moon, gathering my courage.

The Carver was in there, and he didn't know that I was still alive, and that I still remembered him. I woke up from a long nap to the certainty that he had returned. That the Carver was sitting in a slummy bar, wondering where to start up again. His face was leathery and scarred, one eye missing thanks to the explosion that I had caused when I gated myself out of his hellhole. The room had erupted in flames, burning him as he tried to get out, and cremating my mother's body to a charred husk. But it hadn't been enough, and I had been waiting for this day. I had been waiting for the day I woke up, knowing he was near, knowing that I could finish what I had started the day he murdered my mother.

I thought about calling Jason and asking him to go with me, but I didn't want to put him in that position. I knew what I was about to do, and I wasn't going to ask the person who had saved my ass thirteen years before to put himself on the line—either his life, or his ethics. Jason would understand what I was about to do, but this was my fight, my journey. I had a one-way ticket and it wasn't going to be a joyride.

As I slowly entered the monolithic structure, I crossed the line. There was no going back. Hecate's power coursed through my body. I had come to destroy—to demolish, obliterate, annihilate. And I knew exactly where I was going.

The image of a small apartment at the top of an abandoned building flickered in my mind. There were a lot of abandoned buildings in the Junk Yard. After all, it had been built to house fifty thousand refugees and now housed who knew how many members of the UnderCult.

The Junk Yard was a labyrinthine maze of apartment buildings, storefronts, nightclubs, and bars. The buildings were concrete, with a lot of broken windows around. Here and there, a stray dog raced by. There were rumors that centuries ago Seattle had an underground component and while some historians claimed the Junk Yard was built over that area, nobody had ever come out publicly saying that it was true. I had my suspicions that the rumors were right, but I wasn't interested in finding out. I had enough on my hands with the Abominations. The last thing I wanted to do was to deal with the UnderCult.

The streets in the Junk Yard were lit by a series of underground track lights that bordered the sidewalks. The lighting had been installed as a way to appease the Jagulins, who disliked the street lamps and bright lights of the city. But it was still a cage, and the Jagulins wanted no part of it.

I scanned the streets, but I didn't need to get my bearings. Even though I hadn't set foot inside the Junk Yard in thirteen years, I knew exactly what apartment to head for. The Carver was staying next door to where he had held my mother and me. Back then, he had been living in a basement. But now, he was in a top apartment.

I hurried through the night, ignoring the passing comments flung my way from the bogeys and shadow men. Lucky for them, they left it at catcalls only, because I didn't have time to administer an etiquette lesson. Maybe later, I thought. But for now, Xan, prominently sheathed and hanging over my back, kept them at bay.

As I reached the burned-out shell of the building in which my life had permanently and forever been changed, I paused. Walking over to the edge, I stared into the gutted-out basement.

The building had burned to cinders, the concrete imploding into dust.

The only memories I had were a blur of flame, my fury rising as his blade carved deep into my mother's skin. And then—the rolling waves of anger as I reached out to Hecate, drawing her deep into my heart. Then, freeze frame and lurch forward to a roar so loud that it drowned out everything else. And then...I woke up on Jason's doorstep.

I inhaled a sharp breath, letting it whistle out slowly, before I continued to the building next door. A light shone in the top right-hand window. My destination.

Quietly, I entered the building and climbed the stairs, forgoing the elevator. Chances were, it wouldn't work anyway. As I approached the apartment at the end of the hall I unsheathed my sword. When I was at the door, I stood for a moment, gathering my flame into a single white-hot spark, and then I kicked open the door.

Inside, the Carver was waiting, standing in front of a desk.

"I felt you when you were outside my building, Kaeleen," he said. "I didn't realize you survived until now."

He was still bald, but the skin on his head and his face drooped in folds of scar tissue. One eye was missing, and he wasn't wearing a patch to cover it. His speech was garbled from the scars on his neck and throat, his tongue swollen and disfigured thanks to my flame so many years ago. The skin of his entire right side was shiny in that way that burn victims have.

"I've been waiting for you," I said. "I didn't know when you would return, but I've been waiting for the day when I would wake up and know you were here. You forever changed my world. I've come back to repay you in kind."

And those were my last words to him. I swung the sword, aiming for his heart, aiming to obliterate. For some reason, I hadn't expected him to fight back. I suppose I had expected him to be waiting for me to end his misery—to end the misery he had inflicted on everyone. In my delusion, I had created him as remorseful and ready to die.

But he wasn't at that point. Not yet. Instead, the Carver raised his hand and mumbled something under his breath, and a dark form filled the room, shadowy with wings.

I whirled to find myself facing a creature that reminded me of a cross between a giant bat and a praying mantis. As I swung my sword, the creature reached out with feathered, razor-sharp legs and attempted to stab me. I managed to clip one of them with the tip of my blade, but still, it scored my flesh, leaving a long gash on my arm. The feathered tips were actually metal. I wasn't facing a living *creature*, but some sort of creation—a robot, perhaps.

The Carver laughed. "I take it you didn't do your research, girl. I'm a magus. I work with automatons." And he fell back into the shadows, watching as I fought his creation.

The creature was about as tall as I was, so I

wasn't outmatched, but I was having a hard time gaining purchase. Images of the room in which he had imprisoned Marlene and me flashed through my mind. A room filled with mechanisms and gadgets and metalwork that I had forgotten.

Crap. I had thought he was simply human, I hadn't realized that he had magic behind him.

I swung my sword again, trying to lop off the head of the monster, but then realized it would keep coming no matter what— it didn't have a brain. As I darted back out of its reach, I sheathed my blade and instead, reached for the spark of flame in my heart.

As the flame grew, I aimed it at the automaton and let it fly, hitting dead center. An explosion filled the room and smoke billowed through the broken windows. I turned back to the shadows where the Carver was hiding. Dagger out, I raced toward him as he stepped out of the alcove, coughing.

Surprise on his face, he blurted out, "You killed my automaton? How?"

"I may not have realized you were a magus, but *you* didn't realize I'm a Theosian. How do you think your building imploded the night you killed my mother?"

He led out a startled bark. "I thought it was a gas leak—"

I said nothing, simply thrust my dagger deep into his side as I forced my fury and fire into the blade. A glowing cloud of flame raced through the wound. He shrieked but I drove the blade deeper, driving the fire forward.

"I owe you this."

The fire melted into his muscle, fusing fibers and charring his blood. And then I could feel Hecate, riding my shoulders.

"Give him Blood Fever," she whispered.

I wasn't sure what she meant, but I focused on the words and I felt the essence of the disease.

A venom traveling through the blood... A poison that will burn forever until the person dies... Inflammation that will cause constant pain with every heartbeat, every moment blood pumps through their veins.

I withdrew my fire from the blade and instead, channeled the infection into his body. As it kissed his blood and caught hold, settling into him, he shrieked once more before I abruptly backed away.

I turned to Hecate, realizing that we were standing at the Crossroads. She had brought us to the fork in the road.

"I want him dead. I don't want him to ever make anyone else suffer."

"He won't be able to. I promise you, if he even so much as *thinks* of harming anyone—even himself—the Blood Fever will drive him into a pain so deep and gut wrenching that he'll be a whimpering mass on the floor. And on the days when he manages to divert his thoughts to the desire to cause pain, the Blood Fever will make every motion, every single twitch of a muscle, hurt. He will never rest. He will never again know a moment without pain. And he will live long enough to pray for death." She smiled at me, and her smile was the smile of cunning vengeance and steel teeth gnashing in the night. Shadow magic at its most painful. "But the choice is yours to make. A quick death, or a long, agonizing life."

I thought for a moment. My mother hadn't been given a choice. Her death had been steeped in waves of pain. I gazed upon my dark goddess, matching her cunning smile. "Then I'm done. I'm done for now with him, and with the past."

Hecate nodded. "You've been bound to me since your birth, and were marked with my triple snakes. The first rite of passage. Now, you have avenged your mother and walked through my second gate. Time for a new mark."

She held out her hand. I took it, and we were suddenly in her office.

"I give you a gift—a weapon that will never leave you. A weapon that will always return to you, and always burn with your fire. A weapon that will represent your nature and passion. And with it, I give you a new name."

And that night, she tattooed the whip on my leg. Every needle stroke drove into my heart, into my core. But when she was done, I possessed a weapon that would forever be with me. I was marked with my fury, and *Fury* I became.

Chapter 14

I shook off the memories and caught my breath. Once again I was standing outside the gated enclosure of the Junk Yard. But this time, I wasn't after the Carver, I reminded myself. The sleet pounded down hard, the wind driving it sideways. Even though I was wearing a cape over my skirt, the drops were frozen pellets, stinging against my face. If this kept up, we'd have snowfall by morning. It was still early in the season—very early—for snow, but lately the weather had been getting colder. Gaia seemed to be funneling us toward a little ice age.

I gathered my courage and plunged in through the open gates of the Junk Yard. Tam and Jason were waiting in Jason's car a block over, and Queet had stopped shortly outside the gates. He promised me he would be on alert and the moment I called for backup, he'd let Tam and Jason know.

But the truth was—backup or not—until they got there, I was on my own.

Phoenix Rising was on Scissors Street, which ran along the side of the Junk Yard, near the southern wall. Over the past five years, the Junk Yard had only gotten creepier, and as I passed silent building after silent building, I could only wonder who was lurking behind the blacked-out windows now. Were the buildings truly empty, or had the UnderCult grown wide, conveniently leaving the city council unaware?

I walked down the center of the road. There wasn't much traffic in the Junk Yard, but I'd have time to dart out of the way if I needed to, especially given my heightened speed. It was safer to keep away from doorways and burrow-lanes where somebody might try to grab me. Strange women made good targets.

I kept my hands beneath my cape, my left hand playing at the slit with my dagger, my right hand poised over the hilt of my whip. Out of curiosity, I called up my Trace to check whether there were any Aboms around. The Junk Yard seemed a good place for them to gather. As I searched while walking along, a few minor blips appeared and I wasn't sure what to make of them. Abominations usually ran strong signals. These reminded me of echoes. Making a note to ask Hecate about them, I closed out the screen. Sometimes an Abomination could pick up on me as I searched for it, and that was the last thing I needed tonight.

I passed some stores—markets and grocers—

and it seemed odd to see such mundane offerings in the heart of the UnderCult. But magicians and rogues and thieves all needed to eat as much as anybody else, though it left me wondering who in their right mind would open up a store here. I couldn't imagine the owners escaping the grafters who sought out protection money every month.

Finally, I came to the intersection I was looking for. Rift Avenue branched off from Scissors Street, leading deeper into the Junk Yard. I headed north. Phoenix Rising was supposed to be a few blocks up ahead and sure enough, I saw the neon sign over the entrance from a block away. As I neared the nightclub, I could feel the energy spilling out into the streets.

The front door was steel, with the neon sign hanging over a black awning. But the energy oozing out from the nightclub was tangible— palpable and sickly sweet. Magicians who worked on the shadow side had a cloying feel to them, unless they chose to cloak up. But there was no need in the Junk Yard. The Devani never went past the gates.

My stomach lurched as I approached the door. I paused, closing my eyes.

"Queet? I'm at the bar and about ready to head in. Will you let Jason and Tam know?" My whisper-speak was strong, and I could tell that he had received my message. I didn't expect one in return, so I headed toward the door, readying myself to enter the world of the UnderCult.

As I pushed through the heavy steel door, I was surprised to find there was no bouncer waiting to shake down guests. But then I thought about where I was. The Junk Yard was the UnderCult's domain. They wouldn't be expecting the Devani to sneak in, because the Devani would never come here, so why bother with guards on the doors. While the light warriors were ruthless, they wouldn't chance creating a civil war, especially with the corporatocracy backing them.

I tried to blend in, suppressing a cough as clouds of smoke emanated from the side booths. I could smell Opish, Tommy-Tee's drug of choice, along with several others that I couldn't identify and didn't want to breathe in. Opish addiction by the likes of Tommy-Tee was one thing. He wasn't dangerous, just sad and slightly pathetic. But these men—and most of them *were* men by the looks of things—looked dangerous and volatile.

I paused, scanning the room. There were three exits in addition to the front door. Two of them seemed to lead to back rooms. The third had an exit sign prominently placed over it and I assumed that it led to the burrow-lane behind the club. A long counter ran against the back wall, with a plethora of liquor bottles lining row after row of shelves behind the bar. Both sides of the club were lined with booths, most of which were full. A scattering of tables covered the main floor, and a good number of those were taken as well.

I glanced around to see if anybody was looking at me, but only a few people seemed to be looking my way. The noise level was so high it almost hurt my ears, though it only took me a moment to regain my balance as I realized that it wasn't the actual conversation making me wince, but the level of energy running slingshot through the room. Chaotic and feral, it ricocheted off the walls. The forces of the Arbortariam had been chaotic and clear. Here, the energy was murky and dank.

I tried to blend in and slowly worked my way through the crowd over to the bar, where I managed to find two empty stools. As I slid onto one of them and motioned to the barkeep, I pushed my hood back, shaking my hair out.

"What can I get for you?" The bartender looked to be a surly human, though by now I knew better than to assume.

"Brandy." Brandy was a relatively safe drink, barely affecting me. Yet another trait I found handy. Theosians were born with an increased tolerance to alcohol and drugs, unless the drug was specifically formulated to affect our kind. Though I could drink the best of them under the table, I usually didn't bother with alcohol. But here, in a rough-and-tumble bar? It wouldn't look right to order water.

The bartender kept an eye on me as he poured my drink. "You're new." It was a statement, but I could hear the inferred question behind his words.

"You're right about that. I'm new in town. I recently came in from Athens." I had no clue why Athens sprang to my lips, but it would do as well as any city. "I'm looking for a well-stocked magic shop. Know of any?" I figured the best way to infiltrate the UnderCult and to discover whatever I could about the Thunderstrike would be to go where the action was, so to speak.

The bartender grunted. "That depends on what kind of spell components you're looking for. I'd start with Price and Wax—five streets over, on Creighton Avenue."

I grunted back as he shoved my drink in front of me, and discreetly pulled out my cash card from the liner attached to my dagger strap. The barkeep deducted the cost of my drink and handed it back to me, his gaze still locked on my face.

"What kind of magic do you work?" He glanced around the rest of the bar but nobody was motioning for his attention, so he leaned on the counter toward me. A tall, burly man, with hair flowing down his shoulders and the scruff of a beard, he probably didn't shave often, or he was trying to grow out his whiskers. His biceps were huge, and he could probably break my neck with those massive hands of his. Now, I understood the lack of bouncers hanging around.

I decided to answer honestly, in case anybody had read my energy. "Fire and shadow magic. Flame is in my blood."

"Why did you come to the Junk Yard? There are a lot of magical shops around Seattle, especially in Darktown."

"They're a little...*tame*...for my needs." I lingered over the word, forcing as much innuendo into it as I could. I had watched him pour the brandy straight from the bottle, so I took a chance and sipped it. It was actually quite smooth and fiery on my throat. "Very nice. There's always a question about quality when you go to a new bar." I glanced at him over the rim of my glass, holding his gaze. It never hurt to flatter the bartender.

"I'm glad you approve. So, what's your name?" He relaxed.

I was prepared for this question. "Fotia." Fotia meant "fire" in Greek.

"Fotia, huh? That's pretty." Now he was turning flirty. "And where are you staying, *Fotia*?"

I took another sip of my drink, counting to ten before I answered. I knew all the games and I could play them with the best. "Oh, around. I'll be around until I can find out if this city is good for me. It all depends on whether I can find others who share my passion for magic. Back in Athens, they didn't take kindly to the games I like to play."

"And what kind of games would those be?" The voice by my side startled me. I had been so intent on the bartender that I hadn't noticed the man edging closer.

I turned and found myself facing a man in a gray-hooded cloak. He was slightly taller than I was, with sandy hair and startling gray eyes peeking out from within the folds of the hood.

The bartender had moved back a step and I was surprised to see a hint of caution in his eyes. That could mean several things, including the possibility that whoever had joined us could be a powerful magician. He definitely ran magic—I could feel it dancing in the air all around us.

I let my gaze linger on him for a moment before answering in a bored voice.

"I occasionally like to play with lightning." I left it at that. It would be an amateur move to flat-out claim to practice weather magic. I'd seem far too eager and if he was with the Order of the Black Mist, he would immediately pick up on my ploy. I wasn't dealing with stupid people and I knew it.

"A lightning witch, you say? You know, sparks can burn your fingers if you're not careful." The hooded man took a seat on the empty stool next to me. He motioned to the barkeep, who set a glass of a blue liqueur in front of him. I didn't recognize the drink, but even from where I sat I could smell the strength of the alcohol and my nose wrinkled in response. Whatever it was, it was potent.

"Honey, I've burned my fingers so many times I've charred off my fingerprints." I tipped up the corner of my lips in a faint smile. "You have to know how to control the element before you let it out of the cage."

I stopped suddenly, realizing that I was talking myself into a potential corner. What if he wanted proof that I could control lightning? Oh, I had my fire magic—but that wasn't the same thing. Theosian spells worked on a different level than those belonging to magicians and witches.

He leaned closer, a sleazy grin on his face as he slugged back the drink. "Another, barkeep."

As the barkeeper poured the drink, he gave me a sideways glance and rolled his eyes, mouthing the words, "Fraternity brat."

That told me everything I needed to know.

He hadn't been polite because he feared the magician's power. He had been polite because of the man's connections. Chances were, I was sitting next to the son of an extremely influential politician or, possibly, the son of a powerful mage. Which might be useful in and of itself.

"I'll have another, too." I pointed to my glass.

The barkeeper grinned at me and filled my glass, then refilled the man's drink as well. "On the house, you two."

I winked at him, making certain my drinking companion didn't see. Apparently, the bartender thought I was a scammer and he was obviously on my side.

"Tulf, tell her what an upstanding man I am." Gray-hood slammed back his drink again and was starting to sound slurry.

I glanced at the barkeep. "That your name?"

He nodded. "That's what I let them call me. Tulf. And yeah, he's as upstanding as they come... in the Junk Yard." Again, a guarded eye-roll, which felt more like a warning than a recommendation.

"Why don' you come sit with me in a booth, pretty lady?" Slurry was rapidly descending into sloshed. He "accidentally" knocked my brandy over. "You pick a booth. I'll bring you a drink."

I thought quickly. I knew all too well what he was up to. "Tell you what. *You* tell me your name, and I'll come sit in a booth with you. But *I'm* going to bring our drinks while you find us a place that's nice and quiet."

Apparently, he was too drunk to notice that I had circumnavigated whatever plan he had in mind. As he lurched off to find us a booth, I leaned over the counter, whispering to Tulf.

"Tell me, is he trouble?"

"Only if Lord Whinypants gets his feelings hurt. His name is Nat Crayburg and his father is one of the vice presidents for the World Regency Corporation. Nat likes to slum here. He dabbles in sorcery and oh, he desperately wants to be part of the crowd. If it weren't for his father, he would have been dragged into a burrow-lane long ago and put out of everybody's misery."

Ding ding ding! We have a winner. So Nat was tied into the WRC. If I was lucky, I had just found my first real clue in this whole mess. It was up to me to dangle the bait and hope that he took it.

Chapter 15

So, if Nat's father worked for the World Regency Corporation, were they using him to get the Thunderstrike back? Would they be that stupid, now that Lightning Strikes was involved? Was Nat a shill they had sent in, looking for it?

"He was going to spike my drink," I said.

"Yeah, but I would have stopped him. I get too many powerful magicians in here to let any prick attempt to lowjack my customers. I wouldn't have any business left if they couldn't trust that they would leave here the same as they came in. And if you happen to have the power I think you might, I sure as hell don't want you causing hell over some little poser." Tulf gave me a long look, a line of red creeping up his neck. He hesitated a moment, then asked, "What do you want with the likes of him, anyway?"

I debated over my answer. "Information. I'm

searching for something and I am hoping he might know where I can find it. He's talkative, and if he hangs out in the right places, he might have overheard...what I need to know. Does he come in here often?"

"Yeah, but it was sporadic till this week. He's been here everyday, I think." Tulf gave me a nod, but asked no further questions. I picked up the drinks and headed over to the booth, where Nat was waiting. A niggling suspicion made me wonder if he was as drunk as he was acting.

As I slid his drink in front of him, he reached for it quickly, his fingers brushing mine.

"*Whatsyername*?" It came out in one slurry word.

I stared at him for a moment, gauging how to play the game. Mr. Whinypants or not, Nat Crayburg had access to information that I needed.

"Fotia. I'm in from Athens. And what's your name?" I held onto my drink, playing with the glass. I wasn't giving him another chance to drug me. It probably wouldn't affect me, but on the off chance the drug was magical I had no intention of taking any risks.

"Nat. I'm Nat." He hiccupped, but it sounded forced and I knew without a doubt that he was feigning his drunken stupor. "So, pretty lady, what are you doing in town? Tell me about yourself. Where are you staying?"

"Just passing through. As to where I'm staying—I haven't decided yet." I sipped my brandy, then volleyed my own questions. "So, Nat...I'm looking for information. And there's a lot that I'd do to find out what I need to know."

The promise of sex might be the oldest ploy in the book, but it had survived due to its effectiveness. Nat's eyes lit up. Yep, horny as hell—his stare instantly fastened on my boobs before his eyes slowly rose to meet my gaze.

"What do you need to know?" His breath came harshly, and his drunken slur vanished.

I tried to gauge his abilities. He did have power, but he also felt chaotic and untrained. Or, if he *had* trained, his studies hadn't been structured. I wasn't sure what he could do.

I decided to stall. "Let's get to know each other a little better first, okay? Tell me, what element do you work with? What's your specialty?" I needed to know what kind of magic I was facing before I could figure out how to reel him in.

Nat rubbed his lower lip, then took a slow sip of his drink. "All right. If you insist. I have no specialty." He sounded bitter. "You going to walk, now?"

That explained a lot. Witches didn't care what kind of magic people used, that much I knew. And magicians like Jason didn't really either, as long as everything was above board. But among the magicians, specialties mattered. Generalized magic was seen as weak, and a magician without a specialty was considered second-rate, unable to master advanced spells. If Nat couldn't focus his magic into an elemental direction, chances were he had been on the receiving end of a lot of snide comments.

I softened my voice. "You get a lot of flack,

don't you?"

Nat searched my face. "You're not being sarcastic, are you?"

I shook my head.

"Thanks," he muttered, staring at his drink. "I come in here time and again but nobody here will talk to me. They treat me like I'm invisible. And my old man thinks I'm a failure." He sounded so forlorn it was hard not to feel sympathy for him.

My entire plan began to shift gears. "That must be rough. I imagine it's been hard, constantly being rejected."

He swallowed the rest of his drink and I motioned to Tulf for another round. He carried the glasses to the table himself, and cocked his eyebrows as he set them in front of us. I gave him the barest shake of a head and smiled.

Apparently I'd hit a nerve, because Nat immediately downed the drink and whistled to Tulf. "You. Barkeeper."

Tulf brought over the bottles. "Here, you might want these."

I groaned inwardly, thinking of the dent this was going to make on my cash card, but Nat paid Tulf without missing a beat.

"My treat." He filled his glass again. I slid the brandy bottle over in front of me and—in a show of empathy—slugged back my drink and poured another. The fire raced down my throat, but the alcohol had little effect.

"My old man told me if I'm going to practice magic, I'd better do it right. He wants me to use my talent for the family business. I don't want to, but hey, that's what I'm doing."

My ears perked up. Most corporations kept hired magicians on the payroll, but just what part had Nat played in the Thunderstrike's disappearance?

"Bah. Government job...politicians... I just want to work magic." Nat was starting to feel the booze—this time, the slightly slurred speech was for real. I could hear it in his throat.

"What does your father do?"

"Veep for World Regency. He works in research and development." He hiccupped loudly, then downed yet another drink. "That's where I work, too."

I winced. Alcohol seemed to be the ocean in which Nat liked to drown his troubles. "So, what kind of things do you work on?"

"World Regency has a contract with the Conglomerate. We manufacture weapons and armor for the Devani." Nat stared forlornly at the bottle. "We outfit those freaks."

I leaned back in my seat, thinking for a moment. The Devani were perfect soldier material, given their ability to accept orders, and they had very few, if any, emotions. I had never seen one up close, but I knew that they were mortal enemies of the Abominations. They hunted them down when they had the chance, but since the World Tree was located in the Sandspit, we didn't see the Devani often.

"You don't like them?"

"I don't think it's a good idea for the Conglomerate to put so much trust in them. My father would skin me alive if he heard me admit it, but I'm a b...bi...bit of an *ani-christ*." Another drink downed, and his words were slurring for real.

"Anarchist?"

"Yeah, that too."

He was just drunk enough to be talkative. I decided to push a little more. "If you don't want to work for your father's company, why don't you go to work in the Junk Yard? Find a...oh...a magicians' group? Maybe they could help you."

Nat shrugged, staring forlornly at the bottle. "Tol' you...I tried, but they won't have me. I want to work for the Order of the Black Mist, but they've rejected me ever...every time I asked."

And there it was. I let the words hang for a moment before asking, "The Order of the Black Mist. I've heard of them. I've been interested in them, too. I like the way they think." I was going to have to bluff my way through this, but given good old Nat was truly pie-eyed, it shouldn't be too difficult. "So, they have a branch around here?"

He poured himself another drink. "Yeah. And Mr. High-and-Mighty Lyon won't let me attend their meetings, even after I gave him the..." Nat paused. "I did a favor for them. Lyon told me I could join the organization if I played my cards right. But he won't take my calls now and he hasn't shown up here at the bar the past couple nights."

Right then, I knew what had happened. They had used Nat to get the Thunderstrike. How they knew about it was anybody's guess, though I'd wager Nat had opened his mouth about it at some point in an attempt to impress them. Now that they had what they wanted, he was probably on the expendable list, and if he got belligerent enough, my guess was that Nat would probably show up dead from some "unavoidable accident."

I murmured a soft note of agreement. "People use and abuse, don't they?"

"They sure do." Nat hiccupped, then before I could say another word, he slumped over the table. I reached over and felt for a pulse. He was still alive, but when I counted up the drinks he had slugged back, I realized he had just passed out.

I returned to the bar. Tulf was polishing glasses with a snowy-clean white rag. At least Phoenix Rising wasn't the dive I had feared.

"Tulf, listen. I have a question and if you don't want to answer, fine. But...who is Lyon?"

Tulf slowly set down the glass and rag. He glanced around the bar, scanning all corners. "I don't know why you want to know, but you should steer clear of Lyon and his crowd. Dangerous folk, Fotia. They hang out here sometimes, but mostly, they keep to their turf."

"Where's their turf?"

He shook his head. "You don't want to go messing with them, I tell you. The kid over there made the mistake of trying to get in good with them. Now, there's a bounty on his head. I haven't told him because he rubs me the wrong way, and my bar is one of the sanctuaries in the UnderCult. Nobody draws blood in here. But at some point, he's going to walk out of here and somebody will be waiting outside the safety-radius. And then, frat-brat or not, he's going down. And no Devani in the world will set foot in the Junk Yard to find out who did it, regardless of who his daddy is."

I slowly sat down on the bar stool. This wasn't my fight, I told myself. Nat was a screwup and a liability, but I couldn't bring him into the picture. I had learned far more than I had expected to, and it was time I left.

I pulled out my cash card and tossed it on the counter.

"Just tell me where Lyon's territory begins, and keep the brat here until he wakes up, sober, and the hundred-odd cash on that card is yours."

Tulf stared at the card, then shrugged and pocketed it. "It's your neck, but promise me you'll be smart?"

I nodded.

"Lyon rules the Tunnels. You find the opening to the Tunnels, and you find the way into his self-appointed kingdom. But be careful—few who go looking for trouble that big ever return. Whinyboy over there only survived because apparently, he had access to something they wanted. He's not long for the world, though. When they're done with you, they're done."

I let out a long sigh. Tulf had been fair enough with me, and I liked him. I slid off the stool and smoothed my skirt. "Thanks for the conversation and the info. I won't forget your help."

As I headed for the door, I realized that—as dangerous as this bar felt—Tulf could be trusted. I hoped I would see him again.

The temperatures had dropped again, and the sudden emergence from the warm bar into the chill night sent a cold ripple snaking up my spine. Part of me wanted to wander around, see if I could find the entrance to the Tunnels. I knew exactly what Tulf was talking about—the rumors of the underground portion of the city—but I also realized it would be suicide to go looking without backup and some research.

In whisper-speak, I summoned Queet. "Queet, come walk with me. I feel vulnerable."

The truth was, now that I had a little bit of knowledge, I felt terribly exposed. At least, if the Order of the Black Mist questioned Nat, he wouldn't know my real name. He would only be able to tell them about Fotia from Athens...though if they were smart, they might manage to put two and two together. I wasn't unknown, especially in the Darktown area.

"Here, Fury. What happened? Did you find out anything?" Queet sounded almost eager, which meant he really had been worried. When he wasn't all that concerned, his conversation consisted mostly of bellyaching about his state of existence.

"Yeah, but I want out of here before I tell you. We've got research to do."

I pulled up my hood and wrapped my cape around me. Unless they had really good night vision or the ability to sense gender, nobody passing by should be able to tell whether I was male or female, which was the way I wanted it.

"We're almost to the gates," Queet said. "Tam and Jason are waiting."

"Good, because I want to get the fuck out of this neighborhood. I hate the Junk Yard." I paused, then added, "Tulf was nice enough, though."

"Who's Tulf?"

"A bartender I met tonight. I think I can trust him, as much as I can trust anybody in this joint." Another moment, and I added, "At least, I hope I can."

A wave of doubt swept over me. Maybe I shouldn't have asked about Lyon. At least I hadn't mentioned the Order of the Black Mist to him. For all Tulf knew, I might work for Nat's father as an informant on his son's activities.

"You okay?" Queet's voice echoed in my thoughts.

I shrugged. "I'm just spiraling. We're getting involved in something with very deep roots, and it's..." I paused again, not wanting to mention the Order even in whisper-speak. "Wait till we get out of here."

Finally, the gates to the Junk Yard came into view. I hastened my pace, pushing toward the entrance, suddenly fearful that something—the Carver, the Order of the Black Mist, or something even darker—might be waiting to jump in the way. Claustrophobic at the idea of the gates shutting before I could get out, even though I knew they didn't close till dawn, I broke into a light jog. I wanted out of the gated enclosure, away from the intrigue.

"Fury, Fury—calm down. It's all right. I've asked Jason and Tam to meet you at the entrance." Queet sounded worried now.

"I'm just..." I tried to say something, anything, but the fear was so thick around me now that all I could do was run. I shot out between the gates, frantically searching for Jason's car. It swung into view just as I heard a footfall behind me. Terrified, I swung around, only to find myself staring at a couple of leather-clad bikers passing by. They were hand in hand, and gave me an odd, disgusted look as they strolled on by, out of the Junk Yard.

"What a freak," said one of them, loud enough for me to overhear. He turned to give me a snarky look. "Honey, don't play in the streets if you're afraid of the cars." And then, he and his partner moved on.

Realizing I had worked myself up without any good reason, I gratefully yanked open the car door and dove into the backseat. "Get me out of here. Now."

Without a word, Jason eased the car out and we were off, away from the Junk Yard and away from whatever nightmares were lurking in my subconscious.

Chapter 16

"Are you all right? You seem rattled." Jason glanced at me through the rearview mirror. The car was auto-driving tonight, and he turned around to lean over the seat. "Where do you want to go?"

"First, check me for a Trace. Just in case I missed it." I didn't want to chance someone being able to backtrack me to my home—or to Jason's store.

He nodded and reached for my hand. I gave it to him, and he closed his eyes. After a moment, he shook his head. "No Trace. You're clear."

"Good. Then get me someplace safe and warm and bright. I feel like I just climbed out of a cold, dark cave." I huddled in the back, staving off the remnants of the claustrophobia that had swept over me when I was in the Junk Yard. I wasn't sure exactly why it had happened, but I had the sneaking suspicion it was due to my baggage with the Carver.

Jason turned back and plugged directions into the autopilot. As we veered—I recognized the route we were taking, and it would lead back to Dream Wardens—Tam scrambled over the front seat to sit beside me. He held out his hands, silently, and just as silently I took them. A faint warmth radiated through me, as the cold fear slowly began to melt away. It was as if I had stepped out into a sunny day, with the warmth and light filling every corner of my body. The next thing I knew, Tam was embracing me, hugging away the lump in my chest, and then he kissed me, long and slow, and I melted into the lushness of his presence. A moment later, he gently released me and I drew a shaky breath. I was still wired, but the panic had dissolved.

"Thanks." I gave him a sideways smile and he returned it, flicking my hair back out of my eyes.

"My pleasure." He winked.

"What happened?" Jason hadn't said a word during the time, but his voice was a little harder and it flashed through my mind that he wasn't necessarily okay with Tam helping me out so willingly.

"I think I triggered memories of my mother." I pressed my lips together, not wanting to admit it. But it was true. That night would live with me forever, and the flashback triggers were numerous and hard to anticipate.

"Yah, I wondered if it was a good idea. Anyway, tell us what you found out, if anything.

Queet said you came racing out of the bar like a bat out of hell."

"That would be fitting, wouldn't it?" I laughed, relieved to be able to find something funny. "I discovered a lot more than I thought I would. For one thing, the Thunderstrike? I know who stole it and why."

"Hold that thought. We're here." Jason took control of the car, easing it over to the curb. Then he programmed directions for it to return to the parking garage. The moment we got out, it would automatically lock itself and head off to the rental space to wait until he needed it again.

As Jason tapped in the security code and opened the door, I eagerly pushed in behind him. The store was welcoming—it always felt safe to me. I unfastened my cape and swung it off, draping it over one of the counters, and then immediately made a nosedive for the sofa, curling up on one end as I pulled a throw over me.

"I want something to eat. Sweet if you've got it." I headed toward the break room as Jason nodded, then vanished back out the door. I knew he had a key to Up-Cakes. While he was gone, I changed into a pair of shorts that I kept in the shop, draping the skirt over a chair. I changed out my shoes for a pair of boots, and returned to the front just in time to see Jason reappear with a box of cupcakes. Tam poured me a glass of water, and I was finally able to let out a long, deep breath as I leaned back against the cushions.

"All right. Here's what I found out." I ran down everything that had happened and everything Nat had said. "So as far as I can figure out, he gave the Order of the Black Mist the Thunderstrike, trying to buy his way in. They took it, said see-ya, and that was that. Lyon...have you ever heard of him, Jason? You run in magical circles more than Tam or I do."

Jason paled and slowly lowered himself to the chair opposite. "We're all in trouble."

"Why?"

"His name is Lyon Burkenwald. He's from Black Forest, originally, and works with a dark magic that has roots going back to...well...to the first witches and magicians from the original Black Forest area. Strong hereditary magic. I only met him once, and that was enough. It was at a meet-and-greet at the Seattle Magicians Guild. Burkenwald wasn't invited, but he showed up anyway. He's a good six-five, long blond hair, broad shoulders. Looks like he should be wielding a broadsword."

"What did he want, if he wasn't invited?" Tam asked.

"Lyon was trying to drum up support for the Order of the Black Mist which, at the time, we knew nothing about. Since it wasn't authorized by the Conglomerate, we told him to leave. He laughed and said we'd rue the day we ever cast our lots in with the Corp-Rats. His whole viewpoint is based on human supremacy. He believes that most of the gods have outlived their purpose, and that Chaos is the only answer. Basically, he's an anarchist who wants to tear down the governments."

"In other words, he's out to topple one regime and set up another. Like we surmised—he wants to form a meteocramancy." I sucked in a deep breath. "How effective do you think he is at luring in other magicians?"

Jason shook his head. "*Too* good. He's riveting, and has charisma out the yin-yang. He's a born orator, and trust me, he wields an incredible amount of power. But he was cast out of the city several years ago for inciting riots. Apparently, he found his way back in."

"Apparently so. And now, he has the Thunderstrike. Do you think he'll use it?" I was thinking of the tornado in Bend.

"He's not stupid, but arrogant? Most definitely. I think he truly believes that he can go up against Gaia, which is insane, at best. But nobody ever said smart people had to be sane, and nobody ever said that intelligence has to be paired with wisdom. It's all too possible for one to exist without the other."

"Too bad he's smart and crazy instead of not-so-bright but wise." I frowned. "Do you think we should go hunting through the Tunnels for him?"

"He'll know we're coming. The man has a following of ultra-fanatical groupies. I don't know why I didn't put two and two together when Hecate told you about the Order of the Black Mist, but it all makes sense now." Jason started to pace—a habit that drove me batty, but seemed to give him comfort.

There was nothing I could add. I was supposed to recover the Thunderstrike. If I couldn't go down into the Tunnels, I wasn't sure just how I was supposed to do that. My phone rang, breaking the silence. I glanced at the caller ID. *Hecate.*

Frowning, I answered. "Yes? What's up?"

"Are you all right?" She was blunt as usual, right on point.

"I'm okay, but what's wrong? You sound frazzled."

"An hour ago there was a major earthquake on the California Plateau, along the edge of the ocean where the Andreas Fault System is. It wasn't natural, Fury. Lightning Strikes sent out a team. Nobody lives in the area, but there's magical energy all over the signature, and astrigators are pouring out of the cracks. Lightning Strikes will try to contain them, but it's likely some will get through and breed."

"But that's two territories away. And I happen to know who took the disk. It should still be in our area. Surely it can't reach out that far?"

"Don't be so sure. But remember, there are also still three magical grimoires missing. The Thunderstrike isn't the only thing that can disrupt the balance." She paused. "That's not all. A hurricane's formed over on the East Coast. It's heading for the Texicana Gulf. It's a monster, and if it jogs east, it will go right over the capital." Her voice was grim. "Lucky for us, it's so big it's moving slowly. But we have to disrupt whatever is spawning it."

I let out a long breath. "I'd better tell you what I found out tonight. Do you want me to come over to the temple?"

"No, just tell me now."

As I laid out what I had learned, and added in what Jason told me about Lyon, Hecate let out a sigh that sounded about as exasperated as a goddess can get.

"The Fates say that the next few days bring the possibility of world-shaking events. They told me tonight that no matter what we do, we won't be able to catch all the loose threads. Some strands will still break, and there will be long-term repercussions."

I sighed. "For once, can't they just come out and tell us what's going on? I get so tired of the riddles. Seriously, would it be so bad if they said—*Order of the Black Mist, bad. Kill them all. You can find them at the top of a bell tower.* Or, *Lightning Strikes? Needs to move in faster.* Something concrete we could work with."

That made her laugh. "Oh, I wish it were that simple. But you know very well that the Fates can't alter the course of destiny, and are limited to speaking in riddles and generalities. They are allowed that much leeway, and no more. The Norns are bound by the same rules, according to Freya."

I paused, blinking. "You talk to Freya?"

"Yes, why?"

"I didn't know the Greeks and the Norse played footsie."

"We don't, but she and I happened to pass each other on the World Tree...and no, it's not the same branch that's down in the Sandspit. We talk."

I thought for a moment. "What about going to

the Conglomerate? We could tell them about the Order of the Black Mist and Lyon. Maybe they can uproot the Tunnels and drive them out? Isn't it time to enlist some human help on this?" But even as I said it, I knew it was a fool's cause. "Never mind. Ten to one, World Regency was holding that disk for some corporation that's part of the Conglomerate. They probably already know about all this." Thirsty, I stood. If I remembered right, there was some juice in the break room.

"Which is why...watch the sky-eyes, Fury. The Devani seem up in arms, and I gather they were massing on the north side of Croix. There's something going down with the Conglomerate, and I'm not certain what they're up to. None of the gods are. The governments tell us what they think we want to hear, in hopes that we're as gullible as their people."

That the Devani were massing was an issue. They pledged total allegiance to the government. I started to answer when the floor began to sway beneath my feet. Instantly, I was on my hands and knees. Tam and Jason dropped to the floor as well.

The Seattle Fault Complex was as dangerous as the Andreas Fault System. As the sound of thunder filled the room, the floor rippled beneath my hands and knees. From out in the streets, I could hear screaming, and the sound of concrete and brick hitting the ground. Darktown was made up of predominantly older buildings, many of which had already been through the World Shift. How well would they hold? How well would Dream Wardens hold?

The lights flickered once, twice, and then went out as the rumbling continued. The infrastructure wasn't very stable down here in Darktown. I crawled beneath one of the display tables. The crashing of items around us as they rattled off the shelves was a grim reminder that we had too much glass in the shop. As the sound intensified, I pressed my hands to my ears. A moment later—it might have been sixty seconds, it might have been two minutes—the ground slowly ground to a halt.

"Kae? Are you all right?" Jason's voice echoed eerily in the darkness from what sounded like the back of the shop. "Tam?"

"I'm okay, I think." I crawled out from beneath the table, bracing myself for any aftershocks.

"I'm fine." Tam's voice echoed from near me. "Damn it. Be careful if you're crawling—there's glass all over the floor. Found a shard the hard way."

Shaking, I slowly pulled myself to my feet, scraping my knee on some sharp metal object as I stood. I pulled out my phone, but the next moment, there was a light shining in the middle of the shop. Jason stood there, a scroll in hand, the light emanating directly in front of him. I knew it wasn't one of his specialties, so I figured it had come from the scroll.

"How did you find that in the dark?"

"I always keep a couple of them in the emergency kit, and I know exactly where that kit is at all times. Let's take stock. Are you sure you're okay? Everybody to the sofa."

"I just scraped my knee. I have no idea how

bad it is, but it stings a little." As I followed him—and the light—over to the seating area, Tam approached from the other side. A jagged piece of glass was sticking out of his hand, blood oozing down the sides.

"Damn, that looks nasty. Jason, where's the first-aid kit?" I turned toward the far side of the store where we normally kept the healing powders. It was impossible to tell what—if anything—was still on the shelves.

"Never mind, I brought the entire emergency kit. Tam, sit next to Kae. I have to hold the light, so she'll have to bandage you up."

That was one bad thing about some of the lower-echelon light spells. The caster had to keep contact with the scroll as long as he wanted the light to last. Which precluded the use of his hands for anything else.

"You couldn't have picked a better scroll to tuck away for emergencies? Like a Light Up spell, or Daylight?" I didn't mean for my words to come out so sharp, but they did, slicing the silence.

"Pardon me, but I didn't expect an earthquake. I just...threw together some of the things that might come in handy. Now, help Tam." Jason let out a low grumble, then added, "I'll find a better one as soon as you get his hand fixed up. Then we'll go outside and see what Darktown looks like." He didn't sound very hopeful, though.

"Yeah, I'm sorry. I didn't mean to snap. It's been a tense evening already and now this... Anyway, Tam, this is going to hurt when I pull the glass out."

Tam shrugged. "I can handle pain." The offhand way in which he said it made me wonder whether he could negate his own shock and fear the way he could take care of ours.

I found a rag and wrapped it around the glass. No use me cutting myself as well. "Okay, are you ready?"

"Just do it, Fury. I'll be fine," he said softly, leaning in to smile at me. "I promise."

"Okay, then...here goes." I grimaced as I yanked the glass out of his hand. Blood spurted from his palm, but I was ready for it, slapping a thick mound of gauze over the wound. As I applied pressure, the blood oozed through the cloth and spread over my hand. I wasn't squeamish, but it looked to me Tam was bleeding too quickly.

"Don't worry," he said, when I voiced my concern. "Head and hands always bleed profusely. Just apply some antibacterial ointment and then some syniskin to stop the bleeding. It will work on the Fae as well as humans and Theosians."

"Get ready to hold the compress with your other hand while I go find the syniskin and ointment. But I should wash my hands first."

But an aftershock put an end to the conversation, rolling the ground beneath our feet. While it wasn't as big as the main quake, it wasn't easy and light, either. As the room came to rest again without falling down around our necks, I headed for the back room, praying that I wouldn't trip over anything. Jason was up and following me the moment he saw where I was going.

I turned on the faucet and water streamed out.

At least we hadn't lost running water as well as the electricity. I rinsed my hands as best as I could, and then, not wanting to wipe them so I wouldn't get any possible contamination from the towels, I headed back to Tam. I quickly opened a can of antiseptic spray and sprayed the wound as he lifted up the sopping mass of gauze, then with my other hand, I sprayed on the syniskin right over the broken skin. He could wash it later, though I had no doubt the wound would start bleeding again.

As the spray hit his hand, it formed a barrier over the wound and the blood quickly stopped flowing. Little rivulets tried to find their way from beneath the coating, but it adhered so tightly, and contained a natural coagulant, that the blood had no choice but to ooze to a stop.

Once Tam was patched up, I wrapped his hand in fresh gauze to cushion it until we could get him to proper medical care. Then, with Jason's help, we gathered our things from the back room and headed out into the streets of Darktown to assess the damage.

Chapter 17

The first indicator of how bad things were was the screaming coming from the direction of the Monotrain. There were flames coming from north Darktown, flickering into the night sky like an ugly beacon. People were running every which way, escaping into the streets. Some of the already fragile ruins had tumbled completely, but for the most part, to my amazement, Darktown was standing.

Jason motioned to Up-Cakes. "It looks like a total mess in there. But at least the windows are holding, and the building seems secure. I need to call Shevron and tell her not to come down here."

"I believe this section of Darktown was built during a time when Seattle required earthquake retrofitting. While this quake gave us a good shaking, I doubt if it was more than a 6.5. Maybe a little larger than other recent ones, but definitely not one to destroy the city." Tam glanced at his hand. The bandage was still holding. "We should get off the street, though. I imagine the sky-eyes will be out in droves to assess the damage, and if they even suspect that weather magic played a part in this, they're going to be keeping an eye out for anybody with a strong magical signature. Like Theosians," he said, pointedly looking at me. He held as little love for the Corp-Rats as I did.

My phone picked that moment to ring. I fished it out from my pocket and glanced at the caller ID. Hecate again. "Hello?"

"Are you all right? Where are you?" Hecate sounded shaken, and I wondered if anything had happened with the Greenlings, given this quake was most likely magically induced.

"I'm still down at Dream Wardens with Jason and Tam. I haven't been home to find out what my place is like."

"Send Queet. Meanwhile, I want the three of you to find a safe place to stay, ground level, sturdy building. I haven't heard anything from Jerako, in case you were wondering. But Tigra—from Lightning Strikes—is heading out into the city to find the epicenter of the quake so she can figure out whether it was magical or not."

"Want to make a bet?"

Hecate laughed, her voice flat. "I never take a sucker bet. You should text Tigra once you find a place to stay. She's going to want to talk to you about the Thunderstrike."

I asked her to hold for a moment and summoned Queet. "I need you to find out what state my apartment is in." He whisked away without a word, and I turned to Jason and Tam, telling them what Hecate had said. "We need a safe place to stay—she said ground level, in a sturdy building. I sent Queet to scope out my apartment. It's a walkup, but we can stay there if need be."

"We could stay over the shop in my apartment, but I'm not sure I'm comfortable with that, just in case of a bad aftershock. And let's face it, Kae, your building is a million years old. Or at least, it's old enough to be dangerous." Jason glanced back at the building behind us, where his shop was, as if expecting it to keel over on our heads any moment.

"I know a place," Tam said. "But it's in the Sandspit, near the World Tree. You're going to have to trust me, because it's a dangerous path."

I paused. Going into the Sandspit was dangerous to begin with. I almost never set foot inside the gated enclosure, not even when hunting Aboms. "Let's wait till Queet—"

"I'm back." Queet was in full whisper-speak mode, so both Jason and Tam could hear him. "Your apartment building is standing but they've got it flagged. I peeked inside and there are a lot of cracks in your ceiling. You'd better start looking for new dinnerware. I wouldn't chance going there tonight, not even to get your things. However, I'll bet Hecate could bring you your sword and probably a change of clothing. The Elder Gods are good at that sort of thing."

Even with the sobering news, I stifled a snort. Queet was right. Hecate *could* do that, but asking her to run my errands? I'd have to think about that for a minute. But then, reality sank in. I couldn't go back to my apartment, and that meant finding another place to stay. Since Dream Wardens didn't seem all that safe, we might have to give Tam's route a go.

Sighing, I returned to the phone. "Listen, my apartment's a no-go. And Jason doesn't trust Dream Wardens—"

"Good. Multi-story buildings aren't a good idea right now."

"Right, well, Tam said he knows a safe place in the Sandspit. Listen, can you nip into my apartment somehow and grab my sword and some clothes? Thanks!" I hung up before she could say anything. For one thing, I knew that she wouldn't be thrilled about us heading into the Sandspit. For another, I had just asked one of the Elder Gods to fetch my things for me and while I figured she would be a good sport and do it, she'd never let me forget it, either.

Jason and Tam were staring at me, mouths open.

"I'm sure she'll understand. So, I guess we head out to your hiding place, Tam." My phone rang again. As I cleared my throat and answered, Hecate came on the line loud and clear.

"Next time you want an errand girl, call one of the demi-goddesses." Her voice sounded so loud I could have sworn she was behind me.

"I'm sorry. I just..." I paused. Tam and Jason were snickering. I shushed them but at that moment, a tap on the shoulder startled me and I spun around. Hecate was actually standing there, towering over me, carrying a tote bag and my sword.

"Here." She dropped them at my feet. "Satisfied? Now, tell me why you are planning on going into the Sandspit?"

"Because I have a hidey-hole there." Tam winked at her and I rubbed my forehead, groaning. It was bad enough I had acted the way I had, but to have one of my friends wink at the goddess who held my leash was just one step over the line.

But Hecate grinned at him. "Don't you try to put a Come-Hither on me, young Fae. Even though you are a pretty sight, you are." But then, she sobered. "You'd best get moving. This is going to be a long night, with looters out. Tomorrow morning, Fury, I want you to go back out to the Arbortariam. Beg leeway from Jerako. I could tell he liked you. Take Tam with you. We need to make certain the Greenlings don't start tearing up the place until we have a chance to take this Lyon character down. Then, come see me. All of you." Her expression grim, she stood back, crossing her arms over her chest. "Seriously, this could be the beginning of the end. The Fates say whatever happens, it's going to change things around the planet. We're just trying to negate as much of the damage as we can."

And with that, she turned and vanished from sight.

We stared after her for a moment. I happened to glance out in the street. Tommy-Tee was sitting on the sidewalk, looking lost.

"Guys...look." I nudged Jason. "Tommy-Tee."

Jason wandered over and knelt beside him. "Hey, Tommy, what's going on?"

"I don't know...everything blew up. The sky's on fire and Great Mother Gaia is singing her pain." Tommy-Tee stared morosely at the curb. "I can't find my bed. There's only a pile of stones to sleep on."

Jason glanced back at us and I bit my lip. I didn't want to have to look out for someone like Tommy-Tee. He was one of the lost-boys, and would need to be constantly supervised. Tam frowned and shook his head.

"Guys, he doesn't have a place to stay—his flop has obviously been covered up with rubble." Jason was a mother hen. He had taken me in, and now he was worried about Tommy-Tee. He always gave cash to beggars on the street, and I knew that at least twenty percent of his income went to various charities.

I glanced back at the store. "You sure the building won't hold together? We could let him sleep in the back room—lock it so he can't get into things."

"Fury, really?" Jason gave me a scathing look. "Given the chance of a big aftershock, do you *really* want to chance somebody's life in there tonight?"

"We can't stand here and babysit him, though." I glanced at Tam. "What do you say?"

Tam spoke up. "Bring him with us, but make certain he does what we say. Where we're going is someplace only the Bonny Fae know about. I cannot have him wandering around on his own.

He's your responsibility, Jason."

Jason shrugged. "I accept that." He leaned over and whispered something to Tommy-Tee, who held out his hand for Jason to pull him to his feet.

Tam jerked his head toward the shop. "Better make sure it's locked tight and lower the gate."

Jason nodded, heading back inside Dream Wardens while Tam, Tommy-Tee, and I waited outside.

"You okay? The other night you didn't look so good." Tommy-Tee turned to me, smiling. It was the smile of a child. Tommy's brain had been scrambled by way too many drugs.

Relenting, I smiled back. He was a good sort, just broken. "Yes, Tommy. Thank you for asking. You're going to come with us and we'll find you a place to sleep."

"Whatever that thing was, man, it was barreling toward you like a bat out of hell." He laughed, then, and suddenly froze, staring into the street. "You better be careful, Fury."

I frowned, following his gaze. Suddenly, my Trace screen popped up. An Abom was out there, somewhere, and it was moving fast. I tried to pinpoint it, but it kept jumping around on the screen. "What the hell? Tam, an Abom. Tommy-Tee picked up on an Abomination."

Tam reached out to rest his hand on Tommy-Tee's arm. A moment later he looked at me, arching his eyebrows. "We need to talk, but it will have to wait."

Jason emerged from the shop then as the gate

behind him clattered down to protect the store windows. He had activated the one for Up-Cakes, too, and that closed as well. "Ready." He paused. "What happened?"

"Tommy-Tee picked up on an Abomination. I'm trying to pinpoint it."

"You'll have to leave it, Kae, we need to get to cover. The action tonight isn't over yet. I just got word from my sister. The Devani are on the march toward the border between Darktown and Croix. Apparently, the bogeys are on their way into all districts, looking to loot. This night won't end without blood." He motioned to Tam. "Lead the way. I'd bring the car but the autopilot informed me the parking garage is closed down so looters can't get in."

We headed out on foot. Darktown bordered the Sandspit and the Junk Yard. I wasn't sure exactly where in the Sandspit that Tam was looking to lead us, but wherever it was, we weren't likely to be welcome. Add in watching for rogue magic zones and the sky-eyes, and we had a hike cut out for us.

Jason took a call as we headed out, following Tam. "Yeah, I made sure your gate is secure, too... No, you stay there with Leonard... What? Right, the shop is still standing... No, the windows held, at least this go-round. There may be aftershocks. I've got to—what? Really? All right, thanks for the warning. We're not going near there but we'll be cautious anyway. All right. Love you too, sis." He slid his phone back in his pocket.

"Shevron?" It didn't take a genius to figure out

who he had been talking to.

"Right. I told her to stay home. Do not try to venture into Darktown. She said…" He glanced around, then lowered his voice. "She said the Devani are on the move, all right, but they aren't just going after looters. They have moved into north Darktown and are searching some residences."

"They need to search the Junk Yard is where they need to search. That's where they'll find the fucknuts behind this." Our world had already been turned upside down, and now, Lyon and his Order wanted to twist it all up again. Life wasn't perfect, there was a lot of poverty and a lot of corruption, but it was better than what it had been like, from what the history books taught.

We headed south. Darktown—and Dream Wardens—was located on the northern edge of the Sandspit, a few blocks away. As we skirted the 22-U, I noticed that the mall had weathered the quake pretty good, but next to it, one entire wall of the Emporium Plaza had crumbled away. We skirted the buildings, stepping over the piles of rubble that littered the streets, avoiding the residents of Darktown who were dazedly wandering in and out of the chaos.

A sudden movement caught my eye and I flattened against the brick. "Sky-eye."

Tam and Jason followed suit, Jason dragging Tommy-Tee back against the building next to him. We waited while the drone zipped in and out, and then it circled the square once and flitted off to spy on another area. We waited for a count of ten, then relaxed back onto the sidewalk.

"I don't trust them. Not at all." Tam glared at the retreating drone.

"No, but let's face it. The Devani are marching into north Darktown from Croix? They've never bothered to come down here. Not that I can remember. There has to be more going on than we know about." I pushed a strand of hair out of my face. The rain had stopped earlier, but the wind was howling fierce. My sword hung over my shoulder, giving me comfort, and Tam was carrying my duffel bag, the strap slung over his shoulder.

We came to one of the Monotrain platforms and I stared up at the staircase. It was silent, and there were no lights on the top of the platform. Something had happened to the train—I knew it. I could feel it as sure as I could feel the shifting tides in the wind.

"The quake took out the Monotrain."

"I think you're right. I haven't seen one pass by at all, and even though service isn't that great down here in Darktown in the first place, we usually get a midnight train by now." Jason scanned the skies, and I thought he was looking for sky-eyes again, but he put that thought to rest. "I'm thinking of going up—seeing what I can by air."

"No!" My quick response startled even me.

"What's wrong?" Jason glanced up at the sky again. "What are you sensing?"

I swallowed hard. I wasn't sure exactly why I had reacted so strongly, but then, as I let out a slow breath, I knew what had startled me so bad. My inner Trace was singing like a choir.

"A flight-born Abom. I've never encountered one." Panic hit me. How the hell had they become airborne? I had never seen one who could fly, and it hadn't even occurred to me that it was possible. They always jumped to humans—how could a human fly?

"That's not possible." Tam shook his head. "They don't work like that."

"They do now, or my wires are seriously crossed." I shook my head. "Something big is going down and it goes beyond the Order of the Black Mist. I can't figure it out here, though. Hecate is right. We have to get under cover. Something...is coming..."

It was as if a fog swept down to cloud my thoughts. The next thing I knew, I was racing into the intersection. At the center, I whispered the charm, swept my arms over my head to clasp my hands, and boom...landed dead center at the Crossroads.

Chapter 18

The moment I landed on the Crossroads,
I knew something was up. Hecate was there,
waiting, her expression grim. She was decked
out in what I thought of as her *Mother-of-Magic*
gear—long indigo robe with her hair falling to
her feet. In this guise, the jet-black locks were
streaked with white, and three snakes wound
around her arms and neck. They were adders, gray
with a brown leopard pattern running down their
backs. Four feet long, with thick, stocky bodies,
they danced, entwining around her in continual
movement as if they were extensions of her body.
She was standing behind a steaming cauldron
in the center of the Crossroads, and through the
mist, a moon rose darkly behind her, the clouds
streaking past at a ferocious rate.

"My Lady." I dropped into a quick curtsey,
then rose.

"We'll dispense with the niceties at this point. I just found out that the quake *was* magically activated, but it gets worse. The Order of the Black Mist is up to more than weather magic." Before I could ask what she meant, she continued. "They aren't looking to simply start another weather war. There are some doors on the World Tree that did not open when Gaia brought about the World Shift. Even in her anger, she made certain they stayed shut. One of those doors leads to Chaos."

Confused, I tilted my head, frowning. "I thought Pandoriam was the realm of Chaos, where the Aboms come from."

"No, though many make that same assumption. Pandoriam actually feeds off the *energy* from Chaos. The actual *realm* beyond the door is where the Elder Gods of Chaos live. They slumber there, and their dreams alone cause enough disruption in the universe. If they were to wake, it would be the end of all things ordered and peaceful."

I eased myself down onto one of the nearby boulders. "The end of the world—of all worlds as we know it. And for some insane reason, the Order of the Black Mist is trying to open the gateway. Have they succeeded?"

"Not yet, but it's imperative for you to retrieve that disk. The Thunderstrike might be able to help them break open the door—it has powers beyond weather magic, and one of the big problems is that we don't know exactly what they are. The records were lost in the World Shift. They have no clue of what they are doing—of what this will mean. We have to get that disk back before they attempt to use it again."

She paused and I knew what was coming. I didn't want to hear it, but I knew what she was going to say.

"I'm sorry, Fury, but I need to ask you to go after it. If the Order hides out in the Tunnels as you say, then I need you to go down there and find it."

I stared at my feet, my breath catching in my throat. The last thing I wanted to do was go chasing around an underground labyrinth, where Lyon waited at the center. I never questioned Hecate, not since the time she dragged me before Themis, but this time, I felt I had to say something.

"Lady...do you realize what you're asking?"

"I do." She stared at me bleakly. "If the Elder Gods could venture after it, we would. Rest assured, I do not send you into this lightly."

Unfortunately—or maybe it was to our benefit, when I thought about it—the Elder Gods were constrained by how much they could interfere in mortal affairs. Just as the Fates were bound from revealing too much, the Elder Gods could only act indirectly.

"I know you're forced to work through your servants here, and I know it used to be just through your priests and priestesses, until we Theosians came about. I'm not sure what binds you to that, but I do understand that you can't just walk in there and take the Thunderstrike from his hands."

She shrugged. "I don't know where or how

the restrictions began and I'm not sure any of the Elder Gods actually know, but we *all* have limitations, gods and mortals...and Theosians... alike. The gods are allowed to intervene through our servants, we can interact with your world, but if we break the boundaries, there will be repercussions. To ignore the rules is to ask for banishment from this realm. The Convocation of Gods is clear about that."

I wanted to ask where they would be sent, but she sounded so incredibly bleak that I decided my curiosity could wait. "I don't know where to begin. Is there any chance you might have any ideas on where I can find the entrance to the Tunnels?"

A light flickered in her eyes and she brightened. "There I *can* help. Before I brought you to the Crossroads, I asked Coralie to look into the matter. The entrance to the Tunnels is found directly in the northeast corner where the Bogs meet the Sandspit. It's a treacherous area, rife with rogue magic, so you'll have to be extremely cautious."

I nodded. We were headed to the Sandspit anyway, so I might as well make a run on the Tunnels while we were there. "Thank you. Hecate, can you give me *any* more help on this? When we get into the Tunnels, how are we going to find Lyon?"

"Lyon apparently lives near the Tunnel Pike, near the waterfront. He's always guarded by a couple of bog-dogs, so be cautious. They're dangerous and won't hesitate to attack. You're going to want to take them down fast because they are vicious and quick."

Bog-dogs were deadly. They had teeth sharp enough to rip flesh to shreds, and a temper to match. They were hard to train and harder still to domesticate. The government had originally bred them specifically for the Devani to use, but some had gotten loose in the Bogs and had bred into feral and deadly predators.

"Lovely. All right, bog-dogs and the Pike. Anything else?"

She laughed. "You're always angling for a new spell or ability, Fury. I like that about you."

Blushing, I stared at the fork in the road. "Well, at least I'm not over there, trying to make a deal."

"You couldn't even if you wanted to. Theosians aren't allowed to make deals with the Elder Gods. You're bound to obey." Even though her voice was light, there was a hint of warning there.

But if I was bound to work for the gods, I wanted as many perks as I could get. Which reminded me that I had forgotten to thank her. "I found the cash card. Thank you—it helps a lot. If everything is a go on Monday, I'll call about that job."

"Fury, when you're short on funds, you should ask me. I'm not going to heap riches on you—that's neither your nature nor mine, but I don't want you going hungry or worrying about paying your bills. I'll always engineer a job for you, or if you need food, make certain you have the money to buy it. The gods sometimes forget that mortals—or demi-mortals such as yourself—have needs that can only be met in practical ways."

Her voice was gentle and I realized that she really did care about me. Unlike some of the gods who made their Theosians suffer, Hecate didn't use me as joke-bait, for which I was ever grateful.

"I'll find the entrance to the Tunnels. I can't promise anything, but I'll do my best."

Hecate reached in the pocket of her robe and pulled out a glittering disk about an inch in diameter. She handed it to me. I stared at the talisman. Engraved on the disk was Hecate's knot—three snakes, entwined in a continuous loop. The silver charm tingled in my hand.

"Keep this with you. If you come within five hundred feet of the Thunderstrike, it will activate your Trace and you'll be able to track the device."

I pocketed the talisman, sliding it into an inner pocket in my shorts and zipping it shut. It was a gift better than gold, giving what we were facing.

"Thank you." I paused, then asked, "What do you think will happen if I don't get the Thunderstrike back?"

"I think...we will all be in a great deal of trouble. Jerako and the Greenlings will go after it, and Seattle will not be able to stand against their attempts to retrieve the Thunderstrike."

"That's what I thought. I just wanted to hear you say it." After a moment, I shivered. "I'm getting cold." Even in my leather jacket, the Crossroads sapped the life out of me. "Is there anything else?"

Hecate let out a faint smile. "Yes, actually. Sometimes, what's right in front of your nose eludes you. Don't go chasing after daydreams when the reality is much more suitable and willing. Go now. Be safe."

I suddenly slammed off the Crossroads, landing on my knees between Tam and Jason, who were frantically looking around, calling my name.

"Kae! Where the hell were you?" Jason's expression was grim.

"Oof, that landing was rough. Help me up."

Tam took one hand, Jason the other, and they pulled me to my feet.

"Hecate called me over to the Crossroads."

"Are you all right? Was there an Abom loose over there?" Jason asked.

I dusted myself off. My knees were scraped, but that was par for the course. I had more scrapes and bumps on my knees than a kid learning how to freewheel on a bike.

"Yeah, I'm all right. Change of plans, though. I have to head into the Tunnels and retrieve the Thunderstrike. Apparently, the Order of the Black Mist isn't acting on a full deck. They're using the Thunderstrike to try to open the doors to the realm of Chaos."

As we headed toward the outer border of the Sandspit, I told them what she had said. "So, yeah, I need to go to the northwest corner of the Sandspit, where it meets the Bogs. The entrance to the Tunnels is there." I almost asked if they would go with me, but then stopped. This was dangerous and I didn't want to put my friends in danger.

Tam cleared his throat. "I'm coming with you. I won't let you go there alone."

Jason blinked. "Kae, I'm game, too, but do you want us tagging along?"

Relief swept over me. Grateful for the offer, I said, "You're welcome to come, but I don't want to put either of you in harm's way. But...I would welcome the company."

"We're with you, Fury." Tam shifted his weight to one side, and suddenly he seemed to glow, his glamour running strong. I realized it was more than skin deep. Under the night sky, he seemed luminous and regal.

"I don't consider this just your fight," Jason grumbled. "Lyon is getting too big for his britches, and the Order of the Black Mist is dangerous. We're all in this together."

"Right." I glanced over at Tommy-Tee. *Crap.* We couldn't take him. "What do we do about..." I jerked my head toward him. "And our things? I don't want to be dragging around a change of clothes through the Tunnels."

Tommy-Tee didn't seem to notice we were talking about him. He was staring at the sky, his eyes lit up like a kid staring into a candy shop.

Tam gave him a long look. "Tommy-Tee is trapped inside his shadow. He's in there, but it would take a skilled shaman from my people to bring him back out."

That threw me. "You mean there's hope for him?"

With a gentle smile, Tam caught my gaze and held it. "There's hope for a lot of the Broken. Humans just don't know the right techniques and your government treats them like lost causes rather than ask the Otherkin for help."

Otherkin was the term the government used to include all those not of human or Theosian–human blood.

"What do you mean?" I asked.

"Too often, it isn't the body chemistry gone wrong as much as the spirit has gone wandering. We'll head toward the Tunnels after we go where I was taking us to begin with. We can leave our things there, along with Tommy-Tee, and he'll be safe."

As we crossed the last divide separating us from the fences surrounding the Sandspit, my stomach worked its way into my throat. The very aura of the drifting dunes reeked with chaotic magic, and with danger. During the day, sometimes the dunes shifted so you could see the World Tree from the edges, but at night, especially when the clouds were covering the sky with their thick, gray masses, you could barely see your hand in front of your face.

There were no streetlights on the sidewalks that surrounded the two-hundred-acre vortex. They shorted out so often the city had removed them. Instead, a row of lights lined the opposite sides of the streets, leaving the fence surrounding the roiling pit swathed in darkness. But the Sandspit had a glow all of its own. Faint, but unmistakable. The dunes emanated a pale blue light, shifting as the great piles of sands moved in the continuous wind that rattled the area.

As we came to the fence, I stared into what had once been a thriving industrial sector of town.

What had it looked like originally, I wondered. What had it looked like the day before Gaia turned it into a twisted heap of scrap metal, and then— dust and sand? The fury in her strike, the fury of what had happened, hit me to the core. We couldn't face her anger again. One more time and it would be the end of civilization for good. We couldn't chance the Order of the Black Mist raising enough hell so Gaia would rage down and wipe every trace of human and Otherkin off the face of her body.

"We have to find the Tunnels," I whispered, staring into the seething pit.

Tam, standing beside me, slid his arm around my waist. "We will. We'll find them."

"I don't want to go in there. But I have no choice." I had been in the Sandspit a few times, but never very far. Two hundred acres might not seem like much, but when every step was fraught with danger, the prospect of two hundred acres was daunting.

"The World Tree is in there. Think of it, Fury. We have a branch of the World Tree right here. Your ancestors would never have believed it possible. They didn't even know it existed until Gaia uncloaked it."

Something about the way he said it made me stop short. "*My* ancestors? What about yours?" I turned to him. "How old *are* you, Tam? Jason is two hundred and twenty-four years old, but I have no idea how old you are."

"Does it matter? Would it change the way you act around me?" He searched my face and I realized he really wanted an answer.

A funny feeling settled in my stomach. I knew very little about Tam, even though I had known him over half my life now. I realized I knew nothing about his family or background—it had never come up in conversation.

"I like to think I wouldn't react differently. But this isn't the place for a heart-to-heart conversation, is it? We'd better get moving. Jason, do you have Tommy-Tee? We don't dare let him wander loose in the Sandspit. It would eat him up."

With Tommy-Tee in tow, we walked along the fence until we came to one of the openings leading into the magical zone. There were large readerboards warning people of the dangers. As with the Bogs, the boards stated that no rescues would be mounted, no searches made, no recovery efforts undertaken. Enter at your own risk, basically.

I sucked in a deep breath and, because this was my fight no matter what Jason and Tam thought, I was the first to step into the Sandspit.

The shift in energy was immediate. Once through the gate, the winds picked up to a steady, brusque clip. The air shifted, taking on a cool, harsh feel, and stinging grains of sand began to pelt my face. The winds never died in the Sandspit. They never fell silent, but ceaselessly howled, their voices clear with warning.

Here, the elements were alive in a way they weren't out in the rest of the world. They had sentience—and emotion. And tonight, the winds were angry. I could feel the energy surround me, sweeping up my own emotion and heightening it. Something had happened, and the spirits were pissed. Was it the earthquake? Or something different? That, I couldn't tell, but I stopped, wanting to hear what the winds were whispering.

"Can you feel it? The winds are trying to tell me something."

"I can hear it, but I can't make out what they're saying." Tam turned, his back to me. "I'll watch behind us and to the right. Jason, you watch to our front and left. Fury, do what you need to."

Jason took hold of Tommy-Tee's wrist, holding him steady. "Go ahead, Kae. Whatever you need."

I stepped between them so that I was protected and raised my hands. I couldn't go into the Crossroads here, there was no intersection, but I could work with my own magic. Fire and flame wouldn't do much and there wasn't much to exorcise, but my powers of divination would help.

I stretched out, opening my mind to the sounds riding the wind. The voices formed a tapestry of music, catching me up in a melody so faint I could barely hear it. As it began to grow, I opened myself to the sound. Suddenly, I was in the thick, dancing on the haunting tune that rode the currents of air. I whirled in the middle of the voices, which appeared as sparks bobbing and weaving. The dancing lights grew stronger as the voices grew louder, and fainter as they faded out. I drifted with them until the music turned into words, and I could hear what was being said beneath the thrum of song.

> *"The tree is awake, the tree is alive,*
> *The roots are thick, the portals thrive,*
> *The doors that are closed buzz like hives,*
> *As the bleak magician strives...*
> *To open, to open, to open the way*
> *As the threads of destiny fray..."*

Abruptly, I dropped out of my trance. "The winds in the Sandspit know about Lyon and what he's trying to do. Whether they are actual spirits or whether it's an air elemental, I don't know, but Lyon's doing his best to change the path of fate and destiny. Tam, take us to where we can safely leave Tommy-Tee and our things. After that, we have to get to the Tunnels as quickly as we can."

I still had no idea how we were going to infiltrate the Order of the Black Mist and retrieve the Thunderstrike, but I knew we had to— and soon. Or the World Shift would be a pale comparison of what Gaia would rain down on us this time.

Chapter 19

Tam led us into what seemed like an indistinguishable mass of dunes. The sand was ochre in color, but it sparkled with lights, as though somebody had dumped a ton of glitter in it. But as pretty as it was, I knew that glitter represented rogue magic and was hella dangerous. Because let one good gust blow it into your face and *boom*—something was guaranteed to happen.

"Don't scuff your feet. Don't kick up sand. Do your best to take steady, easy steps. Try not to breathe too deeply. It's a bad idea." Tam kept his voice down.

I brought up my Trace and checked for any Aboms that might be in the area, but saw no signs. The aerial Abomination we had seen earlier was nowhere in sight—it was long gone.

"We're clear on Aboms for now, but that doesn't mean there aren't other creatures prowling around here." I shivered. My legs were cold, but it was the Sandspit giving me the creeps.

"This way." Tam skirted a large dune that was mounded over a scrap heap of rusted metal, and turned to the left.

We followed him as he wound through the dunes. I realized I had no idea how deep we were into the Sandspit. From here, none of the exits were visible. The sides of the Sandspit seemed to be swallowed up by unending dunes. We might as well be in the middle of the desert instead of downtown Seattle. The noise of the streets was muffled as well, and I began to wonder if the Sandspit was off in its own dimension, nestled in the midst of the dark city streets.

After a time—it could have been five minutes or it could have been an hour—Tam stopped. He pointed ahead. There, rising out of a crater so deep that its top was almost level with the sand, was the World Tree. The tree was over one hundred feet tall, which meant the crater had to be at least that deep.

"I had no idea it was actually inside the crater. Was that formed..."

"When Gaia shifted the world? Yes. All over the world, she summoned the branches of the World Tree. This tree, and others like it, are just limbs of the one that connects all the realms together." Tam stared at it reverently. "Whether it was birthed out of her anger or her love, the Tree is a beacon to all who travel through the different dimensions and worlds."

"Like the Abominations."

"Yes, it's a beacon for them, unfortunately. And for the Devani, which is equally unfortunate. The two are mirrors, but they are both so far out on their respective ends of the spectrum that they're not really all that different." Tam paused, his gaze darting around the area. Finally, he seemed to see what he was looking for. "Come. This way."

We followed as he skirted the crater. About halfway around it, he paused by one particularly sharp-looking heap of scrap metal and then cautiously approached the edge of the crater.

"We go down here."

"Down?" Jason asked. "We're actually descending into the crater?" He sounded just about as thrilled as I felt.

"We have to, yes. Don't question. Follow single file in my tracks. There's a hidden stair and it is steep and treacherous, so be cautious. Jason, you could probably fly down but I doubt that Tommy-Tee can make it on his own, so if you could stay in human form to help him, it would probably be best." And with that, Tam vanished over the edge.

My stomach knotted. I waited for a moment, then gingerly followed his tracks to the edge of the crater. In the dark, so it was hard to see the path he was taking, except for the luminous glow emanating from the World Tree. The incandescent green light lit up the air. Tam's footsteps leading down the slope toward the crater glittered with sparkles.

Hesitantly, I stepped over the side. Beneath the sand, I could feel the steps hidden under the dunes. They were slick because of the sand, but I was able to follow the sparkling pattern of his steps. I cautiously began to make my way down, one step at a time, holding my breath. A hundred-foot tumble down into a crater of sand would still smart.

"Crap, I hate this," I muttered to myself. But I fell into a rhythm and the descent grew easier. *Take a step. Pause, make certain I'm on a firm foundation. Take another step. Pause.*

The minutes wore away and I lost track of the time because the descent was so slow. There would be no hurrying, no rushing. We couldn't afford to make a mistake. We were so close to the World Tree that I could see the portals from where I was. They were flat against the trunk, swirling vortices of energy plastered against the bark. Where they led, I didn't know, but the last thing I wanted was for some Abomination to come zipping through while I was trying to keep my balance on the side of the crater.

A shower of sand poured around my shoulders, startling me, and I heard Jason's muffled curse from up above. Tommy-Tee muttered something. I didn't look up—I didn't want sand in my eyes—but I could guess what had happened. Tommy-Tee must have slipped and Jason caught him. As we descended farther into the crater, the rest of Seattle seemed to fade. Even thoughts of the quake vanished as I focused on my steps and my breathing.

"Fury?" For once Queet's voice was soft. *"I don't want to disturb your thoughts, but I wanted*

to let you know I'm here."

I was counting the steps by now to keep my focus. The sparkling sand scared me. The glittering grains were rife with rogue magic. For some reason, the thought of falling into it frightened me more than the thought of an Abom coming in off the World Tree.

"Thanks," I said to Queet. I paused in mid-step, not wanting to mess up my coordination. "How long have I been moving? Hours?"

"No, but time in the Sandspit runs oddly. It's not like time outside. Think of it like being out on the Crossroads. You can be there for what seems like an eternity but only a blink of an eye might have passed back here. I'll be quiet and let you finish." And he was good to his word.

I went back to descending the hidden stairs until I happened to glance over at the tree and realize that I was nearly at the bottom. The sound of the winds was cushioned down here, with only a light breeze to shift and move the sands of the dunes. As I stepped off the last stair, Tam was waiting. So relieved to be down safe, I fell into his arms, holding him tightly.

"I feel like I've come through another world," I whispered, my head on his shoulder.

"You have," he said, his words a whisper in my ear. "You're okay, Fury. The descent affects everybody that way. We all feel it when we come down here. You're traveling through history, through layers of magic, through worlds dying and being born. I can't explain it, but you are no longer where you started out. That may sound obvious, but..."

I looked up into his face, shivering as his silver gaze held me fast. I wanted to kiss him, to feel his lips on mine again. His arms were warm around my shoulders and I wanted his fingers to linger over my skin, to caress my breasts, my stomach, my...

"Later. *I promise*. Later." His words shook me out of my reverie and I blinked.

"How did you—"

"I feel it, too. But right now, we should focus on what must be done." And with that, he slid his arm around my shoulders and I turned to face Jason and Tommy-Tee as they stepped off the stairs. Both looked shaken, though Jason more so.

"Everybody okay?" I asked. "I thought I heard someone almost fall."

Jason nodded somberly. "You did. I slipped and Tommy-Tee managed to grab me when my boot slid off a rock. I hope we didn't hit you with too much sand on the way down."

I shook my head, surprised. That Tommy-Tee managed to not only think fast enough to grab for Jason, but actually *managed* to catch him, surprised me. I was suddenly grateful Jason had insisted we bring him along.

"Look at that—the tree is on fire." Tommy-Tee pointed to the trunk of the World Tree.

The tree wasn't actually on fire, but it was glowing with flickering waves of energy—of magic. Green and blue, orange and purple, all entwined like snakes in a mating dance. The flames ringed the trunk, crackling softly in the night. The roots of the giant oak dug deep into the earth, and as I looked down at the roots that trailed near my feet, I could feel the pulsating energy flow through the lignified veins that dug deep into the earth. I knelt, holding my hand over the wood. The radiance swirled around me, catching me up in the warm resonance of magic.

"I could stay here all day and just float in the waves."

Tam and Jason joined me, and after a moment's hesitation, Tommy-Tee crossed to my side. A blissful look swept across his face and he let out a sigh.

"I remember this," he whispered.

"Remember what, Tommy?" Jason tilted his head, seeming as loath to move as I was.

"I remember the night this happened. I remember when the Tree was born."

We all stared at him. Tommy-Tee couldn't possibly remember the World Tree's birth. It had happened centuries ago, long before my time. Long before Jason's time. I wasn't sure about Tam.

"Tommy-Tee, are you *sure* you remember when the Tree arrived?" I asked.

He nodded, the blissful look spreading across his face. "I was down here, hanging out on the tracks with some buddies. The storm...it was terrifying." His voice took on an anxious tone. "We tried to run, and I managed to get on top of one of the railroad cars. Then, the lightning hit, and the world went sky-high as metal twisted and screamed. Everything shifted and a lightning strike hit the yard and formed the crater. The Tree was born that night. I remember crawling to the edge of the crater and looking in, and there it was. The doors opened, and then..."

He paused, holding his hands out toward the tree in a beckoning gesture. "Then I don't remember anything...not for a long time. But I do remember crawling down into the crater. I sat here for a long time. So long that the world seemed to turn to stone around me."

His eyes suddenly clouded over again and he pressed his lips shut, the vacant look returning. He pulled his hands back as a tear rolled down his cheek. "I'm sad," he whispered. "I want... I don't know what I want. I need a hit."

I motioned to Jason and Tam and we moved off to the side a bit. "What do you think?"

"I have no clue except that was the most lucid I've ever seen him. But...and this is a *big* but...can we trust what he said? He seems agitated now." Jason shrugged. "I don't know."

"It's probably time for his Opish. He may have some on him, most of the addicts do. Check his pockets," Tam said.

Jason moved off to help Tommy-Tee while Tam scouted the area. I stood, arms folded, staring at the World Tree. The trunk was at least twelve feet in diameter. Branches sprang out beneath each portal to a network into a set of natural stairs—or rather, limbs that could be used as stairs. It would require some climbing, but as far as I could see, it would be possible to reach any of the vortices from ground level.

Jason found Tommy-Tee's stash and helped

him pop one of the tablets. Opish could be either taken internally or smoked. Most O-Heads preferred the smoke, but we didn't have time for Tommy-Tee to light up. But he seemed to be content swallowing the tablet and a few minutes later, the blissful look returned to his face, only this time it was the bliss created by the drug rather than the magic.

Tam returned. "All right, I found what I was looking for. Follow me."

We followed him around the base of the World Tree, stepping over limb and branch and root. The tree radiated like I imagined the nuclear power plants had so long in the past. All of the power plants fueled by reactors had been torn to bits during the World Shift. As far as I knew, Gaia had negated the radiation in them and now our power was generated by wind, geothermal energy, and solar power.

As we crossed another quarter turn around the gigantic tree, Tam veered to the left, toward the wall of the crater. We followed. There, in the dark of the night, was an even darker mouth of a cave. The opening was only five feet high. Tam ducked inside. I followed, with Jason and Tommy-Tee right behind me.

As I straightened up, I gasped. We were in a large cavern. A twenty-foot ceiling extended farther than I could see. The walls glittered with sparkles of rogue magic that gave off a dim light. I realized that the sand had been compacted. It was smooth and shiny, so dense that it had become hard as stone.

The cavern was empty, as far as I could see, but it didn't *feel* empty.

"What is this place? Does the city know about it?"

Tam shook his head. "No. This tunnel belongs to my people. It leads to a safe space. Don't worry about it collapsing if there's an aftershock. I guarantee it won't."

As we approached the back of the cave, Jason exclaimed as he pointed to the ceiling. Inlaid against the roof of the chamber was a star-shaped pattern of glowing crystals. They were blue and green and they shimmered, brilliant against the dim light that pervaded the chamber.

"What's that?"

"That is the symbol of my nation. The Tuatha de Dannan. What you call the Bonny Fae. We go back farther than the Weather Wars, you know—a lot farther. My people originally came from a land called Eire. We have a history so steeped in magic and legend that it would put modern history to shame if they were to record it right."

"Why don't we know about this?" I asked. "I never learned anything about your people in history class, not even when we studied the cultures of the Otherkin."

"Because the corporatocracies don't want you to. Not only are they leery of the Otherkin—which is why we're banned from holding public office— but they don't want you to know about life before the Weather Wars. You only know what they want you to know. For example—Jason's people? The hawk-shifters? They come from the land of Black

Forest, but from a time when the actual Black Forest existed as a woodland rather than a city. Long before the rise of nations and the rise of technology. The time of the Weather Wars isn't ancient history. The time of the Weather Wars is *built* on ancient history."

At that moment, Tam led us into a narrow passage leading away from the main chamber. As we headed in the general direction that I gauged the Bogs were in, Tommy-Tee suddenly spoke up from behind me.

"I've been here before," he whispered. "I remember this place, too."

As I glanced over my shoulder, Tam suddenly vanished through an opening ahead. I stumbled over a root, catching myself as I came to the edge of the archway. As I peeked in, Tommy-Tee's words vanished from my thoughts.

"Welcome to the Court of the Bonny Fae, welcome to the home of the sons and daughters of the Tuatha de Dannan," Tam said, leading us into a brilliant throne room filled with Fae. As a group near us stopped to stare, Tam inclined his head as a collective gasp ran through the room.

"Lord Tam O'Reilly, Lord of the Barrow! Welcome home, Your Highness," one of the men said, as everyone—man and woman—dropped into curtseys and bows.

Jason and I stared at Tam, who merely winked at me, then strode to the throne in the center of the room and there, he took his place.

Chapter 20

"*Lord* Tam?" Jason stared at him, incredulous.

"I am at that, Jason. Lord Tam, Prince of the Northwest Clan of the Bonny Fae. I'm Lord of the Realm here." Tam sprawled out on his throne like he'd been born to it. Every one of the Fae in the room had cast a reverent eye on him.

As we cautiously approached the throne, I looked around the room. The chamber was so large that I couldn't see the far end. The ceiling stretched beyond my sight, the apex lost among the flickering lights emanating from the walls of the chamber. Furnished with benches and long tables carved from some dark hardwood, the cavern seemed sparse, nothing like I would picture a throne room. Except for the throne itself.

Tam's throne had been hewn out of what looked like black marble, etched over every inch with knot work carvings. What I first thought was Wandering Ivy covered the base, but then I realized the plant growing around the base wasn't sentient. Holly branches broke through the cavern floor to flare out from the other sides of the throne. Crystals—shimmering and clear—sparkled from the back, above where Tam's head rested, and silver spines jutted out to the side along the back, forming a gleaming row of threatening spikes.

"You're a prince?" My mind reeled, trying to take in the news.

"I've been called that and worse," Tam said. He snapped his fingers and two men stepped forward, kneeling at his feet. "I don't have time to stay, but I have a task for you."

"Whatever your will, Lord Tam." The taller man rose, coming to attention.

"One of my friends needs protection while the rest of us are away. You will guard him from harm. He's one of the wandering ones. Keep an eye on him, make him comfortable. If he's amenable, let him visit with the shamans but do nothing that will harm him. We also need you to watch over our things while we're away." Tam motioned for Jason, Tommy-Tee, and me to move to his side. "These are friends of the realm, friends of the throne. Any time they need protection, they are welcome here in UnderBarrow. I present to the court Jason Aerie—hawk-shifter and magician. Tommy-Tee, vagabond minstrel. And Fury...chosen of Hecate."

At that, there was a groundswell murmur ran through the chamber and a ripple swept the word *Welcome* to us from a hundred voices in unison.

"And now, I must be off. Stay safe within

UnderBarrow this night. The ground may not be done with her shaking and moaning." Tam was on his feet again and motioned for us to follow him.

We swept along behind him. I had no clue what to say as we exited through a door on the far left of the chamber and found ourselves in a long passage. Everything had happened so fast that it felt like it was a hallucination. We followed Tam along the barren corridor until he stopped at another door.

"We can go find the Tunnels now. Tommy-Tee will be well cared for until we return." He paused. "What?"

I glanced at Jason, who was grinning like an idiot.

"I can't even begin to form a coherent statement. You lead us into an underground cavern next to the World Tree that happens to be a Fae barrow, and then we find out you're King of the Hill. Then *boom*, we move on again. You expect us to be blasé about it? What is wrong with this picture?" Jason was laughing so hard all of a sudden that I couldn't help but join in. With everything that had gone on, this might actually have been the most disconcerting.

"Jason's right. Should we start calling you Lord Tam now? What's the proper etiquette?" I leaned against the wall, grateful for the chance to blow off some steam. Everything had been so grim the past few days.

Tam glared at us. "I don't know what's so funny. You never asked if I was royalty, and I never had a good reason to tell you." He caught my gaze and held it. "Does it make so much difference to you?"

I sobered, suddenly feeling the weight of his question. While he had directed it at both of us, somehow I knew he meant it for me. I caught my breath and smiled.

"No, of course not. You're still the Tam we've known all these years. Just...more. And just how often do you meet a faerie-tale prince, anyway? This is the answer to a lot of girls' dreams."

He motioned for us to follow him up another set of stairs hidden beneath the sands. As he took the lead, Jason reached out to catch my arm.

"Is something going on between you two?" His gaze pierced my own.

I blinked. He didn't sound all that pleased. "No. Maybe. I don't know. Why?"

"Be cautious, Kae. The Fae...they're different. They can break hearts and walk away whistling a merry tune. They don't mean harm, but they don't think or feel the same way..."

"The same way *what*? The same way you feel? The same way I feel?" I bristled. "Jason, as close as we've been and as close as we'll always be, you need to let me make my own choices. You know what I've been through. You know what my work is like with Hecate. You're my friend, but you're not my father. I lost my father a long time ago."

Jason regarded me for a moment. "I knew him, you know. I met your mother through him. He loved you so much, and I made him a promise when he got sick that I'd do whatever I could to help your mother and you."

I froze. I had never heard him speak of my father. "You knew him?"

"We were friends, yes. He and your mother came to my shop when you were born and the hospital found out you were Theosian. Neither of them had any clue about how to raise a daughter who was a minor goddess. They were terrified that the government would take you away from them." He frowned. "I try not to fill his shoes—you *aren't* my daughter. I don't *see* you as a daughter. But... you were my charge. And you are my friend. I care about you."

Once again, a twinge ran through me. I had tried for so long to ignore my feelings for Jason. Now there might be something real with Tam. I knew Jason was mourning Eileen in his own way, and I wanted to make allowances for that, but why did his words hit me so hard?

Then, with a flash, I knew. It wasn't my crush on him surfacing. No, it was a flashback to my childhood. I had buried my grief over my father's death from the beginning. My mother needed me to cushion the blow for her. Even as a young child I had realized that. With the circumstances around her death, life felt far too dangerous to give into emotions. And it felt like everything that had gone on—that was going on—was threatening to push me into a great vat filled with all the pain and loss I had repressed.

I caught Jason's gaze. "Please...leave his memory in the past. My father's dead. I can't afford to think about my losses right now. You *are* my friend, Jason. As my friend, please don't try to run my life or protect me from one of the few things that aren't trying to kill me. Tam is Bonny Fae, and—apparently—a prince. But he's also *Tam*. And since there's nobody else in the picture, if getting involved with him is a mistake, let me discover it on my own."

Jason's expression went blank, though I thought I saw a flash of pain in his eyes. But he merely nodded, turned, and followed Tam up the sand-covered stairs.

Once we reached the top of the stairs, I found myself totally disconcerted. The World Tree was behind me, but I had no clue which direction we were facing.

Tam pointed to the front and right. "The Bogs are in that direction—northwest. The Junk Yard lies beyond them. We should be able to find the entrance there. But we need to discuss what we're going to do. We can't just barge in. We're going to need to locate Tunnel Pike and be prepared for the bog-dogs."

"Besides my weapons, I also have a talisman that will allow me to Trace the Thunderstrike once I'm within five hundred feet of it." I sat down on a sand-covered chunk of metal. "But I need to rest for a moment. We've been going a long time, and I'm so tired."

Jason and Tam had an advantage on me—shifters, Weres, and the Fae had more resilience and stamina than humans and most of the

Theosians. While I could wipe the floor with most humans in a fight, the fact was that I needed plenty of sleep and time to recharge.

"Are you capable of going in there tonight?" Jason motioned for me to scoot over so he could sit down too.

"I don't know, to be honest. My hand still hurts from the acid burn. I should have looked at it while we were in UnderBarrow. I'm just...tired." I yawned. "You know, if we're going now, I'd better get on my feet."

"We can help, though it's going to take a toll on you in the long run. A small toll, but still, fair warned." Tam motioned to us. "Back to UnderBarrow. We have a shield in there, beyond my throne room, where time shifts. All Fae are capable of shifting time if they're in their Barrows. You can rest, and when we come out, only an hour will have passed. One hour isn't going to make a difference. I should have thought of this while we were there, but my people don't tire easily and I'm afraid I forget about others at times."

Jason nodded grimly. "That's best. We can't afford to go in at low ebb, and to be honest, I'm tired too. Let's go."

"Queet? Can you go tell Hecate what we're doing? We'll be on our way in an hour, but I desperately need sleep." I knew that I couldn't reach her from the Sandspit with my phone—reception fritzed out here all the time. And there was no way it would work in UnderBarrow.

"Sure thing, Fury. I'll be waiting here when you come out in an hour." Queet whirled past, a

ghostly mist in the cool night.

As I dragged myself to my feet, I knew Tam's answer was the only one that would work. I was too tired, and we were in too much danger to go on without rest. Without another word, we followed Tam back down the sand-covered stairs, and re-entered the world of UnderBarrow.

Tam led us down the hall beyond the throne room. This part of UnderBarrow was alive with color and light and shadows that moved by themselves. I felt like I was in some sort of Faerieland. Which, I supposed, technically I was. I could smell fresh bread and stew and the scent of roasting meat. My stomach rumbled. I realized I hadn't eaten in a while, and most of my food had been sugar.

Tam heard the gurgles and laughed, but in a way that made me smile at him.

"I guess I'm hungry as well as tired."

"We can take care of that. We're passing past one of the kitchens. I'll have food sent to both of you." He walked respectfully by my side, and I wanted to reach out, to touch his hand, but was very aware of his status. One simply didn't grab the hand of a king...or a lord, whatever the case might be. Not in his home. Not in front of his people.

Tam showed Jason to his room first. Jason gave me a warning look before closing the door. I knew what he was thinking but shook off his concerns. This was my life, and if I had a chance to find something real with Tam, I wanted to risk it. Jason saw me as a good friend. I could feel it on a gut level, and I didn't expect that to change. All the fantasies of what life would be like if Eileen wasn't in the picture had come crashing with a reality check. And as they shattered, I realized that they were schoolgirl fantasies. Jason had rescued me. I had a case of hero-worship that I'd never fully grown out of.

We stopped in front of a door five down from Jason's room. Tam nodded to one of the servants who had followed us. She was a pretty girl who looked about twelve, but she might have been two thousand, for all I knew. She stepped up to the door and opened it, entering before Tam. Protocol, I thought. Tam seemed used to it. I thought of all the times he had held the door for me and ushered customers out of the shop. The juxtaposition gave me a headache. Who was he, really? How did a Fae Prince go from Lord of UnderBarrow to working on computers in a magic shop?

I followed them into the room and gave a little gasp. The chamber was small but the bed was piled high with luxurious silk covers, and it smelled like autumn and cinnamon and everything cozy that made me want to curl up and nap. A gown was draped over the bed, sheer, the color of the night sky covered with hundreds of twinkling beads. I slowly walked over to it, only to find that the beads were actually metallic thread, embroidered onto the cloth.

"This is...beautiful."

"A beautiful woman should wear beauty to her

bed." Tam slowly approached, as I heard the door shut behind us. The servant girl had exited the room.

"Tam..." His name lingered on my tongue. I wasn't sure what I wanted—what I needed, even, beyond a good night's sleep.

"Hush, and let me talk." Tam reached out and put his hands on my waist. He drew me toward him but stopped short of embracing me. "You need sleep most of all. I'm not going to pressure you into anything. We need to talk. There's obviously something growing between us. Why it emerged now, I don't know. But we have to discuss it, to see where we want to take it. I leave the decision up to you."

I bit my lip, feeling the need to be honest. "I have to tell you something. For years now..."

"You've had a crush on Jason."

I let out a sharp breath. If it was obvious to Tam, then had Jason noticed it? But Tam shook his head, as if reading the question in my eyes.

"I don't think he knows. But I want you to search your heart. He's free now. If you want to pursue him, I'll stand back. But Fury...as close as you are to him, I don't think Jason would be a good match. You admire him too much, and he feels too protective of you. I don't know if he would see you as his equal, precisely because of the fact that he raised you."

I knew he was right. Jason had treated me like a kid—a buddy—too many times and I had done my best to ignore it. But in the past couple days, since Eileen's death, I had felt it more keenly. I was his friend—one of his best friends—and that's what he needed from me.

"Do *you* see me as your equal? I have no clue of how old you are. Jason's always reminding me of how much younger I am. And you...not only are you one of the Bonny Fae, but I find out you're a prince, no less. What the hell are you doing at Dream Wardens, by the way? What's up with that?" Before I realized it, I snorted and slapped him lightly on the shoulder.

Tam laughed then and took my hands in his. "I like variety, and what better way to keep track of the human world than to become part of it? And computers and I...we get along." He paused, then said, "To answer your other question: Fury, you're a Theosian. How can I consider you an equal when you belong to the gods? My ancestors were divine...but you *are* divine. You belong to Hecate. I honor that and I honor who you are and what you do."

I entwined my fingers around his. "Tell me something. Have you looked at me before? Like this? Before you gave me that healing kiss?"

He shrugged. "A few times, but I knew how you felt about Jason. And I knew that if something were to happen between us, it would have to happen in its own time."

"One more question, before I can eat and sleep." I looked up into his eyes. "Do you have a wife? A girlfriend? I don't break up relationships."

Tam leaned down, his lips hovering over mine. "There's been no one for a long, long time."

His lips met mine and I lost myself in his kiss,

drifting into his embrace as he worked my lips with his, nipping them lightly, then sliding his tongue gently into my mouth. I let out a gentle moan, both tired and aroused, wanting him more than I had wanted anybody in a long time. Every fiber of my body screamed for him to touch me, to run his hands over my breasts, my legs, to kiss his way down my body and make me forget the dark night outside.

The room swirled and I broke away, gasping for breath.

Tam wrapped his arm around my shoulders and led me to the bed. "Enough for tonight. I want to make love to you when we have both the time and energy to explore each other. I want you when you are refreshed and feeling strong. Tonight, let the kiss be enough."

I nodded, not wanting to stop, but realizing he was right. I was too tired, and his energy was overwhelming at this moment. I caught my breath, held it a moment, and then slowly let it out.

"Yeah, I guess you're right. And I'm hungry and my hand hurts." I smiled ruefully. "Who would have thought that we would end up here?"

Tam smiled then, held out his hand. "Let me see your wounds." As he removed the bandage, he added, "I thought perhaps, one day, this might happen. I'm glad I kept hope. Now then, the wound looks clean but it's still angry."

At that moment, there was a faint rap on the door. Tam answered it, ushering in the serving girl who was carrying a tray with bread and cheese and sliced meats and fruit, and a mug of hot soup on it.

She set it down on the nightstand.

"Fury needs her hand looked to. Summon a healer. And I should have him look at my own hand, as well." He dismissed her and she ran off to fetch help. Tam sat beside me on the bed. "So, change into your bed gown and then eat while we wait. You can change behind the screen over there." He pointed to a standing hand-carved screen in the corner.

I carried the dressing gown behind the screen, only to find a discreet bathroom there. I wasn't sure how it worked, given UnderBarrow probably wasn't hooked up to a sewer system, but I was grateful for it. I changed, then washed my hands and returned to the bed, to find he had pulled down the covers.

"Get in bed."

I climbed under the sheets, propping myself up against the headboard.

Tam set the tray across my lap. "Eat now."

As I began to eat, he told me what life was like in UnderBarrow until a healer came in. After attending to our wounds, the medic left, along with the serving girl who took my tray. Tam leaned over and placed a chaste kiss on my lips.

"Sleep now, Fury. Rest as long as you need. When we return to the outer world, it will still be nightfall and we'll have lost only an hour."

As he turned to go, I remembered something.

"You said in the long run there's a cost for the time distortion?"

Without losing a beat, he answered. "The more time you spend here, the harder it will be for you to leave. Too many nights spent in UnderBarrow and you won't ever want to leave. And now, love, good night."

Before I could say a word, he shut the door, leaving me alone. The lights played against the walls, illuminating the dark with their sparkles. I slid down, resting my head against the pillows, wondering if I'd be able to sleep. But before I realized it, I found myself sliding into a deep slumber, with no dreams to disturb my sleep.

Chapter 21

I opened my eyes to see the same serving girl as the night before standing by the nightstand next to my bed. She was arranging breakfast on a tray, and as I sat up and stretched, I was suddenly aware of the sheerness of the gown, and the fact that I was displaying my breasts to her. But she merely smiled and curtseyed.

"Your breakfast, Your Grace."

I stared at her. I had never in my life been called anything like that. "I'm Fury. What's your name?"

"Breena, Your Grace." She paused, then whispered, "Is it true? You're one of the *Theosians*? A goddess?"

I blinked. Most people shied away from me when they found out what I was—either because of fear or envy. I wasn't used to being admired. I pulled my covers up and accepted the breakfast tray, which held sweet rolls, hard-boiled eggs, a rasher of ham, fruit, and coffee.

"Yes, I am. I'm pledged to the goddess Hecate." I took a long sip of the coffee and breathed a sigh of relief as the caffeine hit my tongue. I was about to ask Breena what she thought of Tam, but then stopped. That would put her in an uncomfortable position. Servants didn't have the freedom to answer negatively about their masters—not without putting themselves in danger.

She brought me my clothes, all of the ones Hecate had retrieved for me. "Lord Tam said you might want to change."

"Thank you. Lord Tam was right."

As I ate, she laid out my clothing. Hecate had chosen three pair of shorts, a skirt, and several corsets. I tended to wear corsets to provide plenty of support for my breasts when I had to run. There were also two more pairs of boots and some underwear in the bag. Hecate had included gloves and my other jacket, as well.

After I finished eating, Breena took my tray, and I slid out from beneath the covers. She motioned to the standing screen. "I've drawn you a bath."

Part of me was screaming we needed to be on our way, but I reminded myself that when we left, only an hour would have passed. I could afford the time for a bath.

I sank into the water and gratefully let the heat work on the knots in my muscles. Even though I had the luxury to soak, the knowledge of what

Lyon was trying to do weighed heavily on me. Breena knelt beside the tub and gently scrubbed my back. It felt odd to have her there, but it was her job and I didn't want to offend her by sending her away. As soon as I was clean and reasonably relaxed, I toweled off and let Breena help me dress. It felt odd having someone hold my clothes for me and help me adjust my corset but I also knew that was her job and she seemed to take pride in it.

When I was ready, I slapped on a little mascara, some lip gloss, and powder, then started to repack my other clothes, but Breena stopped me.

"Lord Tam said this is to be your room whenever you need it, and I will be your personal maid during your stay. You may leave your things here without worry. No one will touch them. I can have your outfit from yesterday cleaned, if you like." She took the folded garments from me.

I froze. I had my own room and lady's maid in UnderBarrow? I wasn't sure what to say, except to thank her. Very little could silence me, but I wasn't sure what to make of all this.

"If you'll let me see your injuries, I'll check on your dressings."

Again, I silently held out my hand. She removed the bandages. The wounds looked almost healed, with the holes healing over and the angry red marks gone. I tentatively made a fist, then tightened it. The pain was gone.

"Whatever your healer did, it worked. My hand feels almost back to normal."

"You should wear the dressings one more day,

but then I think you'll be able to take them off. Let me redress your hand, if you please."

She set to work bandaging up the wounds again. After she finished, I set to double-checking that I had everything I needed—my sword, dagger, the talisman that Hecate had given me—when a knock echoed on the chamber door. Breena answered.

"Lord Tam of UnderBarrow, milady."

I blinked. I was "milady" now?

Tam swept in, dressed in all black. He was obviously dressed for our mission. In fact, I'd never quite seen him look so hot. He was wearing black leather pants, a black mesh shirt that I quickly realized was some sort of metal that had movement and flexibility, a leather jacket, and boots that made no sound as he walked. His hair had been pulled back in a braid, which made his features look even more angular.

I cleared my throat, moving toward him, wondering how I should act after last night. But he took the reins, reaching out to grasp my hand and pull me into an embrace. He placed a light kiss on my lips and whispered, "Good morning."

I shivered at the sound of his voice. "Morning, you."

"Did you sleep well?"

I nodded. "I feel so much more able to take on the Tunnels now. You're sure we will only have lost an hour in the outer world?"

"I'm positive. Come. Jason's waiting for us." And with that, he led me out of the room and down the hallway to Jason's door.

Once again, we stood on the edge of the crater, the World Tree behind us. As Tam had promised, we exited UnderBarrow into darkness, with the night still feeling as it had when we went in to rest. I pushed thoughts of the room and Tam's kiss to the back of my mind as I focused on what we had to do. Jason had given me a questioning look when we stopped at his room, and I had given him a neutral smile. There was nothing to talk about—at least not now.

"Queet? Are you around?"

"Yes, Fury. I'm here."

"Can you verify that only an hour has passed? Tam says so and it feels true, but…"

"But you need to know."

"Right."

"Tam speaks the truth," Queet said using the faintest of whisper-speak. *"You are less than an hour out from when you went to rest."*

Relieved, I turned to Tam. "I suppose we're as ready as we will ever be. Lead on."

"While we slept, I had my men do some reconnaissance. A ways from the entrance of the Tunnels lies a hidden entryway. It doesn't seem to be watched very carefully, probably because very few people know of its existence. It's a little trickier, but I think it's our safest choice."

"That sounds like a our best option. Is it still within the confines of the Sandspit?" Jason appeared to have acquired a couple weapons since we were in UnderBarrow. He was carrying a long dagger that I had never seen before, and another was sheathed on his belt.

"Not totally, although it edges into the Sandspit. It's in the Bogs. The boundaries between the two are a little nebulous. The fence surrounding the Sandspit vanishes at that point, and no matter how much the city tried to repair that area, the fence kept disappearing. So they finally left it alone, as they did with the main gates into the Sandspit." Tam adjusted the quiver draped over his back. He had a pistol-grip crossbow, a quiver full of bolts, and at his side, a narrow katana.

As we headed out to cross the rest of the Sandspit, a light drifting of flakes began to fall. At first I thought it might be ash from some fire, but when I held out my hand, the flakes melted and I realized it was snowing.

"Winter's early this year."

"It's been coming earlier every year. Climatologists think Gaia is spiraling us into a mini ice age. We're headed in the opposite direction of what was happening right before the Weather Wars," Tam said. "Earlier and colder winters, summers that aren't quite as hot. But unless she decides to speed it along, we won't be seeing glaciers drift into the Pacific Sound anytime soon."

The light dusting quickly became a flurry. I was grateful for my boots. I had bought them specifically because of the traction on the soles—

they held firm while I was running and climbing over things. I was trying to avoid falling over a scattered pile of scrap metal, so busy watching my step, that I failed to see the swirl of sand and snow that rose up behind me.

"Fury, dive to the left. Get out of the way!" Queet swirled past, panicking.

I dove. Queet and I had worked together long enough that I didn't question when he told me to move. When he said jump, I jumped. He might be whiny at times, but when we were out on a mission, he was focused and always on the lookout.

As I ducked and rolled, the edge of the mini-twister of sand, snow, and rogue magic swept over me. Thank gods the main funnel missed me, sweeping past, because even the edges of the sudden cloud stung with a fury. The rogue magic set off my inner Trace, bombarding me with a thousand sudden sparks that clouded my vision. I reeled, unable to come to my feet, as the shock wave rolled through my body.

Tam and Jason were immediately beside me, Tam on my left, Jason on my right. They helped me sit up as I struggled to gain control of the thrumming of magic that darted through my body like shards of glass ricocheting off every nerve. The pain was incredible and I could barely catch my breath. I felt Tam's hands on my shoulders and I tried to stop him, not wanting him to put himself in danger, but Jason grabbed my wrists and held me firm so I couldn't struggle away. As Tam steadily drained the rogue magic, I realized I could breathe again. And then, it drifted off, leaving me charred from the inside out.

"Fury, are you all right?" Queet was whisking around, his whisper-speak almost a shout.

"Hush! Don't shout. My head feels like it just got shoved into a light socket." I struggled to stand. Looking up at Tam, I asked, "How are you? I know that had to hurt because I know what it was like to go through it."

He shrugged, looking pale but pulled together. "I'm all right. I don't take on the full impact, so I can't imagine how horrible that was." He leaned forward, brushing my hair out of my eyes, his fingers stroking my face. He cupped my chin and gently touched my lips with one finger. "How are you? Really?"

I closed my eyes, swimming in the gentle waves of his energy. As I assessed my body part by part, I could feel the rogue magic slowly draining away. Every nerve jangled. I wasn't hurting so much as...just jarred. And yet, there was something familiar about the feeling when I reached out to touch the energy. And then I knew. I was connected to the Sandspit in a way that I had never really thought about.

"My mother went through a full attack when she got caught in the rogue magic wave that generated the change in my DNA. I recognize the energy. I can feel it in the core of my being. It hurt, but it also resonated." I exhaled and shook off the residual twinges. "This...is my birthplace, really, when I think about it."

"She must have undergone a tremendous

amount of pain as the magic seeped into her blood, and into yours." Tam stood back, assessing me. "You think you're ready to move on?"

"Let me make certain my Trace is working. And..." I had a sudden, irrational fear that my whip wouldn't be there—that somehow the magic might have eaten it away. But as I slapped my right hand against my thigh, the weapon coiled into my hands. I turned to the side and gave a practice crack with it. Nothing seemed amiss. Then I brought up my Trace. There were no Aboms near, but the Trace seemed on track and working.

"I'm ready." Once again, I shook off the excess prickles running through my body. "Let's get a move on. Queet, thank you for the warning. It would have been so much worse if you hadn't managed to give me the heads-up."

"I always keep watch for you, Fury. And I will continue to do so." Queet misted into view behind Tam.

"We have to be cautious. It won't be much longer before we're out of the Sandspit, but the rogue magic can stir at any time and if it slams you full on, it can be deadly. People have been fried caught in its wake." Jason ran his gaze over me. "You sure you're ready?"

"Yeah. Let's get a move on." As we headed out again, this time we all kept watch. The flurry thickened into an actual snowstorm, but my adrenaline rush was so high from the rogue magic attack that I barely noticed the chill. I kept my Trace open as Tam led us through the Sandspit. At least if an Abom came in off the World Tree, I'd spot it before it spotted us.

We had navigated around one last heap of slag metal, now covered with a dusting of white, when Tam motioned ahead.

"There's the edge of the Sandspit, where it meets the Bogs. To get to the Tunnels, we would normally take a right. There's no path, but my men scouted the area while we rested and found the landmarks to look for. And before you ask, no one saw them. The Bonny Fae can move like shadows when we choose to. But the secret entrance is to the left a ways, well into the Bogs. Then we jog to the right. The entrance leads into what was an old sewer tunnel. From there, we crawl through a shaft where they broke through to the Tunnels."

"Guards?"

"Only on the main entrance. I suppose they figure nobody in their right mind would venture out into the Bogs, considering they're even more dangerous than the Sandspit, given the bog-creatures and the quicksand."

"Maybe, but I'm not sure which is worse—quicksand or rogue magic. Best to arm ourselves now, before we need it." I pulled out my dagger. My sword was far heavier and while it did more damage, it was more problematic to carry unsheathed. I fought left handed with my dagger, leaving my right hand free to grab my whip. Luckily, I'd been ambidextrous from birth.

Jason readied his blade, and Tam adjusted his quiver to easily reach the bolts. He fit one into the crossbow and set the safety. As we crossed the last stretch of sand dividing us from the Bogs, I went on high alert. This was going to be as dangerous as fighting Abominations, and I had to remember that. Magicians might not be able to devour my life force like an Abom, but they could kill just as easily. Lyon was a freak who had no hesitation about using whatever weapons were at his disposal. We had seen that in the tornado in Bend and the earthquake.

"There," Tam said, pointing to a large barren oak tree guarding the edge of the Bogs. "That's where we jog to the left. We'll have to go directly into the undergrowth, so be cautious. There are patches of quicksand, and most likely they'll be covered with enough snow to be almost undetectable. Shift to single file when we enter the Bogs, and the lead person tests the ground before moving ahead."

Jason turned to me. "Do you want to take the lead, since you have the talisman to help you Trace the Thunderstrike? Or will that matter?"

I shrugged. "A few steps won't matter. The moment it's within five hundred feet, I'll pick up on it. Honestly, with as amped as I am, I'd rather one of you goes first."

Tam motioned to Jason. "I suggest using a long stick to test the ground with. That won't be a problem given all the downed branches and trees."

Jason moved to the front and, as we approached the edge of the Bogs, he cast about for a moment until he found a tall, narrow branch that he could easily twist off a tree. It had broken most of the way through and all it took was a turn or two in order to rip the last bit of bark away. He was about to use his blade to cut off the straggling limbs from it, but I stopped him.

"My sword and dagger are perpetually sharp. Let me save the edge on your blade." I knelt and quickly hacked off the stray branches, then trimmed the top few inches to make it easier for him to wield. "All right. Out of the frying pan, into the fire."

And so, we headed out of the Sandspit and into the depths of the Bogs.

Chapter 22

The Bogs seemed even more creepy under a layer of snow. It was bad enough trying to watch our footing when the weather was good, but the snow hid all manner of deathtraps, from the quicksand to the Wandering Ivy, to the langchamp cannibal plants. Snow also muffled sound and made it harder to hear if any bog-creatures were following us. The rooftop canopy of tree branches didn't stop the snowfall. Given that we were into autumn, the leaves had been shedding off the trees for a couple of weeks.

Since there was no path to follow, we worked our way through the undergrowth. Jason walked a few steps ahead, tapping the ground with the branch. Every now and then he would stop when the branch slid into a pocket of quicksand. In some cases, it was a fist-sized hole. In others, we found ourselves skirting larger patches.

Tam walked behind him, giving directions. Even though we were into autumn and snow was falling, the undergrowth was still thick and green, making it hard to see the ground. The night was dark but the silvery sheen to the clouds gave us a faint light to guide our way. Queet swirled around me, keeping an eye out for bog-creatures as we traversed through the undergrowth.

We had walked for about fifteen minutes when Tam tapped Jason on the arm.

"Up ahead you'll see a huckleberry bush. My men tied a ribbon to it. Make a slight jog to the right of the bush, but not a hard right. We want the large row of cedars on our left until we hit another bend in the road."

Jason paused by the huckleberry bush. A brilliant red ribbon was tied to it, standing out against the background of green and white. He turned a quarter turn and then headed deeper into the tangle, pushing through the bushes, still tapping with his stick. Every now and then he would pause and hold up his hand as he tested the ground to find stronger footing. Another twenty minutes and we came to another ribbon.

"Where to from here?" He glanced over his shoulder at Tam.

"Make another quarter turn to the right. We'll come to a clearing in about fifteen minutes. When we reach it, we'll look for the sewer grate. They didn't mark it in case anyone from the Tunnels decides to use that entrance. We don't want to arouse suspicions."

"Give me a moment to gather my focus. The

constant prodding for quicksand takes a lot more energy than I thought it would." Jason sucked in a deep breath and let it out slowly, closing his eyes. I could feel the currents of air swish past. Hawk-shifters worked with the element on an intimate level. The swirl of wind and snow rose around him as he abruptly opened his eyes and headed out again. One step at a time, he moved forward, prodding the ground, focusing intently as the snowstorm intensified.

I focused on my inner Trace. As we continued, I found myself listening to every sound around me. The sound of the falling snow, the rustling in the undergrowth, faint sounds that could have been distant traffic...all blended together into a collage of white noise.

After what seemed like an eternity, Jason broke through the foliage and stepped to the side. We had found the clearing.

About twenty feet in diameter, the clearing was circular. I wondered what kept the vegetation at bay. Nothing seemed to grow within the odd space. At the center, a grate covered what appeared to be a tunnel. Three feet in diameter, the grate looked set firmly into place. I cautiously knelt beside it, examining the edges. The rusted spots had been loosened, but it looked like it hadn't been opened in a while. Moss had grown over the spots where metal met soil.

I glanced around the clearing. "Snow, but no plants? What's wrong with this picture? The flora of the Bogs usually eats up everything in its way."

Tam cocked his head as though he were

listening to the wind. After a moment, he said, "There's something odd about this particular space. It feels like a force field, but not to keep people out. It's...I think it's to keep the plants out. How strange."

"Maybe they didn't want to have to fight the plants every time they come in through the back door, so to speak," I said.

"No, because this isn't magicians' magic. This is something else, but I don't know what." Tam straightened up, shaking his head. "Something else has been back here, but I can't tell what. For all I know, it could be the work of the Greenlings, although I don't know why they would want to keep this area clear."

"Do you think there are any traps?" While I couldn't read anything about traps on my Trace, that didn't mean the grate wasn't set to trigger.

Jason pursed his lips, thinking. "Let me look. I have a cantrip that may work."

Tam and I backed off. Jason crouched by the grate, pulled off his gloves, and held his hands out, whispering a chant in Cast-speak. A faint blue light appeared at the tips of his fingers and he spread them wide. The light filtered out, rolling over the grate. It blanketed the ground, turning the snow that had accumulated a pale indigo, then settled like a thin layer of gel over the metal. Another moment, and it melted away, the snow still as pristine white as it had been.

"No traps. That cantrip would have shown anything, be it magical or physical. That doesn't mean that once we get into the tunnel, that everything will be safe. But we can at least remove the cover and see what we're facing." He slipped on his gloves again and grabbed hold of the grating. As he began to pull on it, the metal let out a grinding sound. "Damn, it's in there good. I doubt this has been opened for a while. Not long enough to rust up again, but it's stuck."

"Let me help." I slid my dagger back in its sheath. I was strong, thanks to my constant workouts. "Scoot over."

Jason made room, and I clasped my hands around the grate.

"Your gloves good to go?"

"Yeah, they fit snuggly, but have some give in them so I can use my sword when I need to. They'll be fine. Count of three?"

He nodded.

"One...two...three!"

Together we heaved the grate out of the ground, prying it away from the compacted soil. The moment it budged, Tam slid his fingers beneath it and pushed from the other side while we pulled. The grating—which was heavy as fuck—groaned as it yielded to our efforts.

Jason and I rolled it to the side and it hit the ground with a thud. We paused, and I immediately checked my Trace. No Aboms, but that didn't mean we had gone unnoticed. We waited for a moment, but there were no sounds emanating out of the hole, and nobody broke through into the clearing.

"I guess we're good to go." I leaned over the hole, peering into the inky darkness. "I can't even see if there's a ladder. If not, then we'll need rope."

"We'll have to make due with vines, then. Here, let me set a faint light spell to travel down and check."

"Better than that, I can send Queet. He should be able to see and it will save us the chance of a light spell being noticed." I started to summon Queet, but he beat me to the punch.

"I'm here. I heard what you said. Going now. Sit tight till I return."

I glanced at Tam and Jason. "Queet's on it."

The snow was picking up, and I folded my arms, turning my back to the wind so it wouldn't blow into my face. But we only had to wait a few minutes before Queet was back.

"Fury? There's a ladder. See the pile of stones on the left side of the hole?"

I squinted as he gusted to hover over the stones.

"See? Here? The ladder is directly inside the hole against this wall. It goes down about fifty feet, then stops. A four-foot drop and you're on the floor of the tunnel. It's slimy and cold, but no standing water that I could see. But there are presences there. I could feel them. Be cautious. Tell Jason he might want to fly down and wait for you on the bottom."

That made sense. It would give us a guard below, and would save Jason's strength. I relayed to the men what Queet had told me. "Jason, are you willing to go ahead and keep watch?"

He was already stepping over to the hole. "I'm on it. But...you'll be in the dark until I get down there and strike a light. There's no way out of it. To see, we're going to have to have some form of illumination. And magical light is softer than a flashlight."

"Go, then. Queet, please let me know when Jason's set up. Jason, when you get down there and are ready for us, just say 'Ready' and Queet will hear you."

"He can hear me if he wants—I also know whisper-speak. He can communicate with me directly and that would probably be best." Jason snorted. "Hear that, Queet? Talk to me, man. I'm going in." He stood back, a blur of light swirling around him as he shifted form. I squinted against the brilliance and when I opened my eyes again, he was gliding down the hole. His wingspan barely fit. In fact he had to pull his wings back a little to manage, but I figured if he had problems, he would just abort the attempt.

A few moments later, Queet swirled around me. *"Jason's ready. You won't be able to see the light from up here, so he's sending it floating up to lead you down. Don't be surprised when you see a glowing orb of pale blue light dancing near your shoulders. Both of you."* His whisper-speak was loud enough that Tam was nodding along with me.

"Fury, you go first. I'll keep watch from above. That way you'll be protected on both sides."

I snorted. "Tam, given the secrets you've revealed over the past few days, I wouldn't be surprised to find out that you're an incredible fighter, but don't forget—I'm trained to fight. Remember? Abomination hunter here?"

Tam rubbed his forehead, groaning. "I know, I know. I just...you're right. Do you want to take the back, then?"

"I didn't say that, but thanks for not trying to take away the option. The truth is," I said, not wanting to admit it but feeling vulnerable, "this mission scares the hell out of me. I know how to deal with Aboms. The demons aren't easy, but I know what to expect from them. And when I kill one, even if it's wearing a human-suit, I know what I'm fighting. I've never had to face down...*people*... before. Except for the Carver, and he... Oh, he wasn't human. Not in my book."

Right there, I knew what my hesitation was. We were probably going to come up against Lyon or his henchmen, and that would lead to a fight. While I had killed countless Abominations over the years, the fact was that I had very seldom ever hurt an actual person. I knew I could—the Carver was proof—but...the thought of plunging my sword into a human or one of the Otherkin? It rankled. But I also knew that I'd do whatever I needed to do. Hecate was riding me hard—I could feel her energy running through my blood. And mine was in hers from the Blood Bond that had been performed when I was a baby. We were linked far stronger than my oath to her.

As I swung over the edge, a pale blue light hovered right below me, lighting the first rung. It floated up to my side, giving me about a sphere of illumination five feet in diameter. I held my breath for a moment, then slowly exhaling, began my descent.

Fifty feet of ladder meant for a lot of rungs. I lost track of where I was in proximity to the ground. Rung after rung passed under my feet, slick with a buildup of slime and moss. I tried not to breathe too deeply—who knew what spores lurked in the mess of mildew? I tried not to listen too hard—I didn't want to jump at every sound. One foot after the other, one rung after another, I made my way down the ladder through the three-foot-wide shaft.

I had lost count of how many rungs I descended when I tried to find the next rung and there was finally none. I glanced over my shoulder. There, a few feet away, stood Jason, waiting.

"Safe to drop down?"

"The floor seems fairly solid, though slick."

I did a half-twist as I launched off the ladder and landed in a crouch near Jason's feet. As I rose up, a twinge hit my side, but I shifted and it vanished. Turning around, I saw that Tam had been just a few feet above me, and not once had I heard him on the rungs. The man could be silent as the grave when he wanted to. He joined us, lightly dropping to the floor. Jason held up his hand and the two balls of light returned to bounce lightly by our shoulders.

"So, where are we?" I used a loud version of whisper-speak that I knew they could hear.

"I had a look around while I was waiting for you. We're in what was an old sewer line. It runs in two directions but the one over there," he pointed to our left, "is filled in. Totally blocked up from what I can tell. If we duck through that archway to the right, we'll be in the main sewer. That should lead us to the entrance of the Tunnels, and from there...well, we find our way to Tunnel Pike."

"All right. Let me bring up my Trace." I hoped that the Thunderstrike would suddenly appear, but no go. We were going to have to do this the hard way. "Well, let's get a move on then. Let me go first, but be ready for action." I turned, startled to see Tam standing directly in back of me.

His eyes twinkling, he placed a finger on his lips, then pressed it to mine. I slowly wrapped my tongue around the tip, sucking gently for a moment. Then, just as slowly, I slid my mouth away, leaving him hungry. Desire spread across his face.

Jason cleared his throat, looking away. "When you're ready..."

Bringing myself back to business, I nodded. "Ready as I'll ever be." And, swinging in front of the men, I ducked, grateful for the globe of light at my shoulder. Without another word, I stepped into the passage that stretched out in front of us. Ready or not, we were on the move, and I could only wonder if Lyon knew we were headed his way.

Chapter 23

Our footsteps echoed as we headed into the claustrophobic passage. It was barely seven feet tall, and only wide enough for one at a time. I dreaded thinking what we'd do if we ran into some creature here. I'd be stuck at the front, because there was absolutely no way anybody could get around to help me. Hoping that we didn't have far to go before we found the opening to the actual Tunnels, I plunged ahead with only Jason's light to guide my way.

The sounds of dripping water were everywhere. While this sewer wasn't used anymore, the condensation was thick, as were the layers of mold and slime that had built up on the sides of the passage. I held my dagger—it was much more space efficient should I have to use it—and quietly edged forward, my gaze darting from side to side as I searched for the entry.

A noise suddenly ricocheted past us.

"Rat," Tam said.

A light scurrying sound drew my attention to the ground and I saw another massive rat racing toward me. It stopped, suddenly aware of us, stood on its hind feet, and then turned and raced the other way again. I was about to relax when Jason cleared his throat.

"You know, that might have been a rat, but it also might have been a spy. Magicians use rats as familiars quite often because they're small and can easily sneak into places a cat or dog or owl might be recognized."

"Hell. I didn't think of that. Should I go after it?" Secretly, I was hoping he would say no. I didn't want to go chasing after the rat.

"No, because if it *is* a familiar, that would give whoever holds its leash a better look at you. If not, then why waste your energy on a rat?" He nodded, looking over my head. "Let's keep going."

As I moved forward again, I began to feel a shift in the energy. It was hard to pinpoint, but there was something different. The passage was still cold and damp, but the energy deepened, feeling less murky and more sinister. There was a faint threat to it that I recognized, but nothing showed on my Trace. *No Aboms. No Thunderstrike.*

Another ten minutes and I was beginning to feel claustrophobic. The passage was so close and tight that it seemed to be narrowing in on us, and I wanted nothing more than to get the hell out from beneath the ground. I tried not to think about the fact that we were looking for an older, more dangerous subterranean sector of the city.

"There," Tam said, pointing over my shoulder to the right side of the passage. "Is that the entrance?"

Jason whispered something under his breath and another ball of light darted forward, dancing beside what appeared to be a dark opening against the side of the passage.

I hesitantly crept forward, doing my best to keep my breath steady and even. As I approached the jagged hole that had been hewn in the side of the sewer, I could see that it was rough and uneven, chiseled out of the rock that made up the walls of the passage. From where I stood, I could see a vague section of the wall on the other side that looked like brick, and I knew we had found what we were looking for.

"Queet, can you take a peek on the other side and see what's there?"

Queet swiftly gusted toward the opening but suddenly bounced back, the mists of his body swirling from the impact. I heard a faint *snap*, like an electric shock, and he disappeared.

"Fuck, Queet, Queet, are you all right?"

Jason struggled in, finally managing to squeeze past both Tam and me, forcing us to lean against the walls that were cold and slimy and covered with years of buildup. I tried not to cringe, even while I was panicking over what happened to Queet.

"It's a force field. We can pass, but spirits and elementals can't. Queet was repelled by it."

"Do you think he's okay? He hasn't answered me."

"Do you think his attempt set off an alarm somewhere?" Tam asked.

"I don't know. As far as an alarm goes, I don't sense one, and we certainly didn't hear anything. I think the force field is used to prevent these entities from *escaping* rather than from entering. Unlike witches, magicians summon things imperiously. That lends itself to a certain need for control over what you call in, because chances are good the creature won't come voluntarily."

At that moment, I sensed—rather than saw—Queet appear. His energy felt agitated.

"Queet, are you all right?"

"Damned thing disrupted me. I'm...I'll be all right but I'm not going to be able to go any farther with you." His whisper-speak was so low I could barely hear it.

I relayed his message to the others. "He'll have to wait out here. I guess we just go through and see what happens. If they were watching the entrance, they know something's up by now, and if they weren't, then we might as well get in there now while the going is good."

"I concur," Tam said. "Go now, before we lose our advantage."

I steeled myself. *"Stay here by the entrance, Queet, unless something happens so you have to get out of the way. Wish us luck."*

"Luck to you, Fury. And Hecate's blessings."

Any time Queet wished me blessings from Hecate, I knew he was worried. I glanced at Tam, whose soft expression made me want to lean in for a hug, but instead, I turned and crawled through the entrance into the Tunnels.

As I crawled through the hole, I felt a shift in energy. It was probably the force field that I was feeling, but whatever the case, it made my skin crawl. After the disruption with the rogue magic, I really didn't want any more static filtering through my energy field. Thank gods nothing had disrupted my Trace, but I had the feeling I'd be spending days trying to shake off the pinpricks that rippled through my body.

I glanced around. I was in a brick tunnel. Here and there, the bricks had crumbled and I could see rotting wood slats beneath—remnants of an earlier passage, perhaps. The tunnel was at least fifteen feet high, as wide as a city street, and lit along both sides with dim lights attached near the top. There was no visible sign of what their power supply was, but my guess pegged them as magical in origin.

Quickly scanning the length of the tunnel for signs of life, I could see no one. I stepped to one side to make way for Tam and Jason. As we struggled to get our bearings, I remembered what Hecate had said.

"We need to find the waterfront area. That's where Tunnel Pike is."

Tam nodded, closing his eyes as he lifted his nose to the air. "I smell...water...but it's a distance.

This way. To the left."

I glanced at Jason, who had scrunched up his face. I knew that look—he was thinking, turning over our whereabouts in his mind. He was good at visualizing the layout of places like that—very analytical and precise.

After a moment, he slowly nodded. "Yes, to the left, but about a mile from here we will need to jog to the right. That will lead us beyond the Junk Yard, then we turn to the left again. Which means we have a couple miles of walking to do. We'd better get a move on, if we don't want to get caught. I'm doubting the Tunnels are heavily populated, but all it takes is one chance meeting with the wrong person and we're screwed."

"Let's jog. Quicker." I took off at an easy pace, not so fast they couldn't keep up, but certainly quicker than walking. Along the way, I wondered who or what might be down here besides the magicians. The Order of the Black Mist couldn't be *that* big, and from what it was beginning to look like, the Tunnels stretched out for miles. A nasty twinge warned me to be on the lookout for Aboms. I wouldn't put it past them to make their way down here to hide out. *Speaking of,* I thought... and pulled up my Trace screen.

We moved at a quick, steady pace. The going was fairly easy as long as we skirted the debris that littered part of the tunnel. But the passages were wide enough that we were able to find our way around the occasional pile of bricks and broken wood. Some of them were knee-high, while others were taller than I was.

As I swung around one tall pile, a deep growl startled me. I skidded to a halt, dagger in hand, as a gigantic disfigured creature rose from where it had been sleeping. Looking more human than wolf, his features were horribly mangled. His muzzle was a cross between wolf and human, and his hair raced down his back like hackles, but still long and flowing.

I brought up my dagger, but Jason barked out *"Stop!"* and I froze.

"Lycanthrope. Ease back a step, very slowly. Do *not* take your eyes off of it." Jason's voice was soft and cautious.

I did as he said, very carefully stepping back first one step, then another. The lycanthrope's eyes glittered, but he wasn't happy to see us. The creature had a dangerous, chaotic feel to him—it was definitely a him by the looks of his groin—and he eyed us suspiciously, wavering as if unsure what to do.

"What now?" I asked Jason in whisper-speak.

"What now is that we try to ease around him without setting him off. We scoot toward the opposite wall and make it clear we don't want any altercations. Lycanthropes are tough—far tougher than Weres and shifters. We could probably take him on, but I doubt we would walk away without bloodshed, and most of it would be ours."

Jason very carefully edged to the side, then over to the opposite wall, pausing with every step as he kept his gaze fastened on the creature. The lycanthrope's eyes narrowed, the bridge of his brow furrowing deeply. But still, he waited, poised.

Jason began to ease himself along the wall, moving forward at a slow, steady pace.

"He's got a nest over this side of that pile of debris. We woke him up, I think." Again, in whisper-speak. After another moment, Jason added, "Fury, you next."

I followed his lead exactly, moving toward the opposite wall, never letting my gaze drop. Lycanthropes attacked from the back, and they attacked when they smelled or sensed weakness. But there were three of us, and if he thought we had no interest in him or his nest, there was a chance he would let us pass without incident. Tam followed me. We were almost beyond the nest when Jason stopped.

"We have a problem. If we keep going, our backs will be to him. Tam, are you comfortable walking backward for a while to keep an eye on him? If he doesn't follow us, after about five minutes we should be good."

"I'm dexterous enough to walk backward, yes. Just warn me about any bumps or dips." Tam's sword was out, and he eased into position. As we moved along the wall, still opting to remain next to it, he used the bricks for balance.

We continued on, still silent, until the lycanthrope was out of sight. Tam turned around to face forward, and we set off at a good clip. Corridors began branching off each side off the tunnel, leading into dark spaces. I wasn't sure whether we should explore any of them, but Jason seemed determined to lead us forward and I trusted his sense of direction. I didn't expect to find the Thunderstrike until we reached the Pike area, anyway.

After ten minutes, Jason paused and leaned against the wall. He was sweating, but it couldn't have been from the weather. It was colder down here than it was up topside, and if we had been open to the sky, it would have been snowing up a storm.

But the lycanthrope still had me wondering. "Do you think he's tracking us? I can't find him on my Trace because he's not an Abom."

Lycanthropes were like Theosians, actually. I had something in common with him. Both our mothers had been hit by rogue magic when we were in the womb. The werewolves bore lycanthropes, while the humans gave birth to Theosians. I wasn't sure what happened to the other shifter types, or the Fae in similar situations, and I wasn't sure I wanted to know.

"I don't know, but I think we can bet he's not. Just keep alert and let's pick up the pace. By my reckoning, it's almost time we turned right, so Tam, keep your nose at the ready. Can you still smell water?"

Tam inhaled deeply, then caught his breath. "Yes, and it's getting stronger. We're going in the right direction. I suggest that we take one of the next passages to the right."

Jason nodded. "I thought so, too. All right, let's go. Up for another quick jog?"

We took off, back on pace. I made sure my Trace was up, and kept hope that we'd run into the Thunderstrike sooner than later. I didn't want to be too deep into the Tunnels when we found it, without a clear exit nearby. Jason passed three more side-tunnels before skidding to a halt at a four-way intersection.

"This must be a major juncture," he said, then quieted as three men came into view from the opposite direction. They hadn't noticed us yet, they were so deep in conversation. They were wearing long brown robes, and my first thought was the Order of the Black Mist, but Jason suddenly swore an oath and strode out into the middle of the four-way intersection.

"Terrance?"

The man in the middle jerked his head up, then did a double take. "Jason? *Jason Aerie? Is that really you?"*

Jason strode forward, a tense smile spreading across his face. "We all thought you were dead."

Terrance—a middle-aged man with graying hair and broad, burly shoulders beneath the long robe—shook his head. "I had to disappear." He motioned to the other men, who backed off to stand by the entrance of the tunnel they had just come from.

Terrance glanced over at us. "Is that little Kaeleen?"

Jason nodded. "Yes, that's her. That's right, I told you about her before you vanished. And this is Tam, one of the Bonny Fae. They can both be trusted. What about...your men?"

"They're safe, so don't sweat it. What are you doing here? I didn't realize you knew about this place." Terrance was glancing to either side. "We don't want to stay in the open too long. Come, follow me."

"We're on the trail of something big. We don't have much time to talk and we can't be caught down here. But why are you here?" Jason motioned for us to follow him.

We swung in behind Terrance as he led us back the way he had come. Terrance's friends flanked him. We had gone about twenty yards before he motioned to a door off to the left. This was the first passage I'd seen with a door, and to my surprise, it opened into what appeared to be a magic shop that looked a lot like Dream Wardens.

As we filed to the back, entering through yet another door, Terrance motioned to the table and chairs in the center of the room.

"Please, sit down. Fury, Tam, I can tell you're ill at ease so let me introduce myself. Jason may not have talked much about me. I was his mentor. I taught him his magic."

Jason nodded as I glanced over at him. "Yeah, Terrance was my teacher. But we thought you died thirteen years ago. You vanished into the Bogs. The Cast assumed you had come to a bad end. We couldn't pick up your presence."

"I had to break the bonding, Jason. I had to break my connection with the Cast in order to do my job. Everyone needed to assume I was dead. And it's vital that you don't tell anyone about seeing me when you return to the Cast. In fact, this is a sticky problem. You won't be able to hide everything. If they ask you, Mahit will be able to sense the truth."

Now I was totally lost. I knew there was some form of connection between Cast members, but I had never known how strong or how far it linked through.

Jason stared at the table. "I can cloak it. I've become really good at cloaking. I closed off so well that the only inkling I had that my fiancée was murdered came as a migraine." He sounded bitter and I suddenly realized that he was blaming himself for Eileen's death in some way.

"Who's Mahit?" Tam asked.

"Mahit is our current shaman. Terrance was the shaman before him, until he went traipsing down to the Bogs one day and vanished." Jason's voice had an edge to it. His expression was clouded, and I could feel the rumblings of anger below the surface.

Terrance turned to us. "I need to ask you, too, to keep my presence here silent. Nobody here knows that I belonged to the Cast. They think I'm a human magician who happens to have figured out how to shape-shift. They have no idea that my name is Terrance, or that I work for the Crystal Guardians." He lowered his voice. "I go by Bodie here."

"What are the Crystal Guardians?" I had never heard of them.

Tam answered for him. "They're a secret organization run by the Greenlings. They keep a watch on the world order and are, in some ways, connected to Lightning Strikes. They rise above all the laws of the land and answer only to Gaia herself."

Jason let out a slow breath. "What are you doing here...Bodie?"

One beat. Then another.

And then, Terrance slowly said, "We are observing a rising group of insurgents who seek to overthrow everything. Not just the government, but the entire way of life our world has built. They're magicians, and they're powerful. I don't know why you're down here, but you want to be careful and get the hell topside as soon as you can."

It began to click then. I let out a slow breath. Terrance was after the Order of the Black Mist. I knew it—it couldn't be anything else. The Crystal Guardians, the Greenlings...they were all connected. But as I turned to him, about to ask, something stayed my tongue. There was something off-kilter.

At that moment, Tam tapped me on the arm, flashing a glance toward the door. I stiffened as my Trace flared to attention. The Thunderstrike was near, and if the Thunderstrike was near, that meant Lyon and his cronies couldn't be far behind.

Chapter 24

I stiffened, trying to catch Jason's eye. But the Trace was growing louder and closer, and there wasn't any time to waste.

"Jason, we have to go. *Now*." I jumped up. "What we're looking for is within searching distance." I started for the door, but before I reached it, Terrance spoke up.

"The Thunderstrike?"

Freeze-frame.

I slowly turned around, searching his face, looking for signs that this might be a setup, but saw none. "How did you know?"

His voice was grave when he answered. "Think about it. I work for the Crystal Guardians—the Greenlings. *They* know about the Thunderstrike, so *we* know. Jerako told me first thing after you went to see him. We've been after information about the Order of the Black Mist for some time.

That's why I had disappear, Jason. This uprising started far earlier than anybody realizes. The Greenlings suspected, though, and sent us to infiltrate."

"That makes sense. Jerako hinted that they've been watching the group for a while." I closed my eyes, focusing on the trace. "They're coming this way. I don't know how many, but the Thunderstrike is on the move. It's within five hundred yards."

"My guess is they're going to take it out through the secret entrance and set off an aftershock. The quake wasn't natural, as you know, and while it could set off aftershocks on its own, it doesn't seem to have done so." Terrance looked so grim it scared me.

"They're out to finish the job, I guess." I stood, preparing myself for a showdown. "We'd better get ready."

Tam joined me near the door, but Jason wasn't quite ready to follow me out.

"Are you going to stand with us?" he asked, turning to Terrance.

Terrance shook his head. "I wish we could, but we've managed to infiltrate the group. We can't be seen with you, I'm sorry. I wish we could help, but all our years of work would come to naught if I stayed and they found out I was a spy. Even if you take out Lyon, there are others, and the group is growing worldwide. We have a chance to learn so much about them in our position."

"Can you at least give us some advice?" I asked.

After a brief pause, he nodded. "The best advice I can give you is this: Lyon's ego gets the best of him. I've seen it trip him up time and again. If you can trigger it—if you can wound his pride—it will throw him off balance. And he's a powerful magician, but his specialty is fire. He's weak when it comes to the other elements. He specialized so narrowly that it's done him a disservice. Now, please leave before he finds you here. We don't want him associating you with any of our operations."

With that, Terrance and his men quickly moved to the back and—pressing one of the bricks—they vanished through a hidden panel that slid open in the wall. I wondered which one of them owned this place, but it was too late to ask.

Jason stood there for another beat, then turned. "Let's get out of here. We can't jeopardize their operations." He headed toward the front of the shop, with Tam and me on his heels.

"How far are they, Fury?"

"Not far, but they probably won't be able to see us yet if we get out of here now. We could hide and ambush them." I peeked out the door. No one in sight. As I darted toward the opposite wall, I spied an alcove a few yards to the right. "We can hide there."

"Question: Do we kill Lyon?" Tam asked it as offhandedly as if he had asked, "Do you want eggs for breakfast?"

"If we can. But our primary goal is to retrieve the Thunderstrike. They can still cause a massive amount of trouble, but at least this will prevent

the Greenlings from advising Gaia to force another
World Shift."

We reached the alcove. Whatever this place
had been, it was about the size of a study booth at
the library without a desk or holoscreen. It would
barely fit the three of us if we snuggled in together.

"Let me be in front," I said. "I need to jump
clear in case I have to use my whip." And with
that, I slapped my thigh, the whip springing to
life in my hands. It tingled in my fingers, singing
as it woke to life. The energy was solid as leather,
solid as wood, and felt comforting as it thrummed
in my hands. With my left hand, I unsheathed my
dagger.

As we slipped inside the niche, I was shivering.
Again, the thought of going up against actual
humans frightened me—there was a fine line
between fighting someone who really was a
villain—like the Carver—and fighting someone you
arbitrarily decided was your enemy.

The Trace grew louder in my head. I quickly
used whisper-speak to ask Tam and Jason, "So,
should we attack to the front, or after they pass?
He'll be passing right in front of us."

"Rear attack would give us an advantage," Tam
said.

"But only if they don't notice us. If they see us
here, we're stuck. I say go in as soon as they get
close enough," Jason countered.

"That makes sense. I don't want to be lodged
in here if there are enough of them to surround
us. Front attack it is, then." And with that, we fell
silent, waiting.

It wasn't long before we heard the sound of voices echoing down the passage. I tried to place how many people were speaking, but only managed to distinguish three separate voices. Of course, that didn't mean there weren't more. I wanted to peek out, but they weren't close enough yet to engage and the danger that they would see us, too great. It was times like this where I really missed Queet being around.

And then, the Trace began to flash in my mind, a beacon on high alert. I glanced over my shoulder at Tam and Jason, giving them a warning nod toward the corridor. As I tensed, the voices came closer. I tried to pick out what they were saying.

"What do you mean, you're having second thoughts?" The irritation came through the man's voice. "You really think you have a choice at this point? We agreed on a course of action, and we're sticking to it."

"I just think... I heard there were a number of people hurt in the Trips."

"Lowlifes, riffraff, and crazies. Just baggage and the city is better off without them. Now shut up or I'll send you to Weaver."

There was a muffled protest, then silence again.

I froze, waiting. They weren't quite close enough. Another few yards. I held my breath and tensed, then, trusting Tam and Jason to be at my back, I leaped out of the alcove, landing in front of three men and two bog-dogs.

"What—?" The center man was tall, with wavy blond hair. He was wearing a long indigo robe, but his eyes struck me the most. They were cruel—glittering, brilliant blue, icy cold with no hint of compassion behind them.

The bog-dogs immediately bristled and one lunged forward. Without a second thought, I brought my whip down against its side. The creatures were deadly predators, and they were so feral that he must have had them under a charm in order to keep them at his side.

The bog-dog, four feet high at the shoulder, met my whip without blinking as it sliced into its skin. Tam and Jason were in the fray now, Tam taking on one of Lyon's buddies while Jason tackled the other bog-dog.

The bog-dog lunged for my throat and I flipped over its head, grateful for every second I had poured into training at the gym. As I landed, I realized I was in front of Lyon, who was holding the disk. I glanced at it, calculating my chances for a snatch-and-run. My split second of hesitation cost me. He brought up one hand and sent flames pouring out of his fingertips toward me. I began to dodge to the side, only to find myself being launched through the air as the bog-dog turned and bowled into me from behind.

As I landed a few feet away, I realized that the bog-dog had unwittingly saved me from the flames. I leaped to my feet and charged toward Lyon, cracking my whip around to catch his wrist. It put a stop to another bout of flames coming my way as I yanked hard, throwing him off balance.

Jason shouted, and I glanced over to see him slicing into his bog-dog with his blade. As the dog fell to the floor, he raised his hand and called out in a loud voice. The next moment, a vortex of air came swirling down the hall at Lyon. I pulled my whip back and dodged again, turning to see Tam bringing down one of Lyon's compatriots.

Lyon shouted as the vortex hit him, sweeping him off his feet. He dropped the Thunderstrike as he tried to keep himself from falling. I dashed toward it. The bog-dog I had been fighting was racing toward me and I slapped my whip back on my thigh and snatched up the disk in my right hand as I turned to meet the creature with my dagger, driving it deep into the skull of the bog-dog.

I managed to hit it directly on the head, and the creature staggered back. At that moment, Tam appeared from behind, thrusting his sword deep into the back of the bog-dog. Confident he could finish it off, I turned just in time to see Lyon getting to his feet, the look on his face terrifying. He was full-on cracker-cat and crazy-eyed, and he raised his hands, aiming them toward me. This time, a ball of fire began to form between his fingers as a wicked grin spread across his face.

"Oh crap," I whispered, backing away. There was nothing to hide behind, nothing to protect me, and while I worked with fire, that didn't make me immune to it. He was too far away for me to attack with my dagger, and I couldn't let the Thunderstrike get away.

I turned on one heel, breaking into a full-fledged run. Luckily, I could blur myself and speed up. I headed toward the nearest intersection where we had met Terrance. If I could get to the center, it would act as a crossroads and I could shift over.

Lyon was moving after me, and I realized he was keeping pace. Double crap. There was something about him that seemed familiar and as I ran, it hit me—*he* was a Theosian, too.

"Fury!" Tam's voice echoed behind me.

I didn't have time to look back. Instead, I just kept running, trying to veer from side to side. I was coming to the intersection and as I skidded into the center, I brought my hands overhead, the disk between them.

Lyon let out a shout, sending a ball of flame directly at me. As the world began to fade and I shifted to the Crossroads, I realized the ground was shaking beneath my feet. The Thunderstrike must have been set to trigger off a quake and somehow, my actions had activated it. I tried to stop my shift, but it was too late. As the fireball engulfed the area where I had been standing, everything blurred, and the Thunderstrike and I landed on the Crossroads.

I blinked, shaking as I landed on my knees. I dropped the disk in front of me, staring at it in horror. I had no idea how bad the quake was that I had inadvertently triggered and could only hope that somehow, by shifting over, I might have negated some of the impact.

Then I remembered Tam and Jason were

stuck back there with a power-crazed magician and at least one of his toadies, in the middle of an earthquake, and the panic really did hit.

As I slowly pushed myself to my feet and retrieved the disk, I prayed that Hecate was paying attention. She always knew when I shifted to the Crossroads, and I hoped this was one of the times when she'd come checking on me, given she knew what I had set out to do.

I looked around. The Crossroads were active tonight. The spirits were running wild—I could feel them swirling past. Wondering if it had anything to do with the quake, I decided to wait for a bit before heading back. For one thing, if I crossed over right now, I'd wind up back in the Tunnels and I had no desire to face Lyon again. I wasn't sure I could hold onto the Thunderstrike if he tried to get it back.

I headed over to one of the rocks by the side of the Crossroads to wait. As I sat there, a familiar tap on the shoulder made me jump.

"Hey, Fury."

"Queet! Oh thank gods you showed up. Did Jason find you?" I knew there hadn't been enough time for Jason and Tam to get out of the Tunnels, but I couldn't think of any other way he could have known.

"No, actually. Hecate just contacted me and told me to meet you here. She's on the way."

Breathing a sign of relief, I leaned forward, my shoulders slumping as I rested my elbows on my knees as I examined the disk. It wasn't large— only about the size of a small dinner plate, but the damage it could do was stupefying. This disk had been used as a weapon of mass destruction during the Weather Wars, and now, at this moment, I was the only one standing between a reenactment of the disaster and the world.

"Queet, can you...never mind. You can't." I wanted him to go check on Jason and Tam, but he couldn't get into the Tunnels. Worry eating at me, I cautiously turned the disk over, looking for whatever had activated the quake, but it was smooth, with red lights running along the edge, and I couldn't figure out how Lyon had managed to program it.

"They'll be okay, Fury. They're strong and resourceful."

"How did you know what I was thinking?"

"I know how you feel about them—both of them."

"Oh."

I tried to believe he was right. Tam and Jason were both strong, it was true. And Lyon only had one henchman left with him when I had shifted out. The bog-dogs were dead. Surely, they would manage to survive.

"They have to," I whispered to myself.

The faint drone of a funeral march reached my ears. I shifted, struggling to see who was approaching. It wasn't Hecate—she didn't go in for processions, really.

Another moment, and a funeral parade came through. I had seen them before, out on the Crossroads. They trailed past, ignoring me, a group of mourners whom I knew were spirits carrying a ghostly coffin to the center of the juncture. They were dressed in veils, wearing colorful clothes, and they sang and danced as they followed the coffin. Once in the middle of the Crossroads, they set it down at the center and placed a handful of coins on the lid, then stood back to wait.

Oh hell, that meant somebody was coming for whomever was inside and I had a feeling I knew whom. I jumped over the rocks, hiding behind them. The last thing I needed was an encounter with another god of the Crossroads. Especially if it was—

A movement cut my thoughts short.

A tall—incredibly tall—man strode into the center. He was dark skinned, but his skin was almost translucent, and his long black hair, a swirl of tiny braids, fell to his shoulders. His eyes gleamed sparkling yellow, and he was wearing a black suit with a white shirt, and black and white shoes. Atop his head he wore a tall black top hat with a brilliant red rose on one side. His skull glistened from beneath the skin of his face.

Papa Legba. One of the Crossroads guardians.

As I watched, he squatted by the coffin and pocketed the coins that had been placed atop it. Slowly, he lifted the lid and waited. Another moment, and a vaporous form appeared from inside the coffin. Papa Legba stood, then laughed a deep belly laugh full of danger and delight, and held out one finger. He touched the spirit and it wound itself around him in a misty shroud.

The crowd of people fell to their knees, bowing

their heads. Papa Legba tipped his hat to them, laughed again, and turned back to the mists out of which he had stepped. As he entered the cloud, I thought I heard a faint shriek—probably the spirit attached to him—and then they were both gone. The mourners picked up the coffin and began to make their way back the way they had come. This time, they were quiet and somber. As they passed the rocks behind which I was hiding, I couldn't help but wonder who the spirit was whom they had delivered, and what was going to happen to it. Another moment, and the mourners vanished.

I was about to step out from behind the rocks when a familiar voice echoed from behind me.

"I see you were watching the delivery of one of Papa Legba's priests?"

"Hecate!" A wave of gratitude sweeping over me, I turned. There she stood, in full robes and with a faint smile on her face. I held out the Thunderstrike. "I got it back. But I was separated from Tam and Jason. I'm worried about them."

She smiled. "One thing at a time, child. Jason and Tam are waiting for you. But first, please explain to me why you set off an earthquake in Seattle."

And right then, I realized that I hadn't managed to shift over fast enough to stop the quake from happening. I could only hope it hadn't been too strong.

Chapter 25

"I didn't mean to. *Really*. I grabbed the disk from Lyon. I was trying to get away from his damned fireballs, and I decided the only way to escape with the Thunderstrike was to jump over to the Crossroads. The quake happened just as I shifted. I figure Lyon must have—" I stopped as she held up her hand, her smile crinkling into laughter.

"I shouldn't tease you. I know what happened, Fury. I was just attempting a little levity."

Irritated, I scuffed my foot. Her idea of a joke had thrown me into a panic. "Ha-ha. Very funny."

She sobered. "You're right, it's not. But we need any break we can get from the damage and destruction that this device has wrought. You must take it to the Greenlings. They will destroy it. All artifacts from the Weather Wars must go through them first. They log it in, and then consign it into history."

I stared at her. "*All* the artifacts? There are more like this?"

Hecate gave me a faint nod. "Many. The magicians were skilled, the nations rich and wanting to grow more so. They poured their money into their magical weapons because they had grown far more powerful than the technological ones."

"Are they all weather related?" I really didn't want to go through this again.

"Some. Others not. Some are worse—magical weapons of death and destruction. Gaia destroyed a number of them in her wrath during the World Shift, but there are still quite a few unaccounted for, buried deep below the shifting sands." Hecate let out a long sigh. "We do what we can. I will take you to the ferry so you can take this over to the Greenlings immediately. I am forbidden from setting foot on the Arbortariam, as are any of the gods."

"I don't want to go over there alone! And what about Jason and Tam? I have no idea if they're okay." I seldom put up a fuss, but right now, I needed to hear that they were alive and unhurt. Or at least, relatively unscathed.

Hecate let out an exasperated sigh. "Fury, we have to get this device under guard. If I transport you to go look for your friends, there's always the chance that Lyon will manage to steal it back from you."

"What if you take it for me? Let me go help them, and then I'll meet you at the temple and you can whisk me away to the Arbortariam." I held it out to her, pleading.

"Think with your brain rather than your heart, girl. If you go back to the Tunnels, there's the chance Lyon will be waiting. I can't afford to risk your life at this stage of the game." Hecate was starting to look put out and I recognized the fine line between her "*Will you please listen to reason*" and her "*Get the hell in line and do what I say*" mode.

"Can you bring them over to the Crossroads for me?" I finally asked.

"No." The finality in her voice put an end to the conversation.

I paused, then decided to tell her what I suspected. The gods needed to know. "Hecate, I think Lyon's a Theosian. I can't be positive but—"

She looked to one side, as though she didn't want to answer. Finally, she gave me an abrupt nod. "I know. We know. He's rogue, Fury. He's gone off-leash."

"But who was he pledged to?" For a Theosian to go off-leash was almost unheard of, but when it happened, punishment always followed. That Lyon was running around free didn't bode well.

"I can't tell you more, not right now. But yes, he is Theosian. Which means, we aren't done with him yet. But that will have to be for another day. And don't tell anyone—not even Jason or Tam— until I give you leave."

I wanted to press her for more information but she had that look on her face that said, "Don't push it," and I didn't. Abruptly, she vanished without another word.

Queet misted up by my side. "Did you make her angry?"

"Maybe. No. Yes, a little, I guess. I'm good at that, I think. I don't want her angry with me—it never pays to have one of the Elder Gods pissed at you, especially if they hold your leash. But I don't know what to do about Jason and Tam—"

Before I could finish my sentence, I felt myself fading from the Crossroads. A dizzying rush hit me as the fog rushed in waves and swallowed me up.

I blinked as I once again staggered, then fell to my knees. I was off the Crossroads and in Hecate's office in the temple. She was sitting behind her desk, dressed in a black leather pencil skirt and a green V-neck sweater.

"Call your friends. See if they're okay."

I pulled out my phone as soon as I dragged myself onto the sofa. Leaning back, my body ached from both the fight and the jump to and from the Crossroads. Luckily, I hadn't fought an Abom over there, or I'd be passed out on Hecate's floor by now.

Dialing Jason's number, I waited, hoping for an answer. If he was still below ground, chances were reception would be spotty. If not, then... But the call went to his messages. Feeling defeated and scared for him, I tried Tam. Same thing.

Hecate was eyeing me soberly. "They'll be all right, Fury. Trust them. They're both strong and capable. Now, really, you have to get that disk back to Jerako. I can't travel over to the island with you, so I'm assigning a couple of my servants to go along. They'll drive you to the ferry and travel with you. When you get there, they'll wait until you return to the ferry."

And with that, I was hustled out the door with a couple of muscle-bound men guarding me, heading back to the Arbortariam.

I was surprised to see that it was early morning when I exited the temple. Not yet dawn, but close. We had been up all night. The second quake, the one I caused, had been a minor tremor, but the city looked far too damaged and wounded from the first for comfort. While it wasn't leveled, not by any means, and the infrastructure was still standing, everywhere there were signs of debris and damage. It would take a long time cleaning up after this.

The entire trip to the ferry and over the water to the island had me tense and afraid. I was carrying the disk in a plain drawstring sack hung over my shoulder. Nobody would know I had it unless they happened to either grab the satchel and run or it was Lyon or his cronies. But my Trace showed no sign of any Aboms, and Hecate had supplied me with a short-term anti-tracking device so nobody could follow my footsteps.

My thoughts remained firmly with Jason and Tam. I wanted to run off and return to the

Tunnels to find them. With a sigh, I gave up and leaned back, closing my eyes. Sometimes, not having control over my own life sucked. Granted, everybody had limitations, but some days, the realization that my life wasn't my own hit me harder than others. I chafed at the restrictions, but then again, if Hecate were to suddenly free me, I'd have to find a different job. And then I'd just be shackled to somebody else's whims. Nobody was truly free, when I thought about it.

At the edge of the island, I left my escorts and headed toward the force field. There, I saw Zhan, waiting for me. He bowed low and bade me follow him.

Once past the veil, he glanced over to me. "Your heart is sore and your spirit weary. I can sense these things."

"I'm worried over Tam and Jason. I haven't heard from them since I escaped from the Tunnels last night. I'm worried Lyon might have killed them." I was so tired that I felt tears well up. I groaned. The last thing I needed was to be crying right now—it really didn't fit my image, but that didn't seem to matter as the tears spilled over and trickled down my cheeks.

"Poor, beautiful Fury. Let me ease your heart?" The hedgemite drew close and I recognized the same look as Tam had sported on his face when he kissed away the swelling in my hand. I didn't need any more entanglements, especially not with someone I didn't know.

I held up my hand. "That's all right. Thank you, though. I'm just tired. Please tell me I won't have to wait long for Jerako."

"We are going to him now. It's a short walk. Might I suggest you breathe in the fresh air and let it clear your head?"

The snow had hit even here, and the air was bracing. I did as he suggested, breathing out my stress. The very air in the Arbortariam seemed to be healing, and my headache lifted, though I was still exhausted. The sound of the birds echoed faintly around me, and the sky—a pale silvery sheen with blue peeking out—promised a hint of sun. While it was still cold, the temperature felt above freezing and the snow was beginning to melt.

We wound through a short meadow, and then Zhan pointed ahead. There, in the middle of the clearing, stood Jerako. I hurried over to him, wanting to get this over with.

"Hello, young Theosian. You bring me a deadly gift, Hecate says." Jerako's cheeks crinkled, the leaves and branches making up his face moving in a most peculiar way. He sounded more gentle than last time. Almost...*caring*.

I held out the bag. "The Thunderstrike. I don't want to be rude, but my friends are missing and I'd like to get back so I can try to find them."

Jerako laughed. "Ever the rush, but this time, ease your heart. They are with friends, safe and sound. I received word a little while ago. They escaped, unharmed for the most part, though with a few singed hairs, I do believe."

"Are you telling me the truth?" I was suddenly terrified he might be toying with me, but he leaned down—no small feat in itself—and patted my shoulder awkwardly, scratching me with one of his branches in the process.

"I am, young Fury. I am. They are alive and intact."

I let out a garbled sound and dropped to the ground, the tears streaming down my face. Only this time, they were tears of relief. "Thank the gods... Was it Terrance who helped them?"

Jerako blinked. "You know about Terrance?"

"Of course I do. We met him this morning. Last night, rather. In the Tunnels."

"Then yes, it was Terrance. But hush and no more talk about him. The Crystal Guardians are so secretive even the government doesn't know they exist." He poked at the bag. "Please, remove the device from the bag. My fingers are not so dexterous with small knots."

I untied the drawstrings and withdrew the Thunderstrike. "Here, take it and I never want to see it or hear about it again." But curiosity struck me as I handed it over. "What are you going to do with it?"

"We will catalog its presence, and then destroy it. Unmake it, so to speak. Great artifacts are never easily destroyed, but we can usually figure out a way. This is no longer your worry, so you may let it go. I do wish you'd managed to destroy Lyon, but then I suppose the Order of the Black Mist would just find someone to take his place."

"Probably," I mumbled. "He's still a danger, isn't he? Lyon?"

"Lyon and the Order of the Black Mist will be

a danger as long as they exist. And now, I'm afraid you're on his radar. There's only *one* Fury and you're hard to miss. You've saved the city, Fury. He would have used this to level Seattle." Jerako held up the Thunderstrike. "You may not have set out to save the day, but you did."

"Haphazardly and without any conscious idea of what to do," I mumbled.

"Most heroes stumble into their fame. Most heroes don't set out to save the world, you know. Fury, your friends are waiting for you back at the store. Go to them. Rest. But we may need you again. If so, we will contact Hecate. And be cautious. Lyon will not take this loss lightly, and he still lives. But the Crystal Guardians are watching, and so are all of us who serve Gaia."

And with that, he took the Thunderstrike, turned, and strode away, leaving me standing beside Zhan, who had waited in the background.

"Come, I will take you back to the ferry."

Feeling oddly let down, and somewhat numb, I turned and followed him out.

Chapter 26

When I got to the shop, I saw the caution lines had been removed from most of the buildings around, though a few still sported the yellow holograms that kept people at bay. The force fields were electric and produced a nice jolt that put off all but the most persistent—or stupid—of trespassers. But our building had been cleared. I peeked into Up-Cakes, where Shevron and her clerks were cleaning up the jumble of broken glass and overturned baked goods. It made for a sharp, sticky mess. Waving, I left them to their cleaning and headed next door to Dream Wardens.

Sure enough, Jason and Tam were there, along with Hans. Relief flooding over me—I hadn't really believed they were okay—I raced into the shop.

"Thank gods you guys are okay. I was so worried." All the stress and weariness set in, and I dropped to the sofa next to Tam.

He grabbed my hands, leaning in as he searched my eyes. "When you vanished with the Thunderstrike, we figured you went to the Crossroads, but we couldn't be sure. I was so worried," he whispered, his voice heavy, pulling me onto his lap.

Without thinking, I pressed my lips to his and melted into his embrace, grateful to be in his arms again. I lingered in the kiss, feeling a barricade inside me jog from where I'd built it up, keeping my heart protected against the pain that I had learned far too young. Except for Jason and Shevron, I had done my best to keep everybody else at bay, but now that was melting away. Whatever I had with Tam, it was real. Wherever it might lead, I was willing to take the journey.

"I was so afraid something had happened to you, but I couldn't go back, not with the Thunderstrike in hand." I covered his face with kisses, suddenly ravenous for his touch. All I could think about was dragging him off to my apartment.

Jason cleared his throat after a moment. "If you two are quite finished?"

Flushing, I broke away. "Sorry. I was just...worried. About *both* of you. I took the Thunderstrike to the Arbortariam and gave it to Jerako. It's safely away from the Order of the Black Mist. But he warned me that Lyon knows who I am now, and he's likely to come hunting. Probably both of you, as well."

"He's right. When I saw you vanish, you crossed your arms over your head as you shifted to the Crossroads. Tam and I couldn't tell whether the fireball had hurt you, or whether you had dodged the bullet before it hit. But Lyon was focused on you. He was watching you. He's not likely to forget your face or anything about you."

"I took that moment to run his other buddy through," Tam said.

"As Tam took out his companion, I set up another vortex that caught Lyon from the back, and we grabbed the opportunity and ran. We raced back to Terrance's shop. He was there, waiting, and he guided us through the secret entrance. From there, he helped us get out of the Tunnels. Queet met us outside, telling us you had made it safely to the Crossroads."

Restless, I crossed to the window, staring out into the street. "Where's Tommy-Tee?"

Tam joined me. "My people are going to look after him for a bit. They might be able to wake him up, but first we have to ascertain whether that's a good idea."

"Okay, then. I guess...immediate problem solved. But we can't let down our guard. We disrupted big plans, and I doubt Lyon will let that go without retaliation. From now on, keep your eyes open. Because this isn't over." I stared out the front window at the damage. "They are out to bring back the Elder Gods of Chaos, and if they succeed..."

"If they succeed, there won't be anything left but fire and ash." Tam took my hand. "Don't forget, there's a hurricane headed into the Texicana Gulf. I gather that Lightning Strikes is working to disrupt it, but you're right—whether it be through weather magic or something else, the Order of the Black Mist is out to change the world. This won't end until they win or they're dead."

As we stood by the window, looking out into the silvery morning, I realized I was shivering. So much of my life had been lived on unstable ground, and this was no exception. I wanted an anchor. I wanted a foundation—something solid.

Jason joined us. "It will be all right." His voice was low, but raw. "The world can't possibly fall back into the pit that brought on the World Shift... Can it?"

With that question lingering in our ears, we watched the hustle and bustle outside as morning began. The whip on my leg tingled, as did the triskelion tattoo on my neck. Something felt like it was shifting in my body and my aura, but I wasn't sure what. I knew my heart had shifted, though. The proof was in the shape of Tam holding my hand.

I glanced up at him, searching his face. I wasn't sure about him. I wasn't sure about anything. But I'd do what I always did—continue on. Because when it came down to the core of things, wasn't that what we all had to do? Continue on in the face of daunting circumstances? Life was made up of challenges, and if we stopped growing, we might as well be dead.

Deciding to rest in the knowledge that we had at least thwarted one plan to knock the world askew, I drew a long breath and let everything go. Jason wrapped his arm around my shoulders, while Tam wrapped his arm around my waist.

Hans stood to the side, arms behind his back, watching at attention, as we waited for the new day to begin.

~End~

If you enjoyed this book, I invite you into my other worlds—and stay tuned for the November release of FURY'S MAGIC, Book 2 in the Fury Unbound Series. And sign up for my newsletter: http:// galenorn.com/newsletter/ to ensure you always get updated on new releases! You can find out more about all my books on my web site: Galenorn.com and in the Biography/Bibliography at the end of this book.

Upcoming releases

August 2, 2016: Flight From Mayhem (Fly by Night Series—Book 2)
September 27, 2016: Shadow Silence (Whisper Hollow Series—Book 2)
November 15, 2016: Fury's Magic (Fury Unbound Series—Book 2)

Playlist

I almost always write to music, and FURY RISING was no exception. Here's the playlist for the book:

Android Lust: Here and Now
Brandon & Derek Fiechter: Witch's Brew; Night Fairies; Legend of the Dark Lord
Celtic Woman: The Butterfly; The Voice
The Chieftains: Dunmore Lassies
Clannad: Banba Óir; Newgrange
Corvus Corax: Bucca; Filii Neidhardi
David & Steve Gordon: Shaman's Drum Dance
Deuter: Petite Fleur
Dizzi: Dizzi Jig; Dance of the Unicorns
Eastern Sun: Beautiful Being (Original Edit)
Eivør: Trøllbundin
Enya: Orinoco Flow; Cursum Perficio
Faun: Iduna; Rad; Sieben; The Market Song
Gabrielle Roth: The Dancing Path: Flowing; Rest Your Tears Here; Totem; The Calling; Mother Night; Raven
Hedningarna: Chicago; Ukkonen; Gorrulaus; Tullí; Räven [Fox Woman]; Juopolle Joutunut
Huldrelokk: Trolldans
Kerstin Blodig & Ian Melrose: Kråka; Kelpie; Bedlam Boys/Bedlam Girls; Miner Viser
Tamaryn: Violet's in a Pool; While You're Sleeping, I'm Dreaming
Tingstad & Rumbel: Chaco; Peru

Biography

New York Times, *Publishers Weekly*, and *USA Today* bestselling author Yasmine Galenorn writes urban fantasy and paranormal romance, and is the author of almost fifty books, including the Otherworld Series, the Whisper Hollow Series, the new Fury Unbound Series, and many more. She's also written nonfiction metaphysical books. She is the 2011 Career Achievement Award Winner in Urban Fantasy, given by RT Magazine.

Yasmine has been in the Craft since 1980, is a shamanic witch and High Priestess. She describes her life as a blend of teacups and tattoos. She lives in Kirkland WA with her husband Samwise and their cats. Yasmine can be reached via her website at Galenorn.com.

Books by Yasmine Galenorn:

Fury Unbound Series:
Fury Rising (July 2016)
Fury's Magic (November 2016)
Fury Awakened (May 2017)

Lily Bound Series (in order):
Souljacker (March 2017)

Whisper Hollow Series (in order):
Autumn Thorns
Shadow Silence (September 2016)

Fly By Night Series (in order):
Flight from Death
Flight from Mayhem (August 2016)

Otherworld Series (in order):
Witchling
Changeling
Darkling
Dragon Wytch
Night Huntress
Demon Mistress
Bone Magic
Harvest Hunting
Blood Wyne
Courting Darkness
Shaded Vision
Shadow Rising
Haunted Moon

Autumn Whispers
Crimson Veil
Priestess Dreaming
Panther Prowling
Darkness Raging

Otherworld: Upcoming:
Moon Shimmers (January 2017)
Harvest Song
Blood Bonds

Otherworld: E-Novellas:
The Shadow of Mist: Otherworld novella
Etched in Silver: Otherworld novella
Ice Shards: Otherworld novella
Flight From Hell: Otherworld--Fly By Night crossover
novella
Earthbound

Otherworld: Short Collections:
Tales From Otherworld: Collection One
Men of Otherworld: Collection One
Men of Otherworld: Collection Two
Moon Swept: Otherworld Tales of First Love

Indigo Court Series (in order):
Night Myst
Night Veil
Night Seeker
Night Vision
Night's End

Indigo Court: Novellas:
Night Shivers

Chintz 'n China Series:
Ghost of a Chance
Legend of the Jade Dragon
Murder Under a Mystic Moon
A Harvest of Bones
One Hex of a Wedding

Bath and Body Series (under the name India Ink):
Scent to Her Grave
A Blush With Death
Glossed and Found

Anthologies:
Once Upon a Curse (short story: Bones)
Never After (Otherworld novella: The Shadow of Mist)
Inked (Otherworld novella: Etched in Silver)
Hexed (Otherworld novella: Ice Shards)
Songs of Love & Death (short story: Man in the Mirror)
Songs of Love and Darkness (short story: Man in the Mirror)
Nyx in the House of Night (article: She is Goddess)
A Second Helping of Murder (recipe: Clam Chowder)

Magickal Nonfiction:
From Llewellyn Publications and Ten Speed Press:
Trancing the Witch's Wheel
Embracing the Moon
Dancing with the Sun
Tarot Journeys
Crafting the Body Divine
Sexual Ecstasy and the Divine
Totem Magic
Magical Meditations